# Vix and the Boy

## MARY O'DONNELL

POOLBEG

Published 1996
by Poolbeg Press Ltd
123 Baldoyle Industrial Estate
Dublin 13, Ireland

© Mary O'Donnell 1996

Reprinted July 1996

The moral right of the author has been asserted.

The Publishers gratefully acknowledge the support of The Arts Council.

A catalogu·e record for this book is available from the British Library.

ISBN 1 85371 557 3

Cover photography by Mike O'Toole
Cover design by Poolbeg Group Services Ltd
Set by Poolbeg Group Services Ltd in Garamond 10.5/13.5
Printed by The Guernsey Press Co Ltd,
Vale, Guernsey, Channel Islands.

## Acknowledgements

Special thanks to my mother, Maureen, who read this manuscript at various stages, my husband, Martin, and to Kate Cruise O'Brien for her insights and generous advice. Finally thanks to Philip MacDermott for his unfailing enthusiasm and support.

Months later – it seemed like years later – they touched down at Schiphol. During the flight from Kennedy, they didn't do any of the things he used to imagine they would do in a jumbo. Economy class didn't have the scope. All those tired-looking, restless people, Luke observed, to-ing and fro-ing between seat and toilet, blocking the aisles. Then the long queue when one of the toilets stopped flushing, and bulging rucksacks which people dropped anywhere they liked once they were airborne, you'd swear they were going to camp right there in the air over the Atlantic. Why couldn't those eejits sit still for five minutes? He dreaded that Ginnie would trip or fall, or be hurt in some way. Her body, her flesh, which he was now part of, must not be hurt. Suppose one of the engines went on fire? Suppose there was a bomb on board? But no, he wouldn't think about that, especially not about the bomb. That kind of terrorism didn't happen on American planes as they headed towards Europe. Anything Middle Eastern was dicey. Anything that passed through Frankfurt from Africa or Thailand. All the druggy, wonky countries that were still being born, where nobody agreed about anything. People in the West were shagging them dry of everything that belonged to them: coffee, drugs, carpets, trees, ivory, exotic little animals on the verge of extinction. Those were the bomb countries, spitzen-sparken and poppen-korken hell-holes where airports

1

were risks. Anyway, if the plane blew up that would be that. There'd be no more wondering about what to do with the rest of his life, about whether himself and Ginnie could hack it. No worries about whether God existed either, which was fine by him. He'd done the round trip to Heaven a couple of times. Cool, it was. Sheer cool.

Ginnie dozed beside him for most of the journey, her head on his shoulder, her arm slipped casually through his and her thumb caught firmly in the loop of his jeans where the belt slid through. He had to crane his neck continually to avoid his cheeks being tickled by the turquoise fringe of her hair. Once, she excused herself and went off down the aisle clasping a bag of skin-creams and ointments, stiff with sleep and, he suspected, pain. He warned her to be careful, then watched her retreating back and the short blue-and-copper-coloured plait which bobbed at her neck.

He didn't sleep at all on the flight. He read a thriller which bored him after thirty pages. Then he watched a film. Although he'd seen it before he kept watching anyway because of Kim Basinger. His arms and the back of his neck still tingled from sunburn. He'd lazed for two hours by the pool in the overgrown garden of their new US contact, enjoying the warmth and the din of the crickets. He'd drifted through the streets of Baltimore, or down to the harbour. He watched the yachts for hours as they cut across Chesapeake Bay like great white birds. Mick was with Ginnie during the discussions, but took an early flight back to Europe a week before. There'd been a lot of talk, but Luke didn't always catch the drift. Sometimes he wished she'd just sign on the dotted line and let them both get on with enjoying life. But that was selfish, he knew, and at least Ginnie was happy.

The captain cut in just as they approached the West of Ireland, giving details of altitude, European time and a European weather forecast. Luke looked down through a misty summer dawn and saw his own country, or what had been his own country, mizen-lights spreading from dots of trawlers, then the rough fingers of the land pawing the Atlantic. He noted the bumps and knots in the landscape, threads of rivers, puddles of lakes. Postcard stuff but from above. He grunted and shrugged. The Rale Ireland. Butter is the Cream. Red hair and freckles forever. Like hell, he thought, but then something tugged at him. Tears welled up in his eyes. He blinked hard and coughed. Beautiful things always made him seize up as if he was in pain. Especially if he tried to deny the beauty its place in his head. That would pass. He knew it, was certain of it. The main thing was, he could still work things out. The future was there, still safe, and there was plenty of it. It wouldn't run away, it would never again be beyond his grasp.

Sometimes, the sight of Ginnie made him ache in that peculiar way. That aching was something he'd never expected, not when they were in Kerry, running like a pair of mad hares on the beach or through the high ferns on Valentia Island. But now, when she stripped off and he looked at her, when she would expect him to look away and feel pity or loathing, and he could not, did not want to, he knew just how complicated life was. The great things, he'd discovered, didn't always come from where he once thought they would. This woman was beyond him and yet not beyond him. In the past she had been beyond his grasp. Now, he had her, but not as he thought he would have her. She could still – and this he admired – tell the whole world to go to hell. And that included him.

Boy, could she fight her corner. The rows, the shagging

3

rows were something else. Even still. But he couldn't hold his tongue either, which didn't help. That was the way of him. She could let anybody know that their petty rules weren't going to fuck her up, that rules were to be broken and nothing was set in stone. And if she could do that, so could he. One word still bothered him, flung in his face months ago on two different occasions. *Prig.* He'd tried hard not to be a prig. She said that most men would be prigs if they didn't have women to untangle all the rules and regulations for them, make them throw off the rose-tinted specs. It was what he was trying to do, after all. He had to hand it to her. She understood important things, the common and ordinary things which everybody shared. We're all basically the same, she would say, no matter what our culture is. Needs are mostly the same. There's joy and there's pain, we're born and we die. That's it. That's all there is, she would tell him gently. Still and all. It did her no harm if he told her to wise up every so often. Or even to shut up. He had to stand up to her in case she swallowed him up. Mad and all as he was about her.

There was nothing for him in Ireland. His life there was over. But living with Ginnie, who was beyond him and yet not beyond him, he felt he was starting to get the hang of life itself. And love. Stuff like that. And if, as she said, there was birth and death like two slabs of a great sandwich, then they *had* to make the way they lived something special. The filling had to be full and rich and sweet. And responsible, he would add, which only drove her around the twist.

An hour and a half later, they walked down the arrivals hall at Schiphol. Mick was meeting them, had hinted that there were accommodation problems, something to do with an alcoholic in the next apartment, thin walls, thin doors and a balcony the size of a stamp. Not the

Dorchester, he had told Ginnie, definitely not the Dorchester. Not yet, Luke added mentally, but soon, soon.

He felt as if he was on safe territory. Even Amsterdam seemed like home after the US. It was as if he was close to his own kind, whatever his own kind was. After he'd grabbed their luggage – tapestried, leather-bound stuff – off the carousel, he pushed the overladen trolley down the polished hall and felt relieved in the cool morning light. The sense of space. Big yellow signs and arrows to this or that departure gate. You'd need to be blind as a bat not to see them but judging by the dithering groups peering awkwardly around, some people still managed to get lost. Then the snappy groups of dark-suited businessmen. Japanese visitors. The taller, paler people of Northern Europe. Messages came through the intercom in different languages. Sometimes, because he recognised a name, he noticed that a message in French would also be repeated in English.

The airport police frightened him. At first he didn't know why he felt fear in the pit of his stomach. Then he remembered. Something to do with the sight of guns in holsters, dark uniforms and that sure-footed tread as they paced the halls and corridors. It reminded him of the last gig in Ireland, at Malla. There had been security people that night, dressed in black or navy, people with helmets, visors, walkie-talkies. No guns, of course, but still. And then there was the other crowd, a sinister man in a navy suit, the glittering rosary-beads on his arms. That dark cloth was a reminder of something rotten. He remembered a march in the centre of Dublin, a terrible crowd of rowdies, screaming, beating the shite out of one another. Pictures. Laminated posters. A strange, liquid-filled jar, shoved in his face by a blue-veiled young woman with eyes that held his a moment too long, allowing her to beam the concerns of her dark and correct soul to his. His thoughts ran as if down a spiral into the past. From guns in holsters, to the night at Malla, to Hilary Dunne. It still happened so easily. Scarcely a day passed when he did not experience a flashback, or when Ginnie did not.

He took a deep breath and tried to stride more cockily. He hoped he looked OK. He looked down at his jeans and checked that he was zippered. You never know, he thought, feeling shaky and nervous even though Ginnie was with him. He rubbed his right hand along his jaw. Good stubble there, thickening by the month; he needed to shave twice a day to keep it under control. Ginnie didn't like hairy men, neither beards nor chests nor shoulders and backs. If a woman wants that much hair, she should sleep with an ape, Ginnie said. Well, he was in the clear in that department. Like silk, wasn't that what she said? Christ but he was hungry. The smell of croissants and coffee teased his stomach and his tongue, and little pockets inside his cheeks suddenly gushed saliva at the thoughts of breakfast.

"Look," she said quietly, touching his forearm.

"Where?"

"Mick. Over there."

Without looking at her he knew she was smiling. Ahead of them and to the left, Mick puffed along, mopping his brow with a red and white spotted handkerchief. He was wearing small round sunglasses with very black matt lenses. When he saw Ginnie and Luke he waved his polka-dot square at them.

"Hey, love-birds! Welcome to Holland! Howsabout some Dutch pancakes and coffee for brekkers? Yum-yum-yum!"

It was a homecoming of kinds.

# One

## Ginnie

Ginnie used to practise smiling. If the result was too close to a schoolgirl grin, she would try again and again until the effect was more seductive. Less porcelain and more pout, she would tell herself. A cross between waif and wildcat. Vulnerable. Beautiful. But wanton.

In spite of her popularity her doubts increased. It was as if she was retreating, as if her body were a mask behind which she hid and felt safe. The last thing she did before every gig was to check her armpits. The pan-stick had to be smooth enough to conceal any residual stubble, but not so conspicuous as to show under the lights.

A week before the gig at Malla, the gig which changed everything, she had a typical night at the National Stadium. As usual, she promised herself that things would go well. They had to. The backing group was fresh and raw, four youngsters from the wrong side of the tracks, that nebulous place which rock critics loved to romanticise. In a way she came from the wrong side of the tracks too. Middle-class backgrounds and rock music just didn't mix, not even unemployed middle-class backgrounds. But it fooled nobody, least of all the hacks. Bonnie Macbeth from the tabloid *Now!* had her hooks in Ginnie, made a big thing of her origins, took pains to expose the details of her decent but dawdling background. She portrayed her family as hopelessly solid and bourgeois and wondered frequently in print why a nice girl like Virgin was wasting her time with a rock career. "It takes chutzpah. The question is, has Virgin got it?"

Ever since she got into the business six years ago, she'd fought to create the right image. Her backing sound had to know what it was about, even if the sound was pure pastiche. The young fellows in the stadium were sexy, energetic, yet raw enough to leave the eight hundred fans in the hall practically panting for *her* entrance. She listened from her dressing-room, checked her make-up again, cursed as one of the fasteners on her Pap-halter snapped, but carried on regardless.

So what if it fell apart during the performance? Those kids down in the hall would love it! On impulse she snagged a hole in the silk stockings beneath her leggings, checked her armpits again, paused longer than necessary in the wings as her own group built up the intro, then strutted her way across the stage, twirled, skipped and pranced towards the extending platform, her body primed for display.

As the kids roared applause the hairs on the back of her neck prickled, she shivered with excitement, her heartbeat accelerated and the blood rushed to her head. Her hands clammy, she raised her arms gradually higher, more stiffly, as the music pulsed to a crescendo. The bass rhythms heightened, the drums crashed and she swung into the first number as the hall burst with howls that hit her ears like a physical wall of sound, pounding, pounding.

*Baby, the world has its ancient charms,*
*Though Antarctica has blown her head,*
*An albatross has crossed the sky,*
*And the river-beds are dry,*

*Yet baby, ancient charms are there,*
*Though the pimps and tyrants live,*
*Though the camps are full, and the refugees flee,*
*The world has ancient charms,*

*When ah sink into your arms, your arms, your*
*arms . . .*
*Baby you know how ah want your arms,*
*When this weariness is on me,*
*Your hands, your lips, and everything you got,*

*To hold me, caress me,*
*Till ah'm crazy for the soul of love,*
*Dying to drown in*
*The soul of all your charms!*

The sax player cut in and she paused, holding the mike away from her face while she breathed deeply. She was beginning to pant. A million voices screamed back at her. *Crazy for the soul of love!* Ginnie stood with her legs apart, pelvis rotating, then slowly unpeeled the man's black jacket, stripped herself of the loose black leggings and threw her arms up and out until her body was revealed in a shimmering teddy, legs glistening beneath the lights.

She wore suspendered stockings, one of them slightly torn, her buttocks jutted as she posed in impossibly high heels. Two youngsters in the front row jumped forward to catch the garments, and Ginnie laughed aloud as one of them, a teenage boy, actually buried his face in the jacket as if to inhale the essences of Virgin.

Forty minutes later the air was charged with the vibrations of lustful emotion, craven want. She waited for the right moment, when she could build to a finale and really blow their minds. It came like a steady chant in her head, stronger, *fuck me*, stronger still, *fuck me, fuck me!* over and over until she felt herself seized by the sense of her own power before the thousands who had come to hear her sing. She would imagine the unimaginable.

It always did the trick. All she had to do was imagine, and somehow, imagining, some sense of gloating vigour was transmitted beyond her and into the crowd. She no longer belonged to herself. The disembodied power of her voice, the sinuous movements of her body were not hers alone. It was like being on a tightrope over the Grand Canyon, knowing you weren't going to slip, because the winds, the warmth, the kindness of the universe held you in place. That was it. Something beyond her, greater than her, moved in her body and through her music. Whatever it was, the moment was ecstatic. Behind, around, over her head, at her feet – sound, pure, unrestrained sound. And no inhibitions either. This was it, this was surely it, a sound like none other. The heat, the pure heat of it, she was hot, hot, by Christ was she hot and ready, as she would be ready, now and forever.

Then it faded, the synthesiser whined down to silence, the guitars stilled, the guys behind her like statues frozen for one split second in her mind's eye. The kids yowled with delight. Ginnie breathed heavily, her face coursing with sweat, the smell of it rose pleasantly from between her breasts, her smell, her odour, *eau de Ginnie,* aha,

10

possibilities there, a future perfume, and here she was, trying to slow, to slow, to slow down.

One final slow number to whet their appetites, a trick she'd introduced in her latest album – *Climax*. The groupies knew what was coming, the wannabees knew what was coming and Virgin's eyes swept the writhing, undulating crowd. It was the simplest, cleanest, most mutual of gratifications. There they were, bottles of lotus oil at the ready, waving as if to reassure her that yes, they understood, yes, they loved only her, and yes, they would join her for ever and ever Amen!

*I can't say forever, but I'll try . . .*

When the words died again and the air swirled purple, all that remained was the cheering crowd, the smiles, the laughs, the weeping of girls as Virgin took the microphone in her hand and addressed them.

"Thank you so much all you lovely people! . . . It's the truth, *lovely* people, that's what you are!"

They screamed with joy.

"And the truth – if ya really wanna hear it – "

She paused, gasped, wiped her forehead with the back of her hand. The fringe of her hair soaked. She stood still and stared out at them, wide-eyed.

"Phew! It's not easy work I can tell ya!"

They cheered and howled.

"Nothin's easy in this life, Virgin!" a girl screeched from far back. Good-humoured laughter rippled through the auditorium. She went along with it, projecting patience, easy accord that nothing in life came easy.

"Right on, whoever you are, right on! But let me tell you, let me tell you how I really feel tonight, God I feel so *goood* when I look out and see all you lovely girls 'n guys . . . and because I feel good, I'm able to say just how full of *love I feel right now*, love for all you people who've taken the trouble to come here tonight."

She paused again. Let it sink in, she thought, let them absorb it. Let them feel it, believe it. It was no more than the truth. At that moment she loved them with all her heart, and she knew that she had their love too. She possessed them.

"I thank you, all of you. And because I want to thank you, this final number . . . "

The howling rose once more.

" . . . is my way of saying . . . of saying . . . "

More wails, the crying and weeping and laughing among hundreds, faces now candle-lit, incandescent and shimmering as white wax candles were clasped and cradled between hot hands. Rows and rows of them. As far as her eye could see. White, pure white, radiant heat and light.

"It's my way of saying . . . that I love each and every one of you."

She said much the same thing at most of her gigs. Her voice almost broke. Silence fell. Her eyes filled with tears.

"And do you love me?" she called, her lungs powerful.

*"YEESSSSSS!!!"*

"Are you sure?"

*"YEESSSSS!!"*

"Do you mean it?"

*"YEESSSSS!!"*

"OK you guys! Let's *ride!*"

The screaming began again. Immediately the lights swung up, the arc-lights, strobes, reds and blues, the yellows and greens and Virgin was slashed through in a spectra of mauves, pinks and eerie reds.

She began with a series of grunts and whoops, let her

12

torso fall forward as if she was doing a tribal rain-dance, raised her muscular legs to the rhythm and leant into the thud-thud of the bass line.

"*Uhh-uhh . . .* " it began, "*Uhh-uhhh . . .* "

She reeled away from the centre of the stage and opened her thighs, running both hands up until they came to rest at her crotch. Slowly, deliberately, with another *uhh-uhhh,* she notched her forefinger into the hole she'd already torn in one of her stockings and began to tear upwards from the knee until the top of the stocking ripped through and the pale flesh was exposed, tatters of nylon glinting, the paste diamonds in her suspenders catching the light.

Down in the audience, five rows from the back, Luke O'Regan stood up, his pupils dilated. Virgin sang tenderly, imploringly. He watched, straining his eyes to catch every nuance, every chance expression, felt the first stirrings in his groin. He had followed Virgin through every number, felt gooseflesh every time she turned. Every word of her songs seemed addressed personally to him.

She left nothing to chance.

*You know we've only met,*
*Ah'm a stranger in this town,*
*But darlin' just remember,*
*Ah'm a woman not a clown . . .*

She was begging for understanding, for love, for respect.

*The truth is ah could play the game,*
*But baby ah'm through with that,*
*Ah don't want no game, 'cause ah'm not tame*

*And ah can really show you what you want!*
*So baby let me do it to you now,*
*Let me spread myself all over,*
*Let me do it to you now,*
*Can't you feel mah heat, feel mah heat, feel mah heat?*

As she swung into the final refrain, Ginnie knew she was home. Hundreds of inflated condoms tumbled from the darkness high above the lights, they floated down, blue, red, pink, green, stippled and ribbed. Some of the kids grabbed them, others punched them gently back into the air. This moment was hers. They were hers. She made love to each and every one, male, female, just as they did to her. The contract was so simple, so beautifully simple.

*Lemme touch you where you've never been*
*touched before, lemme pour the juice of love,*
*lemme touch you till you glisten,*
*and you're cryin' out for more! More! More!*

Her eyes never wavered as she slipped a small phial from beneath her waistband, flat enough to be undetectable, and filled with oil. Lotus oil was what Mick Delaney, her manager, called it. In fact it was baby oil because she couldn't stand the sweet fug of the real thing, but what the fans didn't know wouldn't harm anyone.

*Lemme pour the juice of love!* she whined and panted, her arousal almost real as she unscrewed the phial and cupped her hand to receive the oil with the reverence of a high priestess. Down below the kids imitated her movements. Those who had been wearing long-sleeved sweaters and black T-shirts had by now removed them.

They stood, smearing oil up along their arms in imitation of Virgin. But she went one step further, as always.

*Lemme touch you everywhere!*

Luke O'Regan gasped. He had no oil and he was too shy to use it. Although he had witnessed the ritual oiling before, he could scarcely believe his eyes as the other kids smoothed on the stuff. The place stank of sweet oil and sweat.

Her final gesture, the one that shocked him to the core, came just as the song reached its climax. One of the group came forward and she thrust herself at him, egged him on, teased him, goaded him to come closer, her hands beckoning, her expression one of undisguised lust. She moved towards him, then just as he was about to touch her, darted back quickly. She moved again, withdrew again. Finally, he caught her, held her and tugged quickly at her breasts. As he did so, two shiny scraps of material came away in his hands. She grabbed the light fabric and tossed them far out. They flickered and drifted, caught in the warm air currents. The youngsters up front fell on them, only to be separated by the security men.

*Lemme touch you, touch you where you ne-eed it!* she sang, her voice rising raucous, higher and higher as she oiled her nipples where they protruded from the cones of her Pap-halter.

Luke struggled to control the insistent hardening within his jeans as Virgin continued to circle each nipple with a forefinger, her expression one of smiling ecstasy. She reminded him of a saint, a picture in his mother's bedroom of a young woman with a crucifix resting on her arm the way other women held babies. The face was the same – radiant, glowing, slightly strange – and there was the halo, except that Virgin's halo was mauve and orange, like a corona flaming out from behind her head and shoulders.

The glorious sound faded, only to be drowned out by a rumpus towards the back of the stadium. Ginnie bowed and bowed again, danced to the left and to the right, opened her arms in an embracing gesture, kissed the air a dozen times, repeatedly murmured her love and thanks through the microphone.

It was time to clear out. The Guardians of Christian Destiny had arrived, once more too late. Luke could see what was happening. In the middle of the final number he'd heard the battering at the doors, picked up the sound of some deep and aggressive chant which came from beyond the building. He glanced back once, saw the security men struggle to hold the crowd at bay. Only when Virgin got to the end of the final number did the chain of uniformed bodies break, distracted by the hysteria and crush of young people who broke into the aisles around them. Offstage, Mick Delaney clenched his fists, furious that a concert had been interrupted once again.

This time, it was a smallish group, led by a man dressed in a blue suit who bore a wooden cross over one shoulder and numerous pairs of rosary beads on each arm. They burst through as Ginnie made her exit. Although he was frightened, Luke booed and barracked with the other kids. Some spat at the intruders. Luke felt sick in the pit of his stomach.

"Close one that!" Ginnie gasped to Mick, backstage. "They're following us all over the fucking country, what're we going to do?"

"Take it easy, honey, they can't do a damn thing," Mick muttered, as he put his arm around her shoulders, "The

16

police are on the way. Listen pet, you were fan-tastic, you have them in the palm of your hand, that's what!"

"Next stop America?"

Ginnie slid from beneath his arm. She was distracted. The Guardians were regular disruptors. Family planning clinics. Literary gatherings. Gay nightclubs. Libraries, entered en masse in order to object to the presence of certain books. Rock concerts. They were there, active but laughed at, derided, especially by the media.

Derision, Ginnie reflected, was not always the wisest response. Even tonight, she thought she glimpsed one of their ridiculous, emotive posters in the half-light, an image of an unformed human waved in the air as the Guardians made their way down the aisles of the stadium.

"America? Maybe. Anyway, let's hightail it out of here. That lot might do more damage than we think."

"Like what?"

"Like banjaxing the bus. You never know, honey." He squeezed her shoulder.

Ginnie was out of breath, exhausted and sweating, beads of perspiration on her forehead and upper lip, her body drenched.

"But trust your uncle Mick!"

He swaggered off to deal with the roadies who had begun to dismantle the amplification system. Pity there was no time for an encore, he thought, cursing the sons of bitches who showed up with increasing regularity at too many of Virgin's gigs.

# two

## Luke

Luke jumped as the alarm-clock rang, then dived to one side of the bed to knock it off, his hand dropping like a dead weight on the chipped metallic timepiece. What he needed, he thought, was a fancy little radio-clock that hummed, something modern and efficient, perhaps with a built-in coffee-maker. Bedroom aero-dynamics, he snorted in half-sleep.

His eyes adjusted to the light and he pushed himself up against the headboard to make sure that he stayed awake, then lay still, on the brink of sleep once again. With an effort, he opened his eyes. He was like a horse. He could sleep on his feet if necessary. When he slept, he died. Sleep meant the colour black, all soft and comforting, cut through sometimes by randy dreams, the kind of unreal stuff that would find its way into those magazines Tod Grimley's father brought in from his trips abroad.

It was June the eleventh. He yawned. He was shagged. He'd cut the silage on their own land over the past two days, working the long swards until after dark, his way lit by the tractor headlamps. But the tiredness came from

18

another source too, a well of despair that floated deep within him. It was as if his entire life were being wasted. And now, morning had come too soon. Work as bloody usual, spuds to be harvested in north County Dublin, the first crop of Queens.

This year, he had to do better than last year's effort. Word had it then that he couldn't possibly take over where Mark O'Regan had left off. But he pushed to hold on to every contract his father had ever had, from the first crops through to July silage, straight through to his favourite time, the grain harvesting from late July to mid-September.

He thought of those months as his flatland time, his attention was trained on the duty and the lust to do everything, change everything. To make things work. Waking then was waking to flatland time. The house was built into a rise, practically the only hump in the land in that area. He could look out and see flatness forever, fields unbroken by hedges, the Dublin mountains a dim grey rumpling to the east; to the west, the black lip which hinted at bog and the conical bump of the Hill of Allen. The air smelt of bog too. Everybody burnt turf; no matter what new-fangled range or burner was installed for heating purposes, people still used turf.

He lived in the bit of Ireland which the teachers at school described in geography lessons as the middle of the saucer. The whole island was a saucer, surrounded by mountains on all sides, and the flatlands in the middle were the equivalent of the middle part that dipped to hold a cup.

His mother always got up to keep him company, wet the tea and see to the fowl. But before he could face the day he would lie back and examine the ceiling. That y-crack which had run through the plaster for as long as he

19

could remember, seemed right-on interesting just then. Someday he would travel every river in the world. That wavering, long crack was a good omen that different experiences awaited him, great waterways, cities, adventure and women. Experience. His favourite word. He thought of the rivers as female, a bit like the women he lived in hope of meeting – the Mississippi, from Minnesota to New Orleans, the Nile Delta, the Moldau, historic and bloody. He'd traced them all on maps like all the female bodies he wanted to run his hands over, again and again, until he found whatever it was he was looking for and would drown himself in it or die.

He wouldn't be a farming contractor forever. He had no intention of breaking his balls in the driving seats of combines and cutters and tractors for the rest of his life. One day he'd pay someone else, a whole team of men, to do that, if it had to be done. Much as he liked being out in all weathers, much as he enjoyed odd moments, like looking back along a headland, observing the sweep of the silage-cutter and the clean sward in its wake, and scatterings of gulls and crows, there were things which he wanted more fiercely.

Experience. Sex.

He was driven, in one form or another, whipped on and on through the present, blistering with anger about the recent past; desire would heap itself like livid coals on his soul until he made a future for himself.

"Luke."

"I'm awake."

His mother moved down the hall of the old stone bungalow, into the kitchen. He loved to listen to the clunking sounds, distant but distinguishable: a low rumble which suggested water gushing into the kettle; the sound of delph being placed hurriedly on the table; a door opening, then shutting with a dull bang.

Sometimes when Luke thought ahead he felt afraid. He didn't fear for his dreams, so much as what had to be lived through first.

He drew back the curtains. June 11th. A pale, limp day. A good day for operating big machinery out in the open.

He missed his father. It broke in him every so often, a deep, raw ache in the chest that could suck the light from a day. Two years before, the old man came in one evening after a day in south Kildare. He ate his dinner, sat back in the armchair for a cup of tea and complained of indigestion, then opened and closed his hands, said he had pins and needles. They'd all been there. Before anybody could move, he keeled over in agony, clutching at his chest.

Luke remembered the hysterical cries, then the silent horror of the younger ones as it dawned on them that their father had simply died in the space of half a minute. His eyes stung at the memory, all he could hear this cool, June morning was the sound of his own voice shouting "Daddy-Daddy-Daddy!", his mother trying in desperation to resuscitate the man, and Mary, who was only fourteen then, shrieking into the telephone at the doctor. In those few moments, his skin palled, then purpled, his lips took on a bloodless tinge.

He died the following morning at the hospital, wired up to gadgetry and drips, with a pace-maker in his thigh.

Afterwards, everything changed. He didn't know who he was and who he could become. He put his plans for travelling the world on the long finger. That was to be before he headed to Dublin to study medicine. He hadn't

21

even done the Leaving and, at seventeen, had begun to take over where his father left off.

"You don't have to," his mother had said. "I can hire someone."

But hiring was expensive; it would mean doubling their work to meet the extra cost or else cutting their income by half. Luke insisted. The younger ones had to be educated and, even if he was young, he was now nineteen. A man. He wouldn't see his mother short.

It was only when he looked back that he realised how shy she was, uneasy in towns and cities, comfortable rearing a variety of fowl which ranged from heavy, plump ducks to speckled guinea-hens, as well as the usual Rhode Island Reds. Her duck liver pâté (Malla Meadow Pâtés) sold well in delicatessens throughout the area.

His nose ran and ran. He blew it and then dressed, told himself that there was no point blubbering. Wise up and forget the past, he told himself, concentrate on the present and plan for the future.

"CYO," he even said aloud, a private acronym: *cop yourself on*.

But worry was an established habit. He opened the bathroom window and looked out across the duck-pens. The wind had dropped, the sky was clearing. Some people could have the life of Reilly on a day like this, he thought. Off to the lakes, scrambling, dossing; fellows his own age perhaps, home from college, or about to set off to America on holiday visas, picking up summer work and new experiences while there. What had they to worry about, with two parents and a working father?

Here he was, stuck at home trying to earn enough lolly for Mary, Ferdia and Tom's education. Mary was bright, but in Luke's view lazy. He'd have to have a word with her at the end of August. If she wasn't prepared to work, there was no sense in her going to that convent school. She was man-mad too. OK, so he was girl-mad, but he was nineteen and she was only sixteen. She had nothing else to do except work hard at school. It was the least she could do. And Ferdia. No aptitude for anything in evidence in his fifteen-year old life. He tinkered around with broken electrical gadgets, but that was the height of it. Tom, the youngest, would probably be all right. At thirteen he'd just finished his first year in secondary school and had come first in the class.

He drew a razor with a harsh swipe along his chin, knowing it was hardly necessary because his fuzz was so fine. But Luke had got into the habit of this particular ritual. It was essential. He used old razors which had belonged to his father. Sometimes he imagined his father peering over his shoulder, as he turned his head this way and that in the mirror. Yet when he imagined him he could never recall his eyes, or what his look would have said. He'd like him to have said something like "Right on, son, you're doin' grand!" but deep down he knew that wasn't his father's style. He wasn't a right-on customer by any stretch of the imagination. He rinsed his face and slapped on a palmful of Eau Sauvage, a present from an aunt the Christmas before.

He and his mother mumbled something to one another. They were quiet first thing in the morning, didn't get involved in too much chat. They were alike in appearance and manner. Her hair was thick and heavy, dark brown, drawn back with a couple of hairpins into a soft French roll along the back of her head. Her eyes were serious – like Luke's, according to the family know-alls who saved such comments for christenings and weddings – hazel

23

speckled with green. But where she was of medium build, he had grown tall. In the past two years his bones had stretched, his wrists had lengthened and his nose had acquired a slightly aquiline form. He was not sure whether this was a good or a bad thing. He didn't want to have a great beak, uncertain of the dividing line between an interesting profile and one that made people think of Concorde. His mother thought him handsome, had noted the nudges and smiles of groups of girls in the town whenever Luke passed by. But then, mothers always found something beyond the beyonds in their children's looks. If he had a girlfriend, she knew nothing about it.

His mother poured herself another cup of tea and gazed out the window while he scooped up the last of his cereal. It would do him good to have a girlfriend, she thought. He lived too seriously. At times she fretted about him, afraid he would become too sensible, an old head foisted on young shoulders. He was still a boy, even if he did run the business.

"Tea?" She lifted the pot.

Luke nodded, bit into a slice of bread. "I'll have to rush," he mumbled, his mouth full.

"Where are you today – near the airport, is it?"

"Ummm. Ten acres of Queens coming in. For Thornley."

"You'd best be along, so."

He gulped down a cup of tea, then pushed his chair back and sat for a moment. They exchanged looks, the mood between them an easy one. Another day, another step forward, and they'd manage, was what that look said.

"I'll get moving too" she said, "I've a pile of livers in the fridge. Mrs de Paor wants three pounds of pâté with plenty of garlic in it."

"Hope you're charging her enough."

"You leave that to me, son. Your mother's no daw when it comes to charging. I've learnt a thing or two in my time."

He lifted the crockery and placed it on the draining-board, filled the sink with water and immersed the lot.

"Leave that, I'll do it. Go on, would you!" his mother ordered.

"See you tonight. Oh, remind Mary that Huddlestons are looking for strawberry-pickers next week. And Ferdia too."

It took over an hour to reach Thornley's place. The tractor and harvester clanked along like unwieldy, slow beasts. He had to put up with stretches of traffic-jams, outer suburban workers trying to make the city in half an hour or less. Cars honked their horns, some took crazy risks by overtaking the harvester on bad bends. One or two drivers gave him the fingers sign, while another went to the trouble of winding down his window to shout that people like him should be off the road by eight o'clock; did he not realise that some people had to get to work? Luke tossed his head and looked away. Why waste his energy and what humour he had on yobs like that. Ignorant yahoo. Probably a Jackeen gone to live in the country. Thought he owned everything. Why were people over thirty so fucking unpleasant when things didn't go their way? They thought they could do what they liked, wherever they liked. They thought they knew everything, fuck them for dickheads. And cunts. Because some of them were women too. They should be rounded up, the dickheads and the cunts, and flung out into the Irish sea, he fumed.

By the time he got off the main roads, his mood had

improved. Isolated by the roar of the engine, he noticed little except how the noise was occasionally penetrated by the drone of a plane approaching Dublin Airport. He checked the inside pocket of his jacket with one hand, slowed to put on his headphones and pressed the switch on his Walkman. Immediately, Virgin's voice hummed in his ear.

*Don't talk, don't talk,*
*just lie here close beside me,*
*a woman doesn't have many chances in this life,*
*so don't talk, because you know ah lo-ove yo-ouu,*
*let me touch you, touch you, touch you,*
*let me hold you to mah bo-ody!*

He'd hold himself to her body all right, just let him at it. He'd had no time to think about last night's concert. Virgin, he thought, oh Virgin! Again, he relived the experience of hearing her sing, watching her dance, the sight of her body, the way she moved, how free she seemed, and the warmth of her voice when she spoke to the audience.

And tonight she was coming to Malla. He was out of his head with excitement. He shouldn't be on the bloody roads at all. For once, he wouldn't have to make a long drive, for once he could just hop into the jeep and actually be at the concert hall ten or fifteen minutes later!

*Virgin. Virgin. Virgin.* He repeated the name quietly as the music played and she howled with pleasure. That was the kind of girl he wanted to meet. The kind he wanted to lay. Not a slag. Not a haughty bitch either. A free spirit, who would love him and adore him and want him to love and adore her. Virgin had it all; she was the proof. There had to be others like her, or maybe just one, that one, special person who could be his alone.

He steered the machine around the turn which led to the farm. A jumbo skimmed low across the fields to his left, making its approach to the airport. Another mile, this time of narrow, poorly surfaced country road. Whitethorn blossom fell like snow in the breeze. It was always like this close to the coast, cooler, breezier, yet the first crops were ready by mid-June every year on these sandy stretches.

He thought again about Virgin, her legs and breasts, how she flung her arms wide in a gesture of open, easy love. She was – he tried to think of the right word – *uninhibited*. That was it. No holds barred there. *Yippeee,* he howled mentally, up and at it, *ya boya!* Just as the tractor rounded the last corner and made to turn into the gap of the field, the harvester caught against a low stone wall. It was nothing but a graze, but it brought Thornley running towards him with a face like the devil. You'd swear I'd driven through it, Luke thought, as he removed his headphones. He hopped down to check what damage, if any, had been done. So much for Virgin. Best keep his mind on work for the rest of the day. Time enough later on for sex. To think about it. *Sex*. He suppressed the word again. It was pure dynamite.

"Sorry about that. No damage done," he called to John Thornley.

"Just as well. I've enough on me plate without havin' to build new walls," Thornley groused.

"Trailer at the ready?" Luke enquired by way of a reminder that he, at least, was set to work.

Thornley nodded. "I'll drive her myself. Start over yonder, on the west side. And mind that hedge. Fella that

27

did this job last year got the grill tangled in them ash-plants. Mind that," he warned.

Luke eased the tractor along the perimeter, over to the far side of the field. It was a massive rectangle, dense with potato plants, a haze of deep green from one end to the other. Thornley followed behind with his tractor and trailer. Luke started up and made straight for the drills, watching as the metal scoops lifted potatoes, plants and clay, then sent the lot thudding along the metal bars of the riddle. It glinted in the sun as dry soil spilled back down again and creamy-skinned potatoes went rattling up the grill to the point where they fell off and into Thornley's waiting trailer.

*Pommes de terre.* Luke resurrected the distant phrase from his schooldays, one of the few bits of French he remembered. Apples of the earth. It always seemed to be an airy-fairy way of describing the good old spud, not half as serious as potato, which was all about being up to your arse in wet clay, planting or picking, till your toenails nearly grew roots. But the French phrase was better, he thought, and didn't remind him of the clatter of steaming saucepans in kitchens on damp days. Somehow, apples of the earth made him think of fruit and good crack, and something which was welcome in people's lives, rather than just spud-ordinary.

He glanced over in Thornley's direction. The man fixed him with a stare. A prickly get. Luke heard he drove a hard bargain, though it was also said that he paid when the job was done. That was the best you could hope for with the big farmers. No easy deals but, occasionally, payment on the spot. Thornley watched him like a hawk, ready to find fault and criticise if Luke slowed the machine.

"Keep her goin, keep her goin!" he shouted roughly, "I haven't got all day to dither!"

Luke speeded up again. He had paused to avoid a hare that darted out from the hedge in front of the harvester. The next field was a meadow. There were probably leverets as well, he thought.

They took no break in the middle of the morning, which suited Luke. He liked to work until lunch and then stop for three-quarters of an hour. It also showed new customers his keenness. By half past twelve they had covered more than half the field. At that rate he'd be finished completely by four at the latest. That would give him an hour and a quarter to get home, plenty of time to prepare for Virgin's concert.

He slowed and waved to Thornley.

"Time we stopped," he shouted. Thornley nodded. His trailer was full for the fifth time, with well-shaped top quality new potatoes.

They strode slowly across to the other side of the field.

"I suppose you're busy from now on?" Thornley asked quietly, hands in his pockets, eyes fixed to the ground.

"I'm fairly well booked up – a few breaks here and there. I'll be working through to the end of September."

"That's not a bad complaint."

Thornley hoisted his trousers up around his waist and glanced at Luke. Not a bad boy that O'Regan, he could see that now. You never knew with young people. Boys in particular. Likely to gad off at the drop of a hat, leave you in the lurch with a field full of grain or spuds.

"You'll be back later?" Luke asked.

"Oh, I'm stayin' put," Thornley replied, "I like to eat out on a good day."

They settled themselves down beneath the hedge. Luke

was ravenous. He opened his lunchbox and wolfed down three sandwiches, stopping occasionally to take a gulp of milk from a carton. Thornley ate more sedately. He slowly inspected the contents of his wife's tin-foil wrapped lunch before he picked up a sausage roll and looked at it, waving it in the air as if he was about to make an important point.

"Grand pastry," he sighed after the first bite. "You're not married yourself, I take it?"

Luke smiled. "No. Nothing like that."

"No. I suppose not. Too soon to be thinkin' along those lines."

"Far too soon."

Marriage! He wouldn't be caught going down that road, not for as long as he could manage it. Even if it did hold certain attractions. Otherwise, people wouldn't be in such a ram-stam rush to get hitched in the first place.

Silence fell between them. It was mild, the whole field lit with contrasting shades and colours, the newly-opened drills a rich, deep brown, the remaining potato-plants sturdy and full-leafed in the sun. Birds swooped low, hundreds of crows, jackdaws, magpies, gulls, even thrushes and blackbirds. They circled and signalled up at the far end of the field, waged raucous territorial wars along the new stretch of spilled earth.

Luke lashed into his sixth sandwich, a tuna and lettuce one which he knew Ferdia had had a hand in making because it was full of mustard. No matter. He took another swig from the carton, swallowed away the burn of too much mustard and settled back. His eyes closed and opened. John Thornley farted quietly, then belched, and opened a flask of tea.

When the smell of the earth had been stirred and

rushed to his nostrils, it was like cutting into a huge loaf of his mother's yeast bread; hot and moist all at the same time. The moment the harvester scooped up the earth, he smelled the wetness of young roots and sun-warmed soil. It reminded him of the smell of himself sometimes. Sappy. Whatever it was, he liked it.

John Thornley drowsed off, mouth open. Luke checked his watch. They had time, another twenty minutes or so. He got up quietly and wandered further along the field to relieve himself. He faced absently into a ditch. Where was life going to lead him? How could he make it a good one? Where in God's name would he ever find a woman?

He had to find a woman. A giddiness, sometimes he thought it was madness, had settled on him in recent months, the like of which he'd never felt before. No matter what work he took on, it was there, eating at him, driving him crazy with desire. Everywhere he looked, he saw women. Big women, slim women, fat ones, thin ones, curvy ones. You could hardly turn without seeing their legs, the curve of calf-muscles, their knees, hints of thighs as their skirts blew in the wind. He remembered an Italian movie on the telly only the week before. He was as desperate as the Italian simpleton in the story who eventually went up into a tree and yelled out all over the countryside for everyone to hear, *'Voglio una signora!',* until this ferocious dwarf of a nun got him to come down again.

At night he would imagine a woman. She had no recognisable face until recently, when he'd tried to give her Virgin's face, but that hadn't worked. For some reason, Virgin played no part in his fantasies as he lay in bed, eyes squeezed shut as he imagined what the woman of his dreams might do, what he might do to her.

He turned and made his way back to Thornley. The

31

older man stretched, hands behind his head, gazed out across the field with a satisfied glint in his eye.

"Want to head back?"

"Ah, take your time son."

*Son.* He'd changed his tune since morning. Luke sat down again and thought. Happiness swept down on him in the way a flight of birds might cut through the garden on a sunny winter day, and all because he was looking forward to the Virgin concert. Soon, Thornley stood and decided that it was time to work. They strolled back through the drills and began again. Time passed in a roar of steady activity, the harvester rattled and clacked, potatoes thudded into Thornley's trailer, cries of gulls vaguely audible above the drone of engines, the clanking of a loose wingshaft on one of the tractors.

As he moved along the last two drills, Luke thought about his father. They hardly knew one another, not really. He wondered what he would think if he could see him today, doing everything he had done, and more. He nearly laughed out loud. Mad for a ride too. Ready to shag a chink in a wall. What would his father think of that? Would he understand? Had he ever been that way? He thought his father would be proud of the way he had managed to keep the business on. Not that the bloody aul business was everything. There were more important things in life, but his father's approval would have meant a lot. When you had to sit down and think about survival, when nobody could advise you, you discovered a lot about yourself, Luke thought. In the past eighteen months a new, unfamiliar mood of independence, which had something to do with his father's death, had taken hold of him. It was, he knew, part of the man he was becoming. It seemed somehow real. He could trust it.

It seemed as if he had little in common with others of his own age. He found it hard not to feel above them, more mature, not to scoff at their hanging on the say-so of parents who could still decide what was best for them. Probably that was how he'd have been too, had his father lived. Summer work around home, then maybe he would have spent time in Europe grape-picking, or in the canning factories of the Netherlands, off the leash for a couple of months. A chance to learn all about Dutch women. Fast as greased lightning, Tod said, even though he hadn't been to Holland.

He turned the tractor again, keeping John Thornley's tractor and trailer within view so that the potatoes would fall neatly off the chute and not over the ground. Thornley was about the same age as his father, he guessed, a more easy-going yoke if his lunchtime performance was anything to judge by. He couldn't ever imagine his father dozing like that in the middle of the day, or eating as slowly as that, as if he really enjoyed his nosh. Thornley would live to be a hundred. With his father, everything had been hurried. Because of this, being around home felt like trying to make the Westport train on a Friday afternoon at Heuston Station. You felt late, late, late, or else not good enough, or not fast enough, whenever he was around. Summer was not the best time to know his father.

Christmas was a different matter. It was their quietest time. Fields of winter corn sprouted here and there, but people were busy fixing up machinery, or they sized up whether or not to invest in new equipment; then there was the annual audit, and more work for his mother as she fixed up the accounts. *That hoor's boot, McNab,* his father used to say, whenever the auditor was due.

Only during the run-up to Christmas Eve would his father begin to relax. The house was chockablock with callers, neighbours with bottles of whiskey wrapped in brown paper bags, gifts in the form of hams, turkey, game which they didn't need, and smoked salmon. The men would sit around drinking and smoking while his mother hovered, filling glasses and re-filling as necessary. It was the time of year when he was most aware of other men. The women were too busy, dashing between house and shop, or stuck in kitchens over steaming saucepans of puddings. It was also the time when he noticed how men hung loose together, how they went about their chat, the slow, neutral introduction to any conversation usually about the weather, milk prices, or the failure of MEPs to think about the needs of places like Ireland, Scotland or Greece. After they knocked back the first drink, things warmed up. The men gossiped away like hens, they spun yarns confident as you like with one another, they laughed and wheezed and argued and drank till his mother marched in to remove the bottles and made moves to start washing glasses.

Last Christmas had been the first without Daddy. It was the worst time he had ever experienced. Everything was normal on the outside, and all the weirder. They'd put up decorations, a tree, a crib with an orange star above the manger. His mother had draped garlands of pine-cones above the open fire and they gave off a foresty smell in the warmth, cracking every so often as one of their wings popped loose. The food had been the same, the table laid with creamy linen, with a golden centre-piece of painted ivy and mistletoe. It surrounded the plaited red candle that threw soft shadows on their faces once it was lit. But nobody sat where Daddy had once sat, nobody would fill that place at the table.

34

Just as his mother had served the dinner, a horrible silence fell that more or less smothered their chat; Tom threw down his fork and began bawling his head off. The sight of him brought on the tears in the rest of them. Soon Mrs O'Regan was sitting with her head in her hands, saying that they must carry on, that somehow they had to carry on, her voice a murmur over Tom's sobs. Luke rose and left the room, dry-eyed but unable to touch his food, followed by Mary, who ran down the hall to her bedroom screaming something about not being able to stand the atmosphere in this kip.

The stillness of that afternoon tormented him. It was as if the whole world was dead. They might as well have been living in a shagging tomb. He gazed out of his own bedroom-window, listened for hours to the silence, the occasional shrieking bird, the sound of a twig snapping in the garden.

Later, when it was dark, the family ate a re-heated dinner and tried to laugh at their earlier behaviour.

"If he could only see us now!" Mary giggled, eyes red-rimmed, digging Tom in the side with her elbow to see if she could make him laugh.

"Just as well he can't!" Luke replied angrily. He didn't expect to be so raging mad, but he knew that at that moment, any soft, loving feelings he might have felt towards their father had gone. It wasn't as if his father had died on purpose or left them in the lurch out of spite. But he *had* left them in the lurch. At least that was what it felt like. Daddy was a selfish get who had never taken the time to get to know them while he was alive. Now here they were, sitting around whining and whinging because he was gone. *Bastard, bastard, bastard,* he repeated silently, and felt relief in the words. He promised himself that they would never have another Christmas like this one, that even if it meant not being at home, he'd prefer it.

Early in January, he picked up some brochures from the travel agent in Malla, winter holiday ones. Maybe that was what he'd do the following year. They couldn't all go but maybe he'd take himself off to the Canaries, or to Austria.

"Hey! Wake up!"

It was Thornley. Luke stirred, then realised that he'd finished the last run almost on automatic, that he'd turned the tractor towards the exit and was staring at the hedge on the opposite side of the road. Embarrassed, he smiled at Thornley.

"Sorry. I was thinking."

Thornley grunted. "Serious stuff, I'd say," he replied archly. "Anyway, we're finished. Grand work. Now . . . we have to have an argument about money."

Luke repeated the sum mentioned when Thornley had phoned a month earlier. The man hummed and hawed and made huge work out of writing the cheque, his hand slow and deliberate. Luke said nothing. He usually let the farmers ramble on about costs, overheads and being run into the ground. His mother said they knew damn well they were getting good value for money, even if they didn't get it for nothing. All he had to do was let them talk on and keep his own mouth shut until the cheque was signed.

"Sound," he said to Thornley, pocketing the cheque after examining it carefully.

"I'll be in touch." Thornley banged his fist against the wing-shaft with such force that Luke thought he'd knocked it off.

The traffic was slacker on the way home. People were

more relaxed, less inclined to blast horns and pull faces behind the safety of windscreens if they were caught behind the tractor.

His ears rang from the constant roar of machinery, and he decided he'd have to start wearing mufflers to save his hearing. By the time he pulled into the yard, a mile outside Malla, he was exhausted, and, again, starving. He yanked on the handbrake, set the machine in gear and hopped out. His arms and back ached from the vibration of the steering-wheel, and he felt a bit spaced out.

# Three

## That Guy in Black

Luke lay in the bath turning the hot tap on and off with his toes. He had plenty of time. Mary was out, so he had the whole place to himself. His thoughts settled once more on Virgin.

Every woman he'd ever fancied became a complete gom compared to *her*. They were only girls, not real women. Before his father died there had been a trail of girls, and any amount of time for fluting around with them; nights out with the fellows from St Brendan's Comprehensive, when something interesting might just happen. He remembered how giddy and tense they'd be, the day before a disco or a party, none of the lads ready to admit just how keyed-up they were, or the real cause of the excitement, but hell-bent on wrestling one another up against the classroom walls, elbow sword-fighting, telling jokes about pussy and cunt and hole and how Tod Grimley got his wool the previous weekend. But it was all show and, he admitted, shifting uneasily in the bath as he forgot to turn off the hot tap yet again, they were pure scared, running yellow at the prospect of having to deal with the girls.

Some fellows got their fathers' cars on loan for the night, which meant female company at least at the end of the dancing, followed by a good fast drive out the country, ripping up and down narrow roads with two or three snogging couples crammed in along with whoever'd pulled the short straw to drive.

A favourite haunt was the ruins of the Westross Castle, and the fields and forests around it. His father once said something about the goings-on there after the Civil War, had disapproved of the burning and ransacking back in the twenties. Luke loved being out there at night, in the ruins, even if the place had just been turned into a leisure park. At night, when the day-trippers and families had gone off home to tea, warm baths and bedtime stories, it was still one of the most secret places. The lake edges were thick with bushes, purple with flowers, surrounded by dry mud paths and strange, funny-looking trees, things which he'd seen in his mother's gardening book but which they never even thought of planting. Then there was the oniony smell at the top of the hill near the castle ruins, wild garlic, his mother said. The giant redwood trees he recognised from a pictorial atlas at home and the bit on California. Here, the redwoods were named after members of the Westross family, who named everything in sight and commemorated everything that died. Even their dogs, a graveyard for bloody dogs, hidden beyond a willow copse.

They'd park at the bottom of the hill and walk to the top, swinging bottles of cider or beer, cracking jokes to impress the girls. Everything, Luke thought, was for the benefit of the girls. Nowadays he wouldn't give a shag about any of them, spoilt, giddy Misses and college girls.

He was jealous of their freedom. But then, up to two years ago, hadn't he felt just like them? Part of the local scene, he was always invited to parties, to raves in big barns out in the country. The invitations began to fall off about six months after his father's death, when he couldn't make time to accept any of them. But he survived. He felt different now, and he *was* different.

Occasionally he ran into Tod Grimley, whose father owned the mill and had been friendly with his own father.

"Well, Luke, any crack?" Tod would say casually.

"Not the kind that'd interest you." Luke would answer. Luke liked Tod. His mother said he was a hound and that sooner or later he'd get into big trouble.

"You're a hound, that's what my mother says. Did you know that?" Luke drawled at him only recently. Tod guffawed.

Tod's father had bought a one-roomed country schoolhouse, long fallen into disuse, just as a place where his large family could hold huge brawls of parties. Old man Grimley was like that, kind to a fault, and free with money. The Grimley parties gave rise to talk, the warm crimson of the specially-installed centre strobes which flickered from the shuttered windows suggesting all kinds of carry-on to the people of the locality. He hadn't taken Ecstasy himself for – how long was it? – a year and a half. Easy as pie. A dream night. He'd danced himself to exhaustion, remembered how easy it'd been, all of them there, arms around one another, dancing their heads off until someone hosed them down with cold water and lined up pints of water. Outsiders, older people, wouldn't have understood. It amused him to figure out just how they got their kicks. Some of them looked as if they were half-dead anyway, one foot in the grave types before they'd even hit forty.

But that must be what it meant to be getting old, Luke

thought, as he stepped from the bath and examined his body before the full-length mirror. He was never going to turn out like them. Hung-up on everything. Afraid of everything from sex to sex. He sniggered. He turned sideways and puffed out his chest slightly, before facing himself again. Dissatisfied with what he saw, he pulled a face and threw down the towel, went to the hot press in search of underclothing, a clean T-shirt, socks. Hound that he was, Tod would be at the Virgin Concert too.

There was one girl though – Kathleen Quinlan. Kathleen's sister was killed in a freak car accident the year beforehand and Kathleen was sad-looking. She didn't laugh in the way other girls did, didn't scream or giggle or stare through him with the sole purpose of mortifying him like some of those bitches did. Luke felt comfortable with her.

One night they'd paired off and she went with him out to Westross Castle. It was stormy, the moon playing games behind a veil of light cloud. There were seven of them in the car, including Tod, and by the time they had reached the summit of the hill and rambled around the lakes and through the ruins until they came to the old wine-cellars, they were in high spirits, their hair tousled by the high winds. Sprawled against the cellar wall, Luke risked putting an arm around her shoulders, felt her boniness beneath his wrist. Once, she turned and he nearly jumped out of his skin when she placed a gentle kiss on his cheek, but by the time he'd got over the shock of it she'd turned away again, so they both sat for perhaps an hour, drinking cider, him electrified to the ground.

Then Tod became restless, and began to score swastikas on the old blockwork. A bit of sparring between himself and one of the other fellows resulted in the empties getting smashed against the block walls of the cellar. The sound of breaking glass seemed vicious in the stillness of the night, in the beautiful aloneness of that place.

Kathleen stood up, her face white.

"Stop it!" she screamed, "Stop it!"

They all gaped as she began to cry and asked Luke to bring her home. Then she told him not to bother, that she'd find her own way home, that she wouldn't have been there in the first place if her sister was alive, because they'd be off somewhere else having a great time and not wasting a night out with a crowd of yobs and lachicos like them.

As he bent over the basin washing his teeth, Luke remembered her small, hurt face; now he understood her rage and exactly why she'd wept. Because her whole life had changed and she was expected to carry on and have fun like every other young person. But it wasn't like that. When someone died, it was like as if a door had got blown down by a storm, and all you could see ahead was the view down this long, long, corridor, a horrible, colourless corridor with a pinprick wall at the other end. You knew you'd go down that corridor someday, whether you liked it or not. That was the thing. That was what he and Kathleen knew now. He was so inept, so cack-handed that he let her go off on her own, stood with his hands by his sides listening to the others asking what the hell was wrong with Miss Prissy.

Five minutes later he pulled himself together and ran after her. She had a good start and must have run, because it took a long time to catch up. She stopped as he caught her by the arm. "Kathleen!" was all he could say just then.

But it was enough, because she smiled and slowed

down and even took his hand. They walked the five miles back into Malla by themselves, let the car pass them half an hour later with its horn tooting and lights flashing, Tod grinning out of the open window at them. It was a long walk. Neither spoke for most of the way. They just walked, and Luke held her hand. Every so often she would squeeze it and he'd squeeze back. By the time they approached the town it was dawn, birds sang and the sun slid up from the horizon like an orange, burning away the mist over the roofs of Malla.

But they made no arrangement to meet afterwards and the latest he'd heard was that Kathleen had left home and taken a flat in the town, near Grimley's mill office, where she worked.

Just as Luke finished, Mary knocked on the bathroom door, an impatient rap which he decided to ignore.

"Lu-uke!" she whined in growing agitation, knocking again, "let me in, I've got to change, I'm in a hur-ry!"

"Coming," he called casually, taking a last look at himself in the mirror. Hair slicked back, his skin was clean-shaven; he flexed his biceps. He wore black denims and a black T-shirt with cutaway shoulders. Feeling – this once – satisfied with his efforts, he opened the door, humming one of Virgin's hits,

*Oooh, it's that guy in black, that guy in black,*
*He's headin' for mah heart and he's never goin'*
*back*

Mary looked at him, a smile on her face.
"No need to ask where you're goin'."
"What of it?" he said defensively.
"Nothin'."

43

She breezed past and bolted the door. "Have a good time!" she sang before turning on the shower.

As he switched on the ignition in the jeep, his heart contracted with excitement, reminding, reassuring him that Virgin was really coming to Malla! Right now she was on her way.

The roads were clogged. Cars, motor-cycles, a van with floral curtains and foreign number-plates and the words *Atomkraft? Nein danke!* beneath the back windows, parked some distance outside the town. The young people walked in groups, droves of them, many dressed in black, the girls skittish and high-voiced, their hair coloured to match Virgin's as they swung along the paths and fields that led to the hall. Every so often the public address system sputtered and spat and a self-important voice could be heard going *one-two-three-testing*. The voice belonged to the councillor who, despite opposition from locals, authorised the event after the owner of the hall – some guy in Dublin – had agreed, and on whose neck the axe would drop if the town was vandalised. Luke laughed to himself. There'd be hell to pay if the roads and pathways were littered with condoms and chip-bags after the gig. They probably would be. He drove past the sign just a mile from the town which proclaimed *Malla. A Good Place to Live!*, weaving the jeep slowly towards the grounds of the Catholic church, where he swung in and braked so fast that it skidded on loose gravel and barely missed smashing into the rear of a highly-polished black BMW.

Out on the streets, he joined up with hundreds of other devotees as they streamed towards the hall. For once, he was part of something; already, the day's crappy details slipped away like an unwanted garment.

The queue which trailed from the entrance had trebled

back on itself, the air whirred with hundreds of voices, footsteps, fragments of music from ghetto-blasters, and over that the clear, unmistakable sound of an early Virgin track, *Lonely Boy*.

Luke chatted with three students who had travelled from Cork for the gig. They'd taken the train to Athlone, missed their connection to Malla and walked six miles that afternoon before finally getting a lift which brought them the last thirty-eight miles of the journey. He was surrounded by strangers, the local kids absorbed into a teeming influx of visitors from Dublin and Galway, others from the North, others again from places he'd never heard of. It didn't matter where they came from. At a Virgin gig, everybody spoke the same language. Everybody was dead-on.

The big hall in Malla was the largest provincial auditorium of its kind, a circular, domed edifice used for political conventions, boxing matches, Feiseanna, beauty and talent festivals and, in recent years, some rock concerts. As far as Luke was concerned, it was the most important building in the country.

Because it existed, Virgin was coming to Malla, like some great bitch of a queen who could save him from disaster. Because of that building, he need not go without the one woman he adored. *Thank you, thank you, thank you, you shower of innocents, little do you know, how little you know!* he whispered, thinking of the councillor, the owner of the hall, the architect who built it back in the sixties and the eejits who financed it, who heated it, who fixed the scaffolding, the seating, the lighting and whatever the hell it took to get Virgin into Malla.

He passed the bouncers, and thanked them and despised them in his head, black-suited security-guards,

45

the evening sun reflecting mother-of-pearl colours on gleaming visors drawn low over their eyes. They hadn't a clue, not a fucking clue, he thought; he imagined them heading off home later that night to wives and children and quiet homes. What did they know about anything! Warm, clammy air wafted across his face – whiffs of perfume, sweat, the circusy funk of sawdust rising from beneath the rows of stacked seating which curved right around the whole building and to either side of the stage. He sniffed again, this time at the sweetness of marijuana and cannabis.

He'd made it. As yet another Virgin lookalike strolled by, he felt again that sharp prod of excitement, a tug of lust that left him hopping for lift-off.

# Four

## Life in the Quarter

Ginnie was the real thing, Mick thought, struggling within a tangle of brown and orange striped sheets. His girl was going to make it like nobody on his books had ever done. He groped for the stool to his left, then realised he was sleeping on a futon, in the new apartment, and that the stool was practically out of reach of where he lay. Eventually, he found his cigarettes and lit up, tried to extinguish the match and lurched around the firm mattress as it fell, still flaring, onto an emerald green quilt. He smashed his fist into the smouldering hole and brushed away the remains of the match.

He rubbed eyes and wondered if he would ever get used to the new living quarters. Chic and expensive as the place was, those white walls took some adjusting to. Hard on the eyes first thing in the morning, especially with a hangover. He was lost without his old bed, taken from his own bedroom at home when the mother wanted rid of it some years ago. Deep as a hammock, it was, it practically wrapped itself around him. And the busted couch, dark yellow velvet with a broken spring or two, that had had to go as well. He could hardly believe it. But he'd allowed himself to be overwhelmed by that young interior designer fella, with his tight backside, graceful gestures, immaculate white-blonde curls and bloody big ideas, advising Mick in the most confidential of voices.

"Trust me, big boy, that thing *has* to go!" he said, tossing a disdainful head in the direction of his old couch. Now he had a black leather suite which, like the futon, was too hard, but also slippery. The only bit of comfort was in the *le Corbusier* lounger, which he'd insisted on.

His thoughts drifted on. Ginnie would need to break into Europe within the next six months. Time was passing. Soon, if he didn't net a solid package, her age would become a problem. Not that he ever said as much. But she knew, they both knew.

Every morning, winter or summer, he woke early. Even if he'd spent half the night in the company of strangers at the sauna. By five am he was turning restlessly in half-sleep, by six he was fully awake and had a pre-breakfast cigarette while he planned the day. In the other place on the North Circular Road, he used to sleep with windows open, whatever the season, and as a result his room smelt neutral, only a hint of his chain-smoking habit lingering in the air. Now however, with the building and renovating that was going on in the warrens of Dublin's Temple Bar, the noise was too much and he slept with windows shut. Behind the avant-garde apartment block, yellow cranes swung loads of precast concrete, the guts of old Dublin were drilled into, ancient leaded roofs were retained, facades propped as rickety interiors were completely reconstructed. Why anybody would want to retain either the roofs or the interiors of some of these joints was beyond him. The area, he sometimes thought, was quite a shabby little quarter made fashionable because certain people had said so.

It was noisy. At night he was kept awake by the clatter of saucepans and crockery from the restaurant kitchen behind the block, or the voices of drunks below on the cobbled streets. Arguments would break out, men and women who couldn't hold their drink screeching stupid, repetitive complaints, airing grudges held secretly against one another and which they would never forgive if they lived to be a hundred.

The thought of Ginnie performing before ten thousand, twenty thousand, even more, made his heart race. The girl had enough ambition, style and talent to make it. There was not the slightest sexual thrill in his imaginings about Ginnie, but it always gave him a depth-charge to think of their earning potential. Manager and star, each needing the other, each helping the other to rise and rise. She was aware of his inclinations. That was why she was so comfortable and confiding with him. Handy. There were no complications where she was concerned. He hoped there would be time for him to find the partner of his dreams. But later. It was always later, when he had accomplished X or Y task. When he had got to where he wanted to be, when success would make him an object of desire to the men he wished would seek him out. But perhaps he'd been making excuses for himself for too many years. Perhaps it was too late. The fact of the matter was that he hadn't met anyone. Women were women, however you looked at it, and that included Ginnie. Though he was fond of Ginnie, no doubt about it. She didn't hassle him. But women could be damn peculiar if you caught them in the wrong mood, that was for sure.

He propped himself on one elbow and ran his fingers through his hair, then looked down at his morning erection. Nothing new there. To do something about it, or

49

not to do something about it, that was the question. In the end he decided against. DIY had never appealed to him, and anyway he had worn himself to a frazzle at the club only the night before. In the showers, in the sauna, in the cubicles. Good God, but he could be a glutton. Down boy, he murmured fondly, stroking his member. He yawned again, then stubbed out his cigarette. But perhaps the gluttony came from his tendency to practise, to insist on – regardless of the lover – what was now called "safe sex". Jaysus, but safe sex bored him. Somehow or other, it took the razor-edge thrill out of love-making. He was insatiable, and he blamed safe sex. Less of that and more of one good lover, no holds barred, no matter how irregularly, and he'd be a happy man.

Some time later he let the shower faucet spill vigorously over his head in the white-walled shower which gleamed with metal surrounds and fittings. Minimalist, wasn't that the word that cunt of an estate agent had used? Still, it was a good buy, cost him the earth, but image mattered. He'd had to move from the North Circular Road to something that fitted a man on the up and up.

Mick was obsessed with a physical cleanliness which sometimes belied his untidy appearance. He was scrupulous about hygiene, about shaving, about smelling just right. The water was scalding hot, as he liked it. The knack was to cool it gradually. Finally, he reached out for his block of Minotaur soap, and lathered himself all over, at the same time fantasising about an advertisement he'd seen on television, which showed this stud soaping himself in the shower, and an animated train running all over the guy's body, caressing those well-tended, tanned muscles. Chuf-chuf-toot-toot. He imagined what it would be like to handle the cheeks of that guy's ass. Tight, very tight. Chuf-chuf-chuf-toot-toot-toot.

He glanced at the soles of his feet to check their condition. All present and correct. Five piggies on each foot, nothing missing. *Jaysus,* but he'd thought that fella from the West was going to suck him to Kingdom Come in the sauna. Had to suck the toes as well, each and every one of them. Well, whatever takes yer fancy, Mick thought, smiling. One of these days he'd have to see to his corns. Nothing gave people's age away so much as the condition of their feet. Corns and bunions and scaly patches could ruin his chances. Not to speak of his gently sagging musculature. But still, hadn't a thirty-year-old told him only last night that he had a lovely body? And him forty-nine? He closed his eyes the better to relive the sensations in the sauna room at *Araby,* the nearness and breathing of so many men, the groans, the whispers, hints and beckonings in the warm pink-lit steam.

His mother's voice sounded in his head.

"You were always water-shy, Mick!" she'd scold, when he was in his twenties and thirties. Well, Ma, I've made up for lost time, he chuckled to himself.

The old woman had gone out badly. He shook his head, examined his feet again, observed the scales of incipient athlete's foot, shook his head and made a mental note to buy some more footspray.

The mother always wanted him to marry. Funny thing though, conservative women avoided him, as if their uptight minds picked up the vibes of homosexuality, although he was to all appearances a non-scene man, definitely not camp in his behaviour. Just as well. He knew too many married men who'd deceived their wives, who pretended to be one thing and played the game of macho husband and father, a spot of golf at weekends, then off to Lansdowne Road for the rugger internationals. All the time they were unable to tell the truth, the poor devils, scared to reveal what they were, trapped in a lie for the rest of their lives.

That was what he liked about Ginnie. She said she got a buzz out of being with him. Plain sailing, she said, and yet you're a real man. She'd also said something about enjoying his male energy, what she called his *charisma*. He knew what he meant, even though he didn't like her talking about "male energy" and "charisma". Always when she was beating her feminist drum, of course. It made him feel invaded. But he thought of her as a friend, even if he sometimes treated her gruffly. He wasn't good at showing his softer feelings, especially to women. But Ginnie understood. She didn't know how to pretend. Even at the height of her fling with Arsebollocks Leo Kilgallen, when she deluded herself about being in love with the politician and entrepreneur, she told Mick she knew they didn't stand a chance of surviving beyond a few years at most. Pity she was still hanging out of him. Kilgallen, by her account, was good in the sack. So big deal, well-hung men were ten a penny, if that was what she wanted why couldn't she find someone in the business, someone who understood what she did? When Kilgallen was with her he was with her all the way, but once he left the country to meet horse-dealers from Saudi Arabia, Kentucky and Germany, she told Mick, he might as well be in Deep Space Nine. Her future, she confided, would probably not include Kilgallen. Wise girl, Mick thought darkly, wise girl. Mick knew that Kilgallen enjoyed the hunt, the kill, and then got bored.

Whenever he thought about the future, or Ginnie, he found himself dwelling on his mother. Ginnie represented real life, the taste of what was possible and what was sane. He'd got his mother into a nursing home after the doctors had diagnosed the worst. Fair enough, he visited her every second weekend, more if he could manage it. Mick's father had run off in the days when a man could desert and little was thought of it. Taking off, bolting for fresh air was something men simply did from time to time. Nowadays, the women were at it too, but nowadays everything was different. If his father had ever returned Mick would have split him with an axe.

His mother had her good moments, even in the middle of the delusions. What else could he do but play along, or at least talk her through the worst of them when she was upset.

He went into the small white and blue kitchen, a towel around his hips, filled the kettle and took a mug from the heap of unwashed crockery that lay stacked in the sink. The place still smelt of fresh paint and grouting. Filaments of copper glinted below the fitted cupboards where the plumbers had worked. The sunshine yellow chrome clock to the left of the hob read nine-fifteen. He looked at one particular unfilled gap in the kitchen fittings and realised that he would have to have a dishwasher installed. He recalled the occasion, while his mother still had control of her speech, when he arrived at the nursing-home only to hear her confide that she'd fallen in love.

"Oh? Who with?" he'd asked as casually as possible.

"You might have heard of him," she whispered, "In your business. A fellow the name of Meat Loaf!"

Her voice was triumphant, her eyes blazed into his, blue, and full of conviction.

"Is that a fact?" he whispered back, his mind turning over possible ways of dealing with the situation.

"Is he good to you?" he carried on, gambling on the fact that the delusion was fully worked-out in her mind.

"Why d'you ask?" she demanded reproachfully, her voice suspicious, drawing back and staring at him.

"Well," he hesitated, "A chap with a name like that, y'know Ma, I'm lookin' out for your best interests."

He was at a loss, breathed out nervously.

"He's good as gold to me son, he treats me properly, he tells me I'm – "

She paused here, pressed her hands together in a praying gesture, "He says I'm a *lady!*"

After the funeral he sat outside the house all night, in his car, relief and loss thundering through him. To this day, he couldn't stand it when people talked about someone going *ga-ga*. It was as if they were written off, fit for nothing but the local dump. Perhaps that explained the attraction which Ginnie held for him, apart from his business interest. She was strong, bright, cheeky, she was sheer power. Nobody and nothing would delude her, in the full of her health, in the end not even Arsebollocks Kilgallen.

He hacked a few slices of brown bread on the black marble worktop, then gazed, without seeing anything, out of the square, uncurtained window that gave a lofty view of the the rooftops along the quays. As long as he lived, he never wanted to see anybody in the state his mother got into. Everything went, muscles, voice, even the strength of her eyelids. She couldn't control her saliva, so she couldn't swallow properly. He hated that gurgling, suffocating sound. That was what did it in the end. She caught a cold, and in her prone state couldn't even cough. The cold turned to pneumonia and in no time at all she was gone, though he'd begged the doctors to end it sooner. But then some people felt they had no right to end someone else's misery. A quick jab would have taken her out of her torment.

Horrible. He stuffed the buttery slices of bread hurriedly into his mouth, slurped back some instant coffee, first fix of the day, and placed the crockery on top of the heap of dishes in the sink. Another time, he thought, someday soon, when he was free, he'd do a major clean-up. In the meantime he had to get on that fax and hustle, confirm gigs, places and fees, the bigger the better. He had to hammer it home to the other sharks that Ginnie was no ordinary sassy singer, that time was money, half in advance. No money, no Virgin, bugger yez all. Simple.

The telephone rang before he had a chance to make his first call. It was Hilary Dunne. He rolled his eyes in exasperation.

"Oh. It's you."

"Hello, Mick . . . when did you get back?"

"Last night. Late."

There was a silence at the other end which he knew to be loaded with expectation. Mick had been meeting Hilary on and off, more off than on, for the past two years.

"I suppose you're busy."

Ya feckin' well suppose right, the thought flashed through his head.

"Can't complain. Business is good, you know how it is . . . " he stalled.

His head reeled. He felt trapped, the way he always

did when women took a fancy to him which, for some reason, straight women sometimes did. Hilary had a way of making him feel that he owed her something. She wasn't a bad woman, if a bit of a puzzle. She had taken him into her immaculate home, just two houses down from his old pad, one night when he was so drunk he didn't know his own name, and sat ossified in the car, outside her front door, incapable of so much as pulling on the handbrake. Lucky for him, Hilary darted out to tell him to move from in front of her gate. She said afterwards, in an attempt at a joke, that the smell of alcohol from his breath nearly straightened the curls out of her hair. Mortified he was, when he woke up on her couch the next morning, clueless as to where he was or what had happened. But he thanked her profusely for her trouble, and thought he would never see her again. But Hilary kept in touch, by heck she did, phoned him once or twice for a chat. God forgive him for taking advantage of her phoney kindness, but it was Hilary who used to keep an eye on his mother, in the days before she went to the nursing home; Hilary would tidy up, Hilary was there in his absence to watch that his mother didn't start wandering through the streets in her nightgown, as happened on one occasion. She had done a lot, he owed her fair and square, she had been around when he couldn't be.

But that time was past. The thing was, the penny hadn't dropped with Hilary that women didn't figure strongly in his life. Not that way. He took her out every so often, not on a proper date, although that was how she interpreted it. But there was nothing in it. Not once did he give her any reason to suppose that they had a romantic involvement. It was just his way of showing gratitude. They had some laughs, well, smiles. She was an odd woman, a bit younger than he. Pity she had no sense of humour.

"What are you up to yourself?" he asked, to give himself time to make up an excuse for not being able to meet her within the next few weeks.

"Nothing much. This and that. I've taken up Judo at the new gym up the road."

Why did she always sound so forlorn?

"Judo? Mmmm."

"Myself and Mrs Kavanagh at the shop had a night out last Saturday. Great crack altogether. I suppose I had a few too many."

She tittered in a girlish voice. It was difficult to imagine Hilary under the influence of alcohol, even on the lowest, safest pastures that skirted the vast Himalayas of drunkenness where he occasionally found himself.

"Ah well. No harm in that once in a while."

"I suppose not," she replied, sniffing.

He didn't want to hurt her, but he wanted a long break from Hilary. Preferably a permanent one. After all, it was three weeks since their last rendezvous, when he'd wined and dined her at a swish country hotel not far from the Curragh. He'd hoped it would be the last such occasion. It was to be the finale to their relationship but clearly, Hilary did not share that view.

"Tell you what, Hilary. I'm busy just now. Expecting a call from France any minute. Can I call you back, say, day after tomorrow?"

The sigh was audible, then the hesitant clicking. He heard her breathing.

"Do that. What time?"

*Shite.* Women. Always wanting to fix definite times, to synchronise things. They'd synchronise their own deaths if they could manage it.

"Say, five-thirty?" he suggested, knowing that he'd be on the road. He wondered vaguely why he did that kind of thing, made promises to Hilary, knowing he would break them, as if he wanted to keep her dangling. But that was the way it was, he supposed. If a woman couldn't cop herself on then that was what happened. He almost took a twisted kind of pleasure in making her suffer. He would have done the same to a man he didn't fancy, if that man kept pursuing him. He would go along with things, make arrangements and then cancel at the last minute, create an aura of unavailability and exclusivity to tease his victim. It made him feel powerful.

"All right. Take it easy. I suppose you're busy promoting Virgin."

Her voice always managed to sound hurt, and *that* annoyed him like hell, especially the way she uttered the word *Virgin,* like it was something despicable.

"You got it. Busy with Virgin," he replied, replacing the receiver before he lost his rag with her.

Much later, he dressed, pulling a brown suede coat over Calvin Klein jeans and a biscuit-coloured Ralph Lauren polo; the soft belt he drew into a knot at his waist. Finally, a suede skullcap, the edge of which was embroidered in brown and orange stitching. He liked the effect and moreover, it covered his bald patch. He stood back and examined himself in the long mirror opposite the bed. Still slightly overweight, with purple pouches beneath his eyes. Cold tea-bags and slices of cucumber laid carefully onto his closed lids for fifteen minutes once or twice a week made no difference. Sooner or later, it would be a face-lift or die. Harley Street here we come. No point having it done in Ireland. You never knew who you'd run into. Laugh-bags, was how the young fella he'd met at *Araby* the night before had described them. He shrugged. They would never meet again. Ships in the night. A nice fella, but he hadn't seemed enthusiastic when Mick suggested exchanging telephone numbers. What could he expect anyway? Not for the first time, he tried to ward off the pain within as he thought of his aloneness.

His mother's relatives hadn't a clue. If they had, he would have been a subject of ridicule and contempt, an easy target for their gloomy assumptions on subjects about which they knew sweet damn all. Born into the kind of glum family that believed only crooks could make it big in this life, he'd proven them wrong with his nose for new talent and an unabashed willingness to work hard. He had them there, he thought. The other business, his anguished search for the man of his dreams, they need never know about. Anyway, he shrugged at himself in the long mirror, who cared? Who ever lost a night's sleep over someone else's problems?

Mick Delaney, talent-merchant extraordinaire, he said mentally, a grin settling on his face as he turned the key to the alarm before leaving the apartment.

He pulled the door behind him, the metal tips of his heels clacking across the Liscannor stone-floored balcony outside, where geraniums flared in the sunshine. As he moved, he accidentally snapped the stem of one of the blooms. Finally, he turned a corner and trod slowly down steps of bare concrete which, in the morning dampness, were slippery. *That,* he thought darkly, was something which he would bring to the attention of the architects, because sooner or later, the tenants in this snazzy block of apartments, would break their shagging necks on the exit stairs. He shook his head as he picked his way down, glancing to the left as he did so; working carefully, pen in hand, a middle-aged fashion designer in the penthouse on the other side was absorbed by his own designs; behind him skeins of wool, rolls of fabric.

# Five

## No More I Love Yous

Ginnie opened the apartment door and breathed in the aroma of Leo Kilgallen. As ever, he was on time.

"Hello, Luscious!"

He bent to kiss her earlobe, then pushed her slowly back into the room.

"Well, howdy stranger . . . hey, take it easy. I'm just up."

"So?"

"I'm cranky, and I'm mad about having to do two gigs I'd nearly forgotten about," she mumbled, trying not to respond to his caresses, to his appearance, and the contrasting odours of cigar smoke and scented male skin.

"Give it up if that's how you feel," he answered.

"Don't even think that."

She turned from him and went into the kitchen.

"Coffee? It's fresh . . . "

"Thanks but no thanks. Got any juice?"

"Oh Buddha, you health-conscious types bug me!"

She rummaged in the fridge, then poured him a tumbler of pineapple and passion-fruit juice. He lay back and relaxed on the couch, a silk cushion at his head. His glance, as he appraised the apartment, was critical. His

61

face registered mild annoyance. He shook his head after taking a sip from the glass.

"You could do with a cleaner, angel."

"I could. No time to organise one. Anyway, I don't like giving orders to people who have to clean up what I'm too lazy to do myself."

"People who aren't used to employing others always say that," he commented drily. "Delegate, Ginnie, delegate. You're going to have to if you continue with your – " He paused and smiled, as if reminding himself to be respectful, "your career."

He flicked through a press release which had lodged between one of the cushions on the couch. *The Virgin Tour*. His face was now expressionless. Her public nomenclature was something he detested because for him it conjured images of Roman trollops, sluts paid to entertain their overlords.

"Hmmm. I'll see. Have to think about it, Leo."

"Do that, sweetie. This place is worth a bomb, we need to keep it properly, you know?"

His tone irritated her. Occasionally, Leo pulled out his trump card, reminded her gently that in the early heat of the relationship it was primarily his money that had bought the place. As a result of his investment, all she had to do was meet relatively small repayments.

"Come here," he called.

She stood and stared at him. "Come here what?"

"OK, OK, I know I've annoyed you, come here, please. Please come to Leo, he's been a bad boy and Ginnie's cross. Sor-ry."

He opened his arms in a contrite gesture, smiled apologetically. Relenting, she sat on his knee, put her arms around his neck and fingered his hair.

"How are things in the great world of politics today?"

He did not reply, busily opened her robe and removed it from her shoulders. It fell to her hips. She sat, pressed kisses to his forehead, down his cheeks, finally to his lips. He hoisted her to her feet, removed the robe completely and, began to steer her towards the bedroom.

"Things," he murmured, "are as bad as ever, or as good as ever, depending on how you look at them."

"That's not saying much. Everything top secret as usual?"

"There are no secrets, Ginnie," he whispered in between kissing her. "But business is business. It's separate from – " he hesitated, opening his hands in an expansive gesture, searching for the right phrase, "from all this. From you."

"Are you in town today and tomorrow?" she asked casually, lighting a cigarette, flicking the still lit match into the fireplace. She missed and the match bounched back and fell on a Chinese rug. His eyes followed her movements and he went to pick up the match, but she caught him by the arm and held him.

"Are you in town today and tomorrow?"

"Until Thursday. Then it's Brussels for a conference."

"So you'd better get undressed, I'm on the road again tonight. Damn. I'd only just lit this."

"That's sex for you. Such an inconvenience. At least we can agree on the need for it. As much and as often," he murmured, placing his mouth around one of her nipples, "as we can arrange it. Which isn't often – " he mumbled between kisses, "now that you're on the road so much."

She ignored the remark. In the midst of lust, it crossed her mind, not for the first time recently, that perhaps the time had come to break for good with Leo Kilgallen.

Afterwards, they lay in silence. It was noon. Morning sunshine had been snuffed out by a rainstorm; the only sounds were the hiss of the traffic on the main road, on the other side of the shimmering beechtrees which overshadowed the apartments at Ruskin Way.

"Some summer!" she grumbled. He squeezed her thigh by way of reply. The immediate need in his groin was satisfied, his mind already elsewhere, navigating the labyrinth of his business and personal life. He would have to put in an appearance at the Dail Chamber later in the day, then zip out to the factory and make his presence felt on the floor.

"So where're you headed tonight?" he asked in a conciliatory manner.

"Malla. The big hall. Rub me."

"Malla?" He shifted his weight slightly, adjusting his arm beneath her head, then reached over and began to knead her shoulder with his free hand. He grunted in discomfort.

"That's one of my – minor interests."

"Oh yeah? You own it? Rub harder. My back."

He sighed. "Roll over. Atta girl. More or less, more or less. Bought it for a song way back in the early eighties."

"I'd like to own property someday," Ginnie said drowsily, "Uhhh – that's great – I'll have to employ someone to massage me."

"I'm sure you will own property, dear, if that's what you want," he replied, thumbing her spine absent-mindedly.

"Do you think so? Really?" She turned and sat up, more alert, then flopped back, pleased at the prospect.

He frowned suddenly. "Now that you mention Malla, it's been a while since I've checked it out –"

"How's Mitzi?" she asked, changing the subject and at

the same time trying to be generous about *his* life and interests, now that he had not dismissed at least one of her dreams.

But she had disturbed his reverie.

"Mitzi?"

At that moment the name seemed remote.

"Oh, Mitzi. She's fine. Bought a new colt at the sales last week. She's working him every day, that kind of thing . . ."

He stretched beside her, then lay staring at the ceiling, his arms behind his head.

"She'll probably go home to Germany for a break in October, if we don't get away in September, that is."

"Keeping in touch with her roots, is she?"

Ginnie found it difficult to curb her cynicism. He blinked and thought for a moment.

"Sure. She's swung a few deals over here for her father. Papa von Heining likes to see her. She's the only one in the family who understands bloodstock. Apart from himself."

He sighed and smiled. "She's a great lady. I'm very proud of her," he added, pleased with himself and his wife.

"I'm sure you are," Ginnie smiled, and the irony of it was lost on him.

She turned from his embrace and sat on the edge of the bed. Talk of Mitzi, even if she'd initiated it herself, invariably filled her with irritation. She scratched absently at the inside of her right arm, her attention idling on the window. It was still pouring.

"I gotta get dressed, Leo. I've a full day," she lied. She was free as a bird until Mick picked her up later that afternoon. That was the point, she was supposed to rest, have fun and let Uncle Mick do the work. But she liked to sound busy and involved whenever Leo talked about Mitzi. He would never see her depend on him, not that way. One thing Ginnie recognised about Leo was that he would change nothing about the pattern of his own life to accommodate her, not one single jot. She'd grown busier in the past year, but Leo didn't notice. He never betrayed the slightest resentment or jealousy about the time she spent on the road. It was as if he did not value her, or the time they spent together. What he did show, to her hurt and fury, was embarrassment. Leo, she knew, was ashamed of what she did.

"We'd both better set to it." He hopped from the far side of the bed. She waited while he showered briskly, towelled himself dry, put on the pair of new, unopened underpants which he always carried in his briefcase, then combed his hair. The ease with which he agreed to leave contributed to her mounting anger. He was like some kind of smart-ass schoolboy, who had gorged himself in the tuck shop. Now he was off to do his homework, or whatever it was he needed to get along in the world.

But she asked nothing of him. She was not about to beg or implore. Either he wanted her or he didn't, but the sooner he decided, the better for both of them. When she thought about it, she didn't know what she was waiting for. But she could wait a little, and she would never ask him to leave Mitzi, not in a million years. That would be a mistake. Anyway, Ginnie wasn't sure she wanted him in that way any more. The real spark between them had died. What remained were glimpses of a man who sometimes, she had to admit, she could not even like. There had to be more. In any case, Leo and Mitzi were two of a kind, just as Ginnie and Leo were two of a different kind. He was an attractive companion, one she could probably *learn* to live with, if such an unlikely development were to take place. But who needed to learn to live with anyone, she thought. What a bore, what a drag. Negotiations and entente cordiales till death do us part. World War Three every few months. No way José. In the meantime, there were songs to be composed and sung, places to go, things that excited her. When she made it big, when she really made it, when she exploded like the new star she was, Leo might think again. But she'd always be the same, wanting to move at the drop of a hat, just as the mood took her, without being constrained by the nonsense of duty. Happiness for Ginnie meant being free to write songs, to sing them, to become famous. Leo would be like a prison warden. She shook her head as she watched him. She could no longer deceive herself. Men like Leo couldn't cope with women like her. Demanding, competitive, aggressive, that was how he viewed them. *That bitch, that uppity slut, I know what she needs.* Wasn't that how she'd heard him describe one of the women in the Dail Chamber? Well, she was better off not caring what he thought, better perhaps if she could unlearn the lessons of all those hours of sheer lust.

He knotted his tie, a red and blue confection of flowers and exotic birds, a complete contrast to the simplicity of his light grey suit and white shirt. He stopped as if something had just struck him.

"Seriously, sweetie. Ever think of getting out of the business? Just answer me straight. No aggro."

She pulled on a pair of jeans, ripped the zip shut and threw him a bitter smile.

"No, I don't ever think of getting out. I'm in too deep, Leo, the fans like me. For Christ's sake, what kind of a question's that? I'm starting to make money!"

"I know, I know, but – " he hesitated, "don't get me wrong, but you're not getting any younger."

"Full marks for tact. Neither are you, and I have a good twelve years on you."

"Don't be prickly, Ginnie. I only mean that you've got to look ahead, to the time when you aren't so young. Most women your age are married and having children. Ot at least they're settled into a reliable career. I'm concerned, that's all."

How come, Ginnie thought, that the people who expressed the greatest concern for one were usually those least equipped to tolerate what one actually wanted?

"I'm happy now Leo, that's what counts. I'm doing what I want. Don't try to stop me."

He turned and began to comb his hair quickly.

"It's like this, Ginnie. I'd like to be able to take you out a little more often. Eh, you know, I'd like to be with you, but you're away such a lot."

"Oh yeah? Who are you kidding? This is the twentieth century, Leo, practically the twenty-first. Are you telling me you'd be happy to have me sit around, cosy in this apartment, waiting for you to put in an appearance whenever Mitzi's away?"

His face flushed. "Don't bring Mitzi into it, that's got nothing to do with you. Mitzi's a great lady – "

"So you said already!" Ginnie snapped. Leo looked at her with raised eyebrows, as if she were suddenly a stranger, an intruder in his life.

"She's also – " he went on primly, "the mother of my children."

His face, when she looked up, was flushed and indignant.

"Oh really? Well, by my reckoning you don't need another mother for more children. Not me anyway."

Not for the first time, she understood why men had always organised themselves into priesthoods of one kind or another, and why they could distance themselves through moralising. They could feel pious about certain things – about motherhood and children – when it suited them of course, she thought. And they could see Mary Magdalene in every woman other than the one they married.

"Don't. Sarcasm doesn't become you," he said.

Ginnie did not reply. She stared past him, over his shoulder and out the window. A dislike which bordered on loathing rose in her just then. To think that it had come to this. He was someone she no longer cared about. He would ruin her if she let him. Not deliberately, not from malice. But by being what he was and expecting what he expected. A place for everything and everything in its place. Quaint, really.

"I know what you want, Leo."

"What do I want?"

"It doesn't matter."

And it didn't. Explaining anything to him would be a waste of energy. He could flip her argument on its head to make her feel indebted to him.

"Tell me. What do I want?" he pressed, grasping her by the wrist, his eyes blazing.

"A kick up the backside," she answered. "Now go wherever you were going. On your bike, to your factory or wherever it is you were going."

"I'll be in touch," he said. "You're not yourself, sweetie. Maybe we can have a rational discussion some other time. Sounds to me as if you've got a touch of PMT. The old menstrual bicycle thing, what?", he smiled. "You mean a great deal to me, you know that, don't you?"

"Spare me. Get lost." She pushed him towards the door.

To fill the silence after he left, Ginnie put on an Annie Lennox CD, went to the fridge and removed a bowl of salad. Her body trembled with rage and the bowl almost slipped from her hands. She went to a cupboard and sprinkled the mixture of endives and chicory with sesame oil, tabasco, some dried chillis and garlic, then sat on the floor, lotus-position, to munch and think and calm down. But Lennox's voice and words were like a steel thread being drawn through her skin. This time, the words felt true. The right words for the right moment.

> *I used to have demons in my room at night,*
> *Desire, despair, desire,*
> *So many monsters,*
> *But now –*
> *No more I love yous,*
> *Language is leaving me,*
> *No more I love yous,*
> *Language is leaving me in silence.*

What Leo really wanted, she thought, munching soberly, scooping the salad with a spoon, was not to have to think about what his feelings for her were. She began to laugh quietly, imagining herself with his crowd, at race meetings, high profile charity functions, tournaments, art exhibitions and all the trimmings that gave life to the chattering classes. Most of all, what he wanted was to know that she was available whenever and wherever he wanted. He would make love to her anywhere, anytime, even with a brown paper bag on her head, as long as she agreed to open her legs, make her breasts available for him to squeeze, and moaned convincingly in between a few strangulated yesses. As long as she didn't measure up in the traditional way of mistresses, he was confused; he was not a man to tolerate elusiveness and rebellion from women other than his wife. He was accustomed to Mitzi's ambition and Mitzi's efficient way of doing things. It was straightforward. He would never want to marry Ginnie, even if he could show her off without disturbing his friends and acquaintances, even if he could present her on his arm like a trophy, a living doll with long, tanned legs, a pleasant smile on her face and an ambition pruned to complement his own. Ginnie knew that, and more, she knew that marriage was for the birds.

She stood up and put the empty salad bowl into the dishwasher, then took a banana, some fresh strawberries, and a kiwi from a boat-shaped glass fruitbowl. Leo would have to learn. She sighed, dropping the fruit into a mixer, pouring yogurt, sugar and some cream and lemon-juice on top. He was pleasant company, generous, skilled and adroit in bed, although the sexual heights to which she had originally climbed with him were waning now, partly because of his automatic assumption that his wants would be hers too. She pressed the button and the mixer turned the fruit to a pinkish pulp. Sex was such an act, she thought, and not for the first time. But she could wait. There were other, more important considerations.

She drank from a tall glass beaker, drew her cheeks together as the slightly tart mixture made her mouth water, then turned her thoughts to the evening ahead. There were lyrics to be checked, she had an aerobics class in an hour's time and she had to return her mother's call.

"Hi, Mum!"

"Virginia?"

"Got your message last night. Great news about Jack!"

"Your father's in a great mood anyway. He'd have burst a blood-vessel if Jack had failed the interview. You know what he's like . . . "

They both laughed, knowing what a stickler Senan Maloney was for formalities, professionalism and the old boys' network.

"I think I got away more easily by being born a girl."

"Perhaps," her mother answered cautiously. "Your father just didn't expect as much. Now he wishes you were married."

"He'll be waiting! And so will you. Poor old Dad. Living through Jack like that."

"'Fraid so, dear. Can't stop himself making plans for the boys. Especially for Jack."

"He might get a bit of a land. Jack won't appreciate Dad sticking his nose in too much." Ginnie tutted. "Oh Mum, I wish things had been different years ago. It all seems such a waste."

"Ah well," Mrs Maloney sighed, "God is good. You threw away the chance of a good career yourself."

"I didn't," Ginnie replied tartly.

"Well, as I said, God is good."

"Oh sure. God's a great fella. God didn't do such a lot for you and Dad when we were small and you were stuck subbing in that primary school or else driving around in the delivery van. With himself at home. *Fenella's Flowers.* Makes me sick to think of it."

"Ah now Virginia, didn't we manage? That's what life's all about, you know. Going the extra mile. Getting along no matter what the odds."

"Maybe. But you could do with a holiday, preferably on your own, without old Whingebag in tow, worrying about

72

his piles and his ulcer, sorting out the problems of the world!"

"Those are unkind things to say about your father."

But they chatted for fifteen minutes. It was an easy conversation which drifted from her father's attitude to Jack, to the long-term effects of Chernobyl, to her mother's discovery of a new recipe for yeast bread.

By the time she hung up Ginnie's humour was restored. She raced around the apartment, picked up clothes and flung them into wardrobes and drawers. Unusually, she pulled up the quilt on the bed, tidied her footwear and dusted the top of the dressing-table.

Outside, the sky had begun to clear. Pale daubs of blue shifted and deepened. The wind fell. She would have time for a jog around the park before her aerobics session.

# Six

## Hilary's Angle

Earlier that afternoon, Hilary Dunne made a few phone calls. Perched in a lavender-scented office just over *Exchange 'n Change,* the second-hand clothes shop which now claimed her time, she dialled headquarters and confirmed the day's assignment.

"When?" she queried, propped in such a way that a wavering trail of cigarette smoke drifted into the dark mass of her hair. Her fingernails were heavily lacquered, and she possessed the tidy, anxious appearance of one who lived in hope of great happenings. Every time the perm in her hair softened and grew out, Hilary would hasten to the local coiffeur to have her curls re-tightened, as if they were screws in danger of falling loose. The jet frizz she considered to be casual, inviting. Girls nowadays, she would sigh, hadn't a clue.

She listened carefully to the voice at the other end of the receiver and nodded.

"This'll be a tough one all the same," she remarked softly, allowing the cigarette to jig up and down as she spoke. Again, she listened.

"Hmmm. I'll try and make it afterwards . . . hmmm . . . oh, you're right, it'll give them a bit of a scare . . . hmmm . . . well, you're the boss . . . "

She turned away and hoiked vigorously to clear the back of her throat.

"Sorry about that. As I was saying, we'll give it our best shot. It's a sell-out, you know that of course . . ."

No sooner had she hung up than she lifted the receiver and dialled again. She spent about an hour and a half on the telephone liaising with companions, people who could be depended upon. The day would come when the world would rush to join them, when they would succeed where other powers had failed.

Below in the shop, the shuffle of footsteps carried up to her room, as people wandered in from the streets to examine the cast-offs of the wealthy. That morning Mrs Leo Kilgallen from The Crescent had sent boxes of stuff around, everything in perfect condition. Hilary had allowed herself first option and poked carefully through the garments before letting Mrs Kavanagh sort them. Designer labels all, worn twice at the most. She sniffed resentfully at the thought, then poured herself a coffee. No wonder Hitler had lost the war against the infidels, with people like that in his country. Corrupt. She sniffed again. The internal telephone rang. Another "emergency" downstairs, good Lord, could none of these so-called helpers be relied on to solve a simple problem? She stomped down the stairs and entered the shop, eyes blazing.

"Now what's the problem?" she asked in a tired, patient voice. As ever, it was a trifle. Some wino had wandered in and asked to be given one of the overcoats on display. Mrs Kavanagh had made a big issue of it. He stood there, offering a pound for a coat marked up at a tenner.

"Let him have it, can't you?" she sighed at the other woman, "I've a lot on my mind at the moment and if you can't run things down here while I do the books I don't know what's going to happen, Mrs Kavanagh, I really don't."

The coat was passed over the counter, Hilary told the man to keep his pound and get himself a good meal, while her assistant tried not to huff.

"The first shall be last, and the last first," Hilary chanted.

"You're not in the schoolroom now," Mrs Kavanagh remarked lightly, concentrating on a box of footwear but unable to resist the taunt.

Hilary looked up slowly. Bad news, she reminded herself as she climbed the cracked linoleum stairway which led to her office, had a way of getting around. A change of career was how she had referred to it, after Tomas got married and left for Australia, even if it was early retirement for reasons of deteriorating health.

Fifteen years in a boys' school had finally worn Hilary Dunne to the quick, until she teetered almost permanently over an abyss of hysteria and psychosomatic illness. Summers for the last five years before retirement had been for recuperative purposes in whatever restful institution would take her. During her final year, when things had grown desperate, she'd met Mick Delaney, whose mother she'd kept an eye on during nights when she couldn't sleep herself. Meeting him had helped for a time, she'd even been able to conceal much of her nervousness in his company. But it was an unpredictable relationship, and he took her for granted, even if he could be perfectly charming and quite open with her when he chose. Most men didn't know how to hold a conversation, hadn't the foggiest about how to talk to a woman. He was in no way like Tomas, she now realised. Colourful, certainly, but different.

She jolted herself back to the present, stung and furious that Mrs Kavanagh had sensed something of her former life. The idea began to niggle that perhaps she knew what had really finished her teaching career; the deliberate campaign against her by a group of horrible boys, the hissing and humming when her back was turned to write on the blackboard, vile notes and letters pinned to her desk on which the most obscene suggestions had been made; cartoons of a highly explicit nature in the back pages of homework copies; a school principal who turned a blind eye to her requests for disciplinary action; finally, an outburst which resulted in her beating a thirteen-year-old boy until his nose bled and four of the other pupils had dragged her off him.

Miraculously, the matter never went to court. She resigned voluntarily, endured a poorly-attended send-off in a hotel, and forsook the classroom for the more harmonious atmosphere of the second-hand clothes shop.

Forget it, she commanded inwardly.

She still went to a counsellor once a month. A non-directive chap who worked from a converted garage in a house in the suburbs. It did her good to get a few things off her chest. The counsellor had given her a tape to play every evening. He'd hoped it would make her dream. She knew he'd misunderstood when she told him that she didn't dream at all. Or if she did, she never remembered her night-time images. The tape, he said, would help her to discover her dreams. The archetypal ones, he said. So she'd stuck the tape on and lain down on her bed. The counsellor's own voice spoke to her, suggested a triangle, three figures held together by a golden thread.

Funny thing was, she began to dream. She saw tigers. They held sabres between their great ruffed paws, as if they were half-tamed and working for people. All around lay mounds of black grapes, except that the grapes were the size of grapefruit and the tigers halved them with their sabres. She had this dream twice, but the counsellor, when she told him, said nothing. That must be what non-directive meant, she thought, and hid her disappointment.

She sipped at her coffee. Before her lay a list of addresses and phone numbers, and a batch of letters and notes which had nothing at all to do with second-hand clothing. She read them carefully, tut-tutting every so often as a mis-spelling leapt out, a poorly-constructed sentence or a malapropism. So many of the people she dealt with nowadays had never, it seemed, learnt how to spell. But they were good, solid people all the same. You knew where you were with most of them, they respected her just as she respected them, because they were united, their goals similar; they were collectively bent on achieving one objective within the coming days if not that very night – the routing of a very great evil from the face of the country, currently endangering the souls of thousands. Tomas would approve, if only he were here!

She would not stand for it, neither would her colleagues in the Guardians, especially the *Magister*. But it was an aspect of her life about which Mick Delaney knew nothing, the motivation for such concealment one of sheer spite. Knowledge was power, after all. Had things shown signs of taking a different, more romantic and companionable course, she would be prepared to forfeit some of her organisational responsibilities. As it was, Delaney hardly acknowledged her existence since that fiasco in the hotel some weeks before, when he'd had the gall to joke about booking a double-room, no less. Only joking, only joking, he said then, when her sense of humour didn't rise to the jest.

Those on the other side must never, ever, realise the complexity and deliberation of the Guardians' vision. Nor indeed its intelligence. Let them feel superior, Hilary mused. It would disarm them.

Her irritation grew, she rocked backwards and forwards and lit another cigarette. The evil-doers would be routed. Hilary Dunne would bear a banner emblazoned in gold and white, she would march behind the leaders of truth and rally the forces which would undo the harm unfolding among the innocent.

The window was open and she moved to close it, but paused, her attention caught by the scene below. She saw it all, the foulness at the centre of humanity. They were all collaborators, even if they didn't know it; just by stepping outside their doors every day, by purchasing evil-looking garments which displayed prominently parts of the body which should never be displayed; by buying that demonic rock music; or by indulging in wild dance practices, pagan rituals which were the undoing of Rome and Egypt, the Chinese Empire and the great rulers, they were drawn into something greater than themselves, beyond the limitations of control.

But today, Hilary decided, was a watershed. This evening, to be precise, something would happen which would change the course of history. That Mick Delaney man would rue the day he'd messed around with her affections, that no-good whelp who was obsessed with the Jezebel would regret the day he'd been born. The Guardians would see to that. The Virgin creature would be an example to every condom-pushing, abortion-and divorce-promoting man and woman in the country. Even if the Guardians had been able to work through the Cumanns on a couple of TDs and got them to vote against the latest Bill, it was not enough. The dam wall was cracking under the pressure of the great weight of so-called progress. Word had it, furthermore, that the hall at Malla belonged to none other than Leo Kilgallen, one of those political wheeler-dealers whose Dail contributions the Guardians had taken note of. Leo Kilgallen was among those who would be singled out. A liberal agenda man, she sneered quietly. Married to a foreigner. That would have something to do with it. But they would get him, up there in The Crescent, they were not done with Mr Leo Kilgallen. They would be there, watching, waiting. Right outside his home.

She went back to her desk and lifted the phone and dialled, then shivered at the prospect of victory. Onwards and outwards my friends, she murmured, before clearing her throat.

"Hello?" Her voice was soft as a dove's.

# Seven

## The Gig at Malla

The road between Athree and Malla was busy. The bus sped along. There were times, like tonight, when something eluded her, when the hard core of determination and ambition served her ill. She needed more time to run through lyrics and choreography. But there was something else too. A loss of nerve. She sat in the bus, pen and notebook to hand, and revised her dance routine, *five-six-seven-eight-and-one-and-cross-and-arms-and-cross again-and-turn-and-jump-and-hips-left-hips-right* . . .

"Stop that. You'll make yourself sick." From the seat behind, Mick prodded her shoulder with his finger.

"Just checking. I need to be sure."

She stopped scribbling, however, sat back and stared out of the window.

So what did she want? To be acknowledged or to shock? And what about that elusive something that ran deeper than self-esteem?

It would be nice to be in a position to retire early to some haven in the sun. As for changing the world, that might not happen, at least not as she once assumed it would, just because she wanted it to.

The Camargue, she thought, or Tuscany. Plenty of Chianti Reserva, Sangiovese with a touch of Cabernet Sauvignon. As the bus jolted and swayed, Ginnie dreamt of sunshine and leisure, a bolthole where she could afford the classic simplicity which went with international stardom. Even some of the most beat-up pop-relics from the sixties found fitting haunts in Ireland, for God's sake, were welcomed as near natives on the strength of past hell-raising, were cosseted in the seclusion of country estates. So why could she not do something similar in a sunnier clime? Be mysterious and private, yet sought-after in the golden years of early retirement. The thing was to be in a position to make choices, and not to be beholden to anybody, especially to Leo Kilgallen.

Her brow furrowed. The truth, she knew, apart from the fact that she did not love him, was that nothing short of a miracle would alter her status as Leo's other woman, that his wife and children would always be there, like monoliths.

He would not leave Mitzi for her, he would not forego a comfortable life, in which his business interests could dominate, for one – no less comfortable – in which Ginnie's interests would require time and attention. But she did not want him to leave. She no longer wanted him at all.

That afternoon everything had become clear as she watched him, listened to him. In the end she found him smug. Insufferable. Now she knew all she wanted to know about most men. Disappointing creatures by and large, difficult in intimacy. She did not expect to meet a man she could both love and like. The pick of the crop was gone.

The remaining ones were either too selfish because women ran after them, too kinky or just interested in other men.

Leo had made her tired and she was too young to be tired. When the affair began after a chance meeting in a restaurant, after a theatre premiere, she'd felt able to cope, to keep her distance from the domestic aspects of his life and regard herself as uninterested in Mitzi's doings. There was no sense of burden, only excitement, sheer, white excitement.

That first evening in the *Mirabelle*, attended by white and gold uniformed, gloved waiters, surrounded by humorous, gently drunken friends, it had seemed easy, obvious. She knew and he knew that they would meet again, without Mitzi, his tall, fair, German wife of ten years. If anything, she'd felt tolerance for Mitzi, a bond even, had taken secret pleasure in what she knew would be their future sharing of one man. If only for a time. That evening, it was an effort to pay attention to her theatre companion.

As she guessed he would, he tracked her down. Another restaurant meeting, this time deliberate, a cosmetic preliminary to the main business of the evening. Leo did not disappoint. He was the best lover she'd ever had. They didn't make it as far as the bedroom of her small apartment, but wrestled one another up against the wall of her living-room; she unzipped him hurriedly. His mouth was warm and moist, needy, hungry. As he pressed against her, she felt herself open up. Swiftly, he hoisted her till her legs clasped his waist.

"Put me in!" he moaned.

Not for the first time in her life, she almost laughed, this time at the notion that size *did* matter.

That first evening, their love-making took the form of

blind attacks on one another, in the shower, on the floor of the sitting-room, on the kitchen table and in bed. She had switched on the gas fire and the flames threw wall-shadows which criss-crossed with their own shadowy images, so that the sitting-room became a theatre of movement and shade, their skins dusky gold in the dim light. As his tongue moved down along her stomach, then down lower, stroking her thighs, then up again until he had buried himself in her pubis, she cried out. It was a cry that bordered on tears, because with the sexual release came something else she understood all too clearly. With completion, loss.

Within a month, they'd bought a new apartment, jointly-owned, a luxury, two-bedroomed penthouse more in keeping with Ginnie's aspirations.

"You deserve it!" he whispered, when the contract was signed.

But things changed. As her attachment had come about in small ways, his gradual detachment should have been predictable. The unexpected, amorous phonecalls, bouquets which used to arrive after her gigs, the hastily scribbled notes which he found time to write, and that first, devastatingly powerful one after their second meeting, the words *I love you, L.* – everything slowed to a trickle, and eventually ceased. Leo rarely phoned.

She closed her eyes as the bus swung out suddenly to overtake three cars. If there was going to be an accident she didn't want to see it. There now. Creeping anxiety about nothing. A sure sign of exhaustion, a loss of balance before she had fully come to anything in the world. And she *had* to make it in just the right way. Lately, she felt like throwing a tantrum, like letting fly, wanted to get angry at someone about some discontent she could not quite identify. How was it one of those magazine psychologists she'd read recently described over-tired brats of children? Didn't the phrase go something like "total disintegration of personality", when a child just exploded with tiredness and rage and was incapable of coherent social behaviour? That was how she felt. On the verge, teetering on the edge between controlling her own life and being controlled by it. Not a safe place to be, she thought. No doubt she should see someone, some self-styled pop-psychologist, or would be advised to do so if she told anyone how she felt. But she didn't want to be rebirthed. She didn't want to cut any ties, or scream primally. She didn't want to finger-paint her way to forgotten childhood traumas, neither did she want to tell all to some non-directive pisspot guru.

What irked most was the frequency with which the words *I love you* passed Leo's lips, as if they were the great absolver when she displayed signs of discontent. Despite claims of undying love and affection and friendship, nothing now would convince her of their truth.

She would not give up singing or performing for Leo. Nobody had the right to make such a demand. Flowers were one thing, letters and kisses too, but action was something quite, quite different, the only proof she needed. And Leo would never act in her favour. Which was neither here nor there now, more a matter of pride. She admitted to a sense of pique.

The bus swept up to the hall's stage entrance. Her eyes smarted with unshed tears. The place was packed. They had come in droves. Why could she not enjoy it? Why did she always have to lag behind enjoyable moments? Was it a disease, she wondered, this habit of pleasure in retrospect? Everything looked rosy when she looked back.

Oh yeah-yeah-yeah, that, oh that was fantastic, God it was great, oh yeah, remember that! She blinked quickly and searched her hold-all for a mirror. This was how she'd arranged her life so far. She had never bothered herself with cosy outings with friends, saw no point in keeping up contact with people from her home town, or visits to relatives. Settling down, as it was called, was for the birds. Settling down to what? You could settle down to business but you never settled down to love. It was not for settling down to, so much as getting unsettled about, and that unsettling, when it happened, made life worth living. She liked to think that the pressure to mate in captivity through marriage had lessened. But if she was unhappy with the present arrangement she had nobody but herself to blame. Now that she thought about it, she wasn't unhappy, so much as lost. Skewed off the path, her own path. So why this emptiness? As she stepped down from the bus, she blew up from her bottom lip to flick the fringe out of her eyes. Not the absence of marriage, of that she was certain.

As the group unloaded their gear, one of the young chaps whom Mick had signed on for the summer carried her bag to the dressing-room. There was no shortage of helpers at this time of year, with all the students out from school and college, plenty of youngsters who fancied their chances in the music business, even working on the periphery as dogsbodies. Most lost interest after one season, so the turnover of casual hands was constant.

The first thing Ginnie did once inside was to locate the lavatory, take her cigarettes, sit down and have a smoke. To her surprise, it was as Mick had said, Athree had been a sell-out. They'd mobbed her before, during and after the gig. Now she wanted to hear the slow swish of silence.

Out on the corridor his voice rose confidently over that of the house manager. They were enjoying a good laugh, which indicated that money had changed hands in advance, something guaranteed to make Mick happy. They were doing well. One more year, even six months, and she'd be ready for a European launch. She imagined herself two years on, internationally acclaimed, beneath the heat of the lights at Wembley, or Berlin's Deutschlandhalle, saw herself even further afield, in New York's Madison Square, or San Francisco; there would be open-air concerts drowning the cricket-filled clamour of the American night, hot, steamy performances in which her talent would be recognised. That'd show them. She thought of her mother's acquaintances, women who could barely conceal the fact that they felt sorry for Irene Maloney, whose daughter had gone off with some hippy New Age types in the early eighties and hadn't settled down since. It was pathetic that such people should matter, that what they thought should matter. She knew that. But that was a private truth. Nobody need ever know.

She flushed the lavatory in the pink-tiled cubicle, washed her hands hurriedly. Something different was being asked of her. She felt it keenly, as if her efforts threatened to yield nothing but discontent. Yet such feelings never assaulted her on stage. There she reigned, a great, energetic, singing heroine who could look out with love, accepting devotion, adulation and joy with fitting dignity, born to it.

"Everything A-OK, pet?"

Mick put his head around the door of her dressing-room. She nodded. The period directly prior to a gig was not the time to start expressing doubts.

"Great," she replied, lining her left eyelid with kohl.

87

Mick disappeared, hurrying down the corridor to attend to the drummer who could be heard howling because some nerd had knocked against one of his African drums, damaging the skin.

"Hell, man," he screeched at a boy helper, "we've got to do the Udu Chant sequence so mind where you shove your great spats!"

At the sound of his voice Ginnie smiled, then turned to consider her costume. Best thing would be to open the gig in the black toga which could be slowly peeled off to reveal a purple chamois leather basque. The effect, according to Mick, was riveting, and according to one newspaper critic, "one of startling, near-naked sybaritism".

In the auditorium, Luke O'Regan was seated six rows from the front, determined this time to have one of the best views in the house – not too close or he'd get a crick in his neck, but near enough to see her as she was, perhaps even the texture of her skin, or the hairs on her head. Until now her hair had been nothing more than a maroon halo viewed from a distance. This time, he might even catch the expression in her eyes. Around him, the other kids sat or stood. Everybody was talking, murmuring, humming, and further back a sort of Mexican wave took hold of the crowd as they chanted *Jubilation!*, a high-energy number which had entered the British charts the previous year. A girl right next to him sat with her Walkman on, eyes closed to the scene around her. As he surveyed the hall he realised that he was dressed like every other male present, then felt slightly foolish and finally, despondent at his utter, mobbish anonymity. He was no different from the hundreds, thousands of others who had converged that evening on the hall.

Suddenly the lights blazed and the stage area was
bathed in a fluid spill of pink and yellow. The band
emerged and jauntily took their positions. Sound levels
soared in anticipation of Ginnie's entrance. While the boys
warmed up, the kids warmed up too, their voices rising
and falling in unison. On the corridor, she paced up and
down. As she listened, she knew that this time something
was not quite right. She felt uneasy, as if tonight she was
going to cock-up. There has to be a first time. Sure. Sure.
A first time. She snapped her fingers impatiently. There has
to be a first time, she tried to reason, when things will not
run smoothly, when the causal factor is intangible. That's
it, that's it, a fatal convergence of some kind. She turned
and paced, turned and paced, then fell into the rhythm of
the warm-up numbers as the sound blasted at her and the
walls vibrated and her insides vibrated with a mixture of
lust and anxiety and anticipation.

"You're on!" Mick's voice, somewhere close by. She
was on, she was on, she would do it again and again, she
would touch them where they needed it, their balm, their
hope, just as they would touch her with their rapture! No
time to stop now, no time to slow up, and no desire to
either, she was on her way, she would make it, she had to.
She moved forward and waited for the right moment,
counting mentally, her hips and shoulders automatically
picking up the tempo, the music crushing and expanding
within her head, taking over, possessing her blood and
energy and fear.

So maybe she was a pussy-thrusting little tart, but – she
breathed in and out, felt fear in her bowels, flexed her
arms till the muscles bulged, then rolled her shoulders
forward and back – to hell with the dissenters, she
thought, to hell with the cowards.

Although she panted, her entrance was slow and measured, not the usual pounce towards the microphone. The kids gasped and whistled their approval as she glided out in a black toga, her ankles circled by plaits of golden leather.

Luke gaped, riveted by the slender creature who began to sing for him alone. He watched her mouth, how it opened to reveal small, white teeth, a pink tongue, lips large and plump. Those lips! He swallowed as lust seized him, his eyes continuing their exploration; the strong shoulders, one of them bare, the breasts hidden within the soft folds of the black garment, her narrow waist and the hints of buttock that revealed themselves as she moved; a knee to thigh gash in the toga revealed stockinged, suspendered legs, the creamy flash of skin above suggested eternity.

But two ice-breakers were enough and abruptly the mood changed, tearing him from his reverie. Ginnie began to strip to the rhythm of *Jubilation!;* the music rose to a frenzy that she met easily, powerfully. The fine velcro separated and the sides of her toga parted to reveal the familiar Virgin, resplendent in purple chamois leather, her breasts pointed, a glittering suspender-belt anchored on her hips.

*Jubilation! Jubilation! That's the word ah want to shout,*
*'Cause you have a way like nobody ah've known before,*
*You're the man who makes me, man who takes me,*
*Man who makes me a wo-om-ahhn!*

She swung into her dance routine, rotated her hips, dropped her torso forward and peered through parted legs at the audience. It was an upside-down crazy world of colour and cannabis smoke, strange bobbing heads, mouths which opened and shut like the mandibles of insects as the kids screamed and waved. She straightened to turn, went into a double-spin before landing like a cat on both feet.

The old magic was working, they sang with her and to her, but now again, she felt that incongruity, an oddness. As she went through the motions, gyrating for an imaginary lover, she could not decide what had happened. The lyrics came too automatically, yet they sounded cool once her voice was broken into strands of differing intensities by the synthesiser and transformed into a passionate call for the fulfillment of desire, love, freedom. Those old, old words. New to every generation, a discovery stumbled on by every young explorer lost on the voyage to the land of liberation.

*Don't let them grind you down,*
*Only fools bring down the grey,*
*Open your mind to jubilation!*
*Come with me, be with me,*
*We can have it all the way! Way! Way!*

As at every concert before, the condoms began to float down the air, they dropped from the balcony in festoons, beribboned in mauve, red and bright green. She called out to the unknown lover, the unencountered one with whom she would head for the stars.

A sudden movement to her left, in the wings, caught her attention. She threw her body in that direction and sang on, surprised to see Mick waving his arms in agitation. He shook his head as if something was amiss, then made a slashing movement across his throat with a forefinger, the signal that she was to break at the end of

91

the number. As the last chords faded, she stood and addressed the audience. The sweat was pouring off her, so that her entire body glistened beneath the lights.

"Look here, all you lovely ones, thank you, thank you, thank you for coming here tonight. I am so honoured to see so many dear faces . . . and mah goodness, wow! WOWEEEE! You all know the words too! But lemme tell you something . . . right now, Virgin needs a little quickie break, if you get mah drift . . . "

The crowd whooped and cheered. She watched as they suddenly moved as one, surging spontaneously into an undulating Mexican wave. In that moment they were no longer rational individuals.

"Uh-huh," she nodded significantly at them. "So you good people just sit back and enjoy the sound the guys are gonna make. I'll be right back," she gushed, blowing kisses in the air.

Mick almost dragged her into the wings, his face white with panic.

"No time to lose, we've had a call – serious stuff, a bomb-threat – some fucking nutcase but we've got to take it seriously – "

"Ah, don't be ridiculous Mick, it's happened before – you mean to say you cut my act on account of some *headcase*?" She was incredulous. "You can't mean it. Look, I'm going back out and don't stop me. I'm telling you, Mick, it's nothing, these people are full of hot air, they'd never risk a bomb!"

She shook her head, then patted him on the shoulder.

"Ginnie, we're pulling the plug on this gig. Now beat it. Ginnie, believe me! The press is on its way."

For a second, she hesitated, then turned from him and made to re-enter the hall.

*"Don't!"* he shouted.

It was too late. Before she could change her mind, the whole stage burst up beneath the band, threw her back with such force that her body slammed into a wall. Her head lashed against the concrete surface and the world went black.

In the auditorium, the kids went hysterical. Luke barely missed the impact of the blast, as masonry, rigging, guitars and electronic equipment hurtled through the air. Flames crackled beneath the stage, the lead guitarist lay injured and unconscious and as Luke climbed over the legs of a crowd of screaming girls he yelled at them to come on, to bloody move themselves if they wanted to get out alive. One of them, a complete stranger to him, froze in horror, pointed at the stage, stuttered. Others bent double, gasping in the fumes. Instinctively he turned and caught the girl who stood in shock, the smell of urine rising around him as he dragged her after him. Hundreds crammed the exit doors; all six doors were jammed with bodies. Two of the six were chained and padlocked, and could not open under the pressure of bodies. The youngsters poured in a crush through the other four exits, but even so the crush was too much, and the smaller, the weaker ones, youngsters of fourteen or fifteen, stumbled and fell and were trampled on. The two jammed exit doors were closest to the stage, and remained chained as the crowds pushed up against them, desperate for escape, desperate for air. Terrified wails rose, unlike any synthesiser, any experiment in sound; kids retched, or cried for their parents, promising divinities that they would be good, they would study hard, whatever.

The more ruthless had decided that there was only one way out, much as Luke had done, by climbing over the shoulders of others.

"Up! Get up and crawl over them! Fight!" he shouted at the girl. He hoisted himself up over someone's shoulders, ignoring screams of "Get down ya bastard, get off me fuckin' back!", ignoring the sight of what looked like twenty or thirty young people whose bodies had already been trampled, and lay unconscious. Come hell or high water, he was going to escape, he hadn't finished with life yet, not by a long shot. He glanced back in the direction of the girl, but already she was trapped, lifted off her feet by the surrounding crush.

He crawled over the backs and shoulders of others until he reached the door. Nothing would have stopped him, not the clinging hands that reached out in desperation, nor the cries of panic, nor the fists that tried to batter him off the packed, suffocating human bridge as boys and girls completely lost their nerve or went under in the crush.

By the time he fell out the doorway, the fire had spread like a blow-torch to the high ceiling. His lungs hurt. The side-wings and flats blazed furiously, and as he glanced back he noticed, as if he were observing a silent video, or something in slow motion, a body on fire.

"Oh Jesus, oh Jesus don't let this be happening. Let me out. Let me live. Oh God," he sobbed, rolled away from the exit and onto the grass.

Outside, five fire brigade units arrived. Ambulances screamed down the road, blue lights flashing. All around, people his own age or younger stood or sat in silence, others wept and held one another, trying to offer comfort where there was none.

"But my sister's in there!" one girl wailed, "I have to find her, where's Anne?" or "Me Da didn't want me to come here, said it was a bad scene. This is a punishment."

Luke held his head and listened, then closed his eyes in

an attempt to obliterate the scene. His shoulder was cut, splinters of wood had lodged in his right arm. He began to pick at them absently. The group, he thought, must have been burned alive, the whole lot of them. He shook his head and gasped. Virgin! His heart tightened. Where was Virgin? Virgin? What was happening to her? Why has this happened? Why did good people die, why did they go away like this? He too began to weep, slammed his hands to his ears by way of blocking out the sounds of distress, wept for his dead father as he had not yet done, in huge, shivering, gulping sobs. Out of control, a storm of grief and anger spilled through him as never before.

Mick had dragged Ginnie away from backstage as soon as her body hit the wall; gagging, he hauled her the length of the smoke-blackened corridor and, manoeuvring his own bulk through the stage door, laid her, unconscious, on the grass near the bus. Then, holding a handkerchief over his mouth and nose, he rushed back in an attempt to rescue the band from what was still a minor fire. But by the time he reached the stage area he couldn't even see, so dense were the clouds which coiled from gaps in the smashed stage. One of the guys began to scream crazily, then burst through the smoke, his back on fire, the stench of burning flesh carrying up Mick's nostrils.

He acted quickly, managing to pull off his own jacket and throw himself on top of Pete, the drummer, and rolled him around and around until the jacket stifled the flames and all that remained was a black, moist mess. Pete passed out and Mick dragged him out and down the steps, placing his body alongside Ginnie's, near the bus. She began to stir, moaned, then rubbed her head slowly.

"You're all right, Ginnie pet, you're safe. Stay there – I'll be right back – there's a fire inside honey, I've got to get the others – "

The place was engulfed. He watched as the flames crackled and roared, as the draught which gusted down the narrow aisles of the auditorium fanned them more fiercely still. He never realised before that fire had a voice, or how ferocious its power. Suddenly, he bent and vomited, knowing the world to have been blasted apart. His whole body was in the control of his guts, yet in the midst of heaving and puking he had a vague sense of being finished in Ireland. He wiped his mouth with his sleeve, swallowed hard to stem the rancidness in his stomach. He felt faint, weak. He wanted to die but instead staggered on shaking legs back towards the bus and saw that the newspaper people had arrived, recorders and notebooks ready. Bonnie Macbeth from *Now!,* he groaned, recognising her thick red hair, and stoop-shouldered Bob Farrelly from one of the Sundays. He imagined them, faces set at the prospect of a scoop, breaking their arses to get the best hook on the disaster.

The sight of the hacks made him groan, but instinctively he decided to deal with them. Let them ask their questions, he thought, still dazed, as he moved around to the crowd at the front of the building. Fuckit, this was only the calm before the storm. Again, his mind swam. This wasn't what Ginnie was about. Her music was special, a very personal statement. That's what she'd called it in a radio interview, " . . . a personal statement. But the problem is, in the public's mind, you are your image, your musical image, and I think that what I project is only an extension of me. It isn't the real me. Well, maybe some of me, but not the full story."

Try as he would, he could not escape the sound of

panic-stricken screaming all around as the kids continued to pour out, some bleeding, others burnt, some with the clothes stuck to their skin where the flames had caught them, the print of a floral shirt or a polyester lace top melted onto flesh. He, Mick Delaney, was guilty, guilty, guilty.

The double doors of the ambulances swung open and medical teams moved in. Gradually, the fire-fighters brought the blaze under control. Luke knew from threads of sentences he overheard that some of the kids had been trampled to death, or had suffocated in the crush.

He pulled himself up off the grass and stepped over bodies, people in shock, shivering, weeping, or just staring up at the sky. He wondered if he would ever stop shaking, if the world would ever look bright again, if he could ever take pleasure in anything as long as he lived. His hands touched against the side wall of the building as he made his way to the back, and found himself confronted by the Virgin Bus. The silver-grey deluxe touring model was blackened with smoke towards the rear, caught in the powerful draught that billowed from the stage door.

A movement held his attention, the sight of a woman who struggled to raise herself off the ground but kept falling back. He heard her mutter, then fragments of swear-words, each time she collapsed again. He approached cautiously. Her face was concealed by her right arm, but he recognised the outfit despite the smoke-blackened limbs and the singed remains of her ponytail. As he leant over, she dropped her arm.

"Who're you?" she mumbled. Luke didn't answer. Words wouldn't come. She'd had a knock on the head, bruising, superficial cuts. Suddenly he was petrified. Virgin, whose beauty and strength had sustained him during the past dark winter, whose every word and breath he followed with the hunger of the affection-starved, lay right there before him and beneath him, vulnerable as he could never have imagined, scarcely aware of his presence, and all he could do was open and shut his mouth. She was smaller than he had imagined.

He bent down, saw the pulse in her neck flicker rapidly.

"My name's L-L-Luke – " he stammered over her face, "I-I've come to help y-you – "

He waited while she absorbed that. This time she looked at him, tried to focus her eyes. The pupils were unnaturally large and luminous, and she blinked frequently, as if unable to see him clearly.

"Where's Mick?"

"Mick Delaney?" he probed.

"Manager," she replied, turning her head aside, "Mick Delaney, I think he pulled me out."

"Lucky for you. He's around the f-front. There were a lot of people in there."

At this, she began to cry weakly, just lay and blubbered at him, the words "So sorry . . . " squeezed from her throat at intervals. He was afraid to lay a hand on her, terrified he might hurt.

"Everything's going to be OK now," he soothed. "The ambulances are here. Fire's practically out. The kids are safe," he lied.

"Really? Are they safe?"

He nodded.

"I want to get away from here." She raised herself on one elbow, this time able to bear her own weight. "I've got to get out of this place."

"Maybe you'd better stick around. You need a doctor, that's a bad knock on your head," he urged, wondering why he always had to say the sensible, reasonable, responsible thing.

"No," she insisted, "I'm all right now. I can manage, just help me up." Her voice was stronger, and she gripped his arm in order to pull herself forward.

"Please help me."

Without another word between them he made a decision and lifted her to her feet. Immediately her legs began to buckle, so he caught her in his arms and carried her to the bus. The door was wide open. He hoisted her up the three steps, manoeuvred carefully lest he should knock her head or cause further injury. She hadn't noticed the unconscious drummer stretched on the grass only yards outside the bus, or the black, raw mess of his back. As gently as possible he placed her on one of the seats, made her lie back and stretch out. A plan formed in his head.

It was crazy. It would never work.

He pulled at the seats on the far side of the vehicle, ripped two of them loose, then rigged them so that she had a full-length bed on which to rest.

Without pausing he left her there and sat into the driving-seat. Her eyes were closing, but he caught what she said.

"Drive on, James, and don't spare the horses!"

The key was in the ignition. He turned it, released the air-brakes, revved and took off just as another ambulance turned the corner, its blue light flashing. Luke swerved, the other vehicle blared at him, but he pulled the bus well clear and drove straight through a wooden fence on the perimeter of the tarmac. The bus jolted across a stretch of

99

grassland avoiding the hold-up in the area outside the big hall, and burst once more through a fence.

It split and ricocheted in all directions. He knew he'd lost his reason. The bus careered down the road, and he knew he'd had it, he was fucked for good; he was stark, raving mad. The police would be after him in no time, what was he doing, what possessed him to do such a thing, he thought, accelerating, then locating the headlights as he headed for the churchyard. Street lights flashed yellowly, he saw the road's damp sheen, and how the place was packed with curious people lured out by the commotion up at the hall. His breath came in gasps, his hands were clammy and gripped the steering-wheel as if frozen solid.

Outside the church, all was quiet. He pulled up in the middle of the road, left the engine running and rushed back to where she lay, wide awake again, her eyes watchful as he approached.

"Oh, Buddha–Buddha, who are you?" She slurred the words. He rubbed his forehead in astonishment, felt panic in his stomach.

"Luke. You asked me to take you away."

"I did?" She began to giggle. "Well then, take me away – Luke – or whoever you are!"

"Come on then." Carefully, he removed the seating from beneath her legs, reached forward and lifted her again. This time, she could stand.

"We need to hurry. I've got a jeep here. We'll use that."

She didn't object, but gripped him tightly as they stepped out of the bus. Rather than waste time walking, he lifted her again, but this time threw her over his shoulder and tried to sprint across the yard. She giggled again, a light ripple behind his head.

"Wow! What have we got here, King Kong?" she tittered.

He searched his pocket for keys, found them, opened the jeep and helped her into the front seat, then strapped her in.

"Where to?" he asked quickly, pulling out through the gateway on the other side of the yard.

"The city."

As he drove off he accused himself, over and over again. Eejit. Wanker. Madman. Basket-case. Thoughts of the next day's silage-cutting flickered across his mind, and the week's pre-booked contracts. God knows what time he'd get back to the farm, and where the hell was he going with this one, anyway? As he hadn't the foggiest idea, he decided to concentrate on driving. Getting from point A to point B in one piece. About an hour and a half of hard roadwork should have them in Dublin. His arms trembled and relaxed, trembled then relaxed again as his terror subsided and the distance between the silver bus and the horror of Malla increased.

They sped along in silence. It began to drizzle, the windscreen wipers cut to and fro in a light hum as tunnels of hedgerow whizzed by and they finally turned onto the M50. He checked his watch. It was only one o'clock, but it seemed as if months, even years had passed since he'd entered the auditorium. Virgin began to shiver. He looked at her, scantily clad and freezing cold, her teeth chattering, and pulled over quickly.

"Here!" He dragged an old wool blanket from the back seat. She draped it carefully around her body. Shocked, out of control, he couldn't believe his luck, teetered between horror and a weird excitement. Or was it pride? It was as if he'd caught something wild, something he'd

101

longed for. He had her. Right there. In his jeep. They were driving to fucking Dublin, he was with the woman of his dreams and he had her, *her,* wrapped up in a tattered blanket there beside him. He'd rescued her, hadn't he? Even if Mick Delaney got there first, he'd removed her from a lunatic hole, for all he knew the whole place might have exploded.

She became talkative. "Where are we? Don't know how it happened. Freakish, man!"

She rubbed the windscreen with the back of her hand. Luke had turned the heating system on but it only steamed up the windows.

"Sure," he said.

"I had a feeling, you know. Hey Luke!"

He stared at the road, driving hard.

"Not that I'm psychic or anything – but I felt outta myself all afternoon. Weird. "

"You'd need to be one of those clairvoyants to beat what happened back there," he jabbered, then swallowed. His mouth was dry.

"Things haven't been so good for me. Personally, I mean," she confided.

The woman was raving, delirious, Luke thought.

"We're getting near the city. Where d'you want to go?" he asked.

"Do you know Ruskin Way?"

"Haven't a clue."

He followed her instructions, circled one roundabout three times as she tried to remember which turn-off he should take, then trailed slowly along tree-lined avenues, past darkened homes or groups of young people out for the night. Once, at the traffic lights in Terenure, he noticed, to the left, a police-car perched at the junction.

When it didn't move he almost panicked, imagined himself watched and under suspicion.

"It's OK, Luke. Only a speed trap. The Guards have to do something to pass the nights. As if Dublin isn't busy enough." She chortled gently to herself.

He was still nervous. Now that he was in the city he was tormented with anxiety.

"Here. Pull in to the right," she said.

"Here?"

It was a red-bricked apartment block, surrounded by mature beech trees, the shrubbery below them impeccable and dewy. He drew in across a cobbled surface and spun the jeep into the first vacant space.

"You live *here?*"

He didn't know what he'd expected. A mansion? Possibly, but not an apartment block, no matter how luxurious. It seemed so ordinary.

"This is it." She pulled at the door-handle. He reached over and opened it for her, then caught the smell of smoke from her skin, which reminded him yet again of Malla. He hesitated.

"OK so," he paused, "I'd better disappear, I've done enough damage for one night."

It was ridiculous, what he'd been toying with. The very idea! Once and for all he'd get a grip on himself and face up to responsibilities and commitments. Time to cut, to leave Virgin to sort out her own problems. It looked as if she wasn't short of them.

"You're all right now?" he asked, staring at her.

"I think so." She fidgeted with the blanket as she stood in the open air, a tattered woman in a filthy leather outfit.

"Come in for a while. You've had a rough time too," she coaxed. "Come on, I want you to come in!"

He hesitated, bit his lips, then turned towards her again. She was so persuasive, even like this, with half her hair singed off and her face stained – like a refugee or someone just released from captivity in the Middle East. He licked his lips and swallowed, his mouth still dry. For the first time, he realised how thirsty he was. Parched, in fact.

He hopped from the jeep and followed her. They didn't speak in the elevator, just stared at one another as awareness and curiosity gradually replaced panic.

The door of the apartment sprang open gently. He stood and peered in after her. She switched on a lamp and again, he followed. Her movements were jerky as she fixed ornaments, adjusted pictures, flicked lights on and off and checked windows, finally running into another room which, from the sounds that ensued, he took to be a bathroom.

He waited. The room was huge, decorated in pale green, with a dark and shining wood floor on which lay heavy silk rugs in dark blue, yellow and green. Comfortable furniture, he noted, wide armchairs, warm, yellow lamps and little lit alcoves in which small clay and metal figures were placed. The walls were crammed with paintings. Some of them looked as if the painter had just fired the paint on the canvas and then messed it about with a knife and fork.

"It isn't always this tidy," she called from the bathroom. "I had a brainstorm today, did a real clean-up!"

When she came back, she'd cleaned herself up too. Now he could see her face, and the massive bruise above her right eyebrow. She wore tight satiny leggings and a loose tunic threaded with gold stitching. He did not know how to speak to her. She pointed to a chair and said that he might at least sit down and relax, or have a drink. She couldn't stand having to listen to Mick just then, she said, couldn't bear any more of it.

"I'm tired of the whole scene. I knew something was wrong but I thought I was the source of the problem, you know? My singing or something, not a bloody bomb!"

She threw herself onto the sofa and began to shiver. Luke managed to lift his feet from where they had taken root. He wanted to comfort her. He knelt in front of her, on the floor. It was like watching himself from a distance, as if he were operated by remote control.

"Does your head hurt?"

She nodded.

"Perhaps you should call the doctor. Just to be safe."

"Over there in the yellow book – no, not that one, the small leather one. Doctor Ryan's the name," she sniffled.

But then she changed her mind. "On second thoughts, I don't think it's necessary. Really. Thanks all the same. I'll be fine if I can rest."

"I'll go then," he said.

She looked up at him, a yellow oriental lamp behind her. She was barefoot. His heart somersaulted. But then he remembered the scene at Malla. It broke through his mind in waves that stopped him from merely enjoying the sight of her. He still heard cries and screams, smelt the stench, sniffed fear as it burst through the evening's pleasure. He held his breath and began to tremble.

"Luke? Would you stay the night? Would you?"

Relief surged through him and he breathed out again. There was no decision to make. It was so very easy.

"You want to change out of those things? I have spare trousers and shirts. They might fit."

She led him to the bathroom and he went through, not

listening as she pointed to the shelves of thick towels, then left him by himself. It was steamy, with gold mouldings; a square bath inlaid with small black and green squares fitted into the centre of the room, with steps which glittered along the edges. To the left, in one corner, lay the jacuzzi and to the right, a wash-basin rose like the head of a flower from a long, grooved, transparent stem. A tracery of blood clung to the floor from where Ginnie's feet had bled when she'd stepped from the shower – and she'd forgotten to turn off the water. It hissed and steamed. On impulse he bent and touched the blood, ran his forefinger through the small map-like shape, and thought *This is her blood, this is Virgin's blood*. But he heard a sound from outside the bathroom and jerked suddenly upright, then felt foolish. The shower door was patterned with long, elegant flowers in red and turquoise glass. He stripped and stood beneath the faucet, thought back to his bath only hours before, when he'd been full of anticipation, and so different, a totally different person.

The water gushed over his head and Luke stood, eyes shut tight, no longer knowing or caring what was going to happen next. A cleansing heat enveloped his skin, calmed him. Tomorrow, or the days after, did not matter. He would stay with Virgin this one night, and why not, she had asked him, she had needed him.

A hand appeared above the door of the shower.

"You'll need these," she called. Towels. A light dressing-gown, gold and black. Five minutes later he stepped out and dried himself, then fleetingly imagined himself as her husband while he pulled on the robe. This was how the man she would marry might look, he speculated, then grinned at his big mug in the mirror.

The problem of who exactly the garment belonged to

struck him next, but something warned him that right then this wasn't essential information. He stepped from the bathroom and entered the living-room. Virgin was stretched out on the sofa. She smoked a joint, gazed absently at the ceiling. A bottle of whiskey on the low table had been opened and she poured a liberal amount into two ice-filled tumblers.

"Help yourself," she said. "And perhaps close the curtains too?"

He tugged at the fabric.

"Try the sides – the cord, the cord!"

Embarrassed, he obeyed, then turned and faced her. The whole thing was a bad idea; he should get dressed and out of the apartment like a bat out of hell. This wasn't his scene. It was all wrong for him.

"Sit down. Relax. I don't bite," she drawled, an amused expression on her face. He was about to insist on leaving. His mouth opened but the words wouldn't come. Instead he sat obediently in the chair opposite, picked up the glass of whiskey, then took such a large mouthful that he nearly choked and half the liquid slobbered down his chin. Again, she regarded him with amusement, though also with curiosity. Neither spoke for a time. Luke's face flamed with embarrassment, he felt like an invader, even if she'd invited him in.

He concentrated on sipping the fiery liquid, which he normally never drank. He wished he could have ice-cold water instead, but was afraid to ask. She might think him a youngster.

"So what brought you to Malla?" she said lightly, in a tone which made it clear that she thought Malla was a dump. She held her glass to one side, swirled the contents idly.

Again he faltered, conscious of not having a stitch on beneath the robe; thoughts of what his mother or Mary or Ferdia would think drifted across his mind.

"I came to see you. What else?" He shrugged. It sounded so cut and dried. "And I live there."

"Smoke a joint?" she said in a near whisper, before bolting forward in surprise. "Jesus! You live there? In Malla?"

"No thanks," he shook his head as she offered him a reefer. "Yeah, I live in Malla." He gave an apologetic laugh. She continued to study him and he squirmed beneath her gaze but at the same time tried not to let his discomfort show. Fuck her, but it was like being under a magnifying glass.

"Curiouser and curiouser!" she murmured, "I mean, you being from that place and all that. A true *local!*" she laughed gently.

"I haven't missed any of your gigs," Luke said gruffly. He wished she'd stop harping on about Malla. He felt like an insect in a glass case, pinned down and exposed by her attention. She raised her eyebrows and pulled the corners of her lips down in an expression of surprise. She was so adult, so sure of herself.

"They tell me you're not alone," she tittered. "At least my manager does – Mick – says the groupies are on the road every bit as much as we are."

"I'm no groupie!" he spat, nettled. She bit her lip and again turned her eyes on him. Her expression showed amusement mingled with contained curiosity. It was as if she expected him to explode if she asked the wrong questions.

"Sor-ry. I said the wrong thing," she said immediately. "I'm truly sorry. I have a big, careless mouth."

"OK. No offence taken," he muttered.

She swung her legs off the sofa, and refilled his glass. He noticed the shape of her calf muscles, swathed in fine satin leggings.

"To your health, Luke."

"To your music," he countered, and he knew he sounded defensive. She crossed the room, raised her glass and emptied it. The gesture weakened him. She held one hand against the small of her back, drawing the light fabric of the tunic against her buttocks, and he imagined the shape of the body beneath it, as if he'd never before seen it undressed or exposed. Quickly, he looked away amd swallowed another mouthful of whiskey. His head was in a whirl. Dizziness and warmth whisked him far from his earlier mood. Jesus Christ, but he was beginning to *like* himself!

His eyes followed her as she went into her bedroom, then casually removed the tunic, beneath which was a light, silken, red vest. He looked away. Women just didn't do that type of thing, not in full view of someone they hardly knew. But when he looked again, it seemed the most spot-on thing for her to do.

Now she observed him from the doorway, smiling. He looked into her eyes in a way he'd never have been able to if she were performing; they were huge and black, the pupils dilated. The bruise on her forehead pulled her right eyebrow into an unnaturally high arch where the flesh was swollen, but she was as beautiful as ever – older, sophisticated, kind. She knew everything, he could trust her. She could tell him things. His head lolled against a cushion as she approached, then removed the glass from his hand, clasped the hand and held it in her own. She might as well have placed it in a blazing fire, and he shrank back, unable to respond to the gesture. Yet he was aroused, shifted his position, pulled his hand back, crossed his legs and told her in childishly offended tones that she shouldn't do such things.

"Luke," she whispered, letting him withdraw, "Luke, I'm sorry, I'm a crazywoman sometimes, and I'm half drunk. Or maybe it's the joint. You're drunk too, only you're the sensible one, and you haven't ever drunk much whiskey before, have you?"

"Only after my father died," he said carefully, wishing his lust would disappear and that for once in his life he could feel sexually neutral. His tongue felt slow and heavy behind his teeth.

"Long ago?"

"Two years."

"Both mine are alive. I have a brother your age. Jack. And three more brothers. Jack's just been accepted into university. He's a lot younger than me. The folks think it's great."

Luke nodded, his eyes closing. Well for him, able to do what he liked because he didn't have to work. He'd heard it before.

"So what do you do? Are you working? You must be. Your hands are firm – strong hands, strong hands," she mused.

He drew his fingertips in to conceal bitten fingernails and what he saw as a pair of awkward paws that drove machinery and lifted and dragged things from one place to another. Hers were tanned and long, the cool hands he'd noticed as she'd reached towards him in the dark back at Malla.

But he answered her questions, his confidence growing, his thoughts taking shape. He began to speak easily, told her about home, his mother, about Mary,

110

Ferdia and Tom, released captive worries as he described how anxiety about the future often kept him from sleep.

"You miss your father," she said.

"I miss him. Ground's gone from beneath me." He shrugged his shoulders, his expression transformed from relaxation to fretful anger.

"Life. Still. He sounds as if he was OK, your old man. *My* father, who is very much alive, lost his job when he was forty-three and we've all had to suffer for it since."

Luke said nothing. She sounded cruel.

"Things have been tough in this country for a long time," he said by way of softening things.

"In more ways than one. Some unemployed people give me a pain. Always whinging. Full of self-pity. Want to solve the world's problems and haven't even the means to solve their own. That kind of thing. He was hard to listen to, my father. Still is at times. I feel sorry for my mother. And for Jack. He feels he has to do well at university for Big Daddy's sake."

"What does he think of you? Your father, I mean."

"Not much. But he doesn't say that much either, because he knows I'm hitting the big-time and will be bigger. He knows I won't listen anyway."

"You sound very – " he searched for the right word, "strong."

She tossed her head in response. "I'm never really sure where I'm at either – you know, you're up there, night after night, some nights you cover two gigs – tonight was one of those – and even though it's great while you're doing it, something's missing. Like a piece of a giant's jigsaw puzzle, and I can't find it. Yeah, that's life."

She sat on the arm of the chair, her arm draped along the cushion behind his head. He could smell her skin, and when he looked up he saw the pulse in her neck, watched as it throbbed, more slowly now, no longer the rapid flicker he had observed earlier.

"But – but you're doing something that counts. I'm just doing what any eejit could do. I don't even want to do it," he protested. How could she speak about something being missing from her life, when she had everything – fame, adoration, talent, beauty, God she was beautiful!

"Is that your real name? Virginia shortened to Virgin?"

"Virginia Maloney, that's me. But everybody calls me Ginnie. Why?"

"I wondered. Just that it's an old-fashioned name, like something out of a book or – something historical – like the American Civil War."

"Luke is an ancient name though – straight from antiquity, and the Bible, right?"

"I had an uncle Luke, that's all," he said, "and it rhymes with puke!" he added drunkenly. His voice was slurring, his mouth felt numb, his tongue an obstacle to free speech. Ginnie refilled his glass. *Ginnie.* He pondered the word.

"Ginnie. I like that!" he laughed.

"That's the last one. Or else you'll have a sore head tomorrow," she said firmly.

"I don't care, I don't care. Not in the least. Because I – "

He couldn't go on. He reached up and tugged at her arm. The gesture was light. She stopped, surprised. She squeezed his shoulders, and again, his head lolled back in the chair. Already succumbing to sleep, his eyes closed.

"Yeah. I know," she whispered, wary of drunken sincerity, whirlpool sentences, simple words and flowing adoration. She tiptoed to the bedroom, fetched a blanket and draped it over him. The last thing she did before climbing into bed was to unplug the telephones to prevent Mick, Leo or her mother from disturbing her. Not that she need have worried about Leo Kilgallen.

# Eight

## The Leo and Mitzi Show

That night, the fire at Malla got priority on the radio news-bulletins. Fifteen young people died, mostly from suffocation and smoke inhalation. Pete, the drummer whom Mick Delaney had dragged free, was in the burns unit of a Dublin hospital, and thirty-two other burn victims were admitted on the dawn of June the twelfth.

In thousands of homes, telephones rang throughout a night which never gave up its bright summer horizon, as relatives checked and re-checked with the police, trying to establish whether their sons or daughters had been among the casualties.

The night grew warm and humid. A south-westerly airflow swept in over the country. In Malla, few went to bed, the streets thronged with helpers and curiosity-seekers, gawkers and journalists.

Mick Delaney had no idea what had happened to Ginnie. Thoughts of kidnap occurred amongst a myriad wilder possibilities such as the one that she had perhaps regained consciousness and re-entered the hall only to perish in the fire. His initial attempt to deal with the press came to nothing. He was shocked and confused, and one of the paramedics eventually sedated him.

To add to his confusion, Hilary Dunne turned up in the middle of the night, breathless with concern. Her face drained of colour, she made her way towards him. She placed her hands on his shoulders. Instinctively, he withdrew from her touch.

"Oh thank God, thank *God* you're safe! I heard it on the news – got straight into the car and drove down the minute I heard – my God, what a dreadful thing to happen, but you're all right now, aren't you?"

"I'm fine," he said with the invincible calm of one carrying a Diazepam injection in his system. "Good on you, coming all this way."

She beamed at him, patted his shoulder, then began to caress his hair.

"What a thing to happen! Who'd have imagined it!"

Drugged though as he was, Mick wanted to shake Hilary off like an insect, but she kept stroking him as if he was a shagging pet. Her eyes were so distant. She kept looking up at the sky, her face intense. He shook his head and rubbed his eyes. The dreadful thing had taken place, that was the point. Ginnie was missing, all those kids were dead, the place was a shambles and questions would be asked. The questions didn't bother him. He could face what would be thrown his way, but the feeling that in some way he was responsible was not dulled even by the sedative shot.

"Those poor kids. Those poor kids," he moaned softly. Hilary stood beside him, squeezing his shoulders every so often. Her hands, she realised, did not work the way she wanted them to. Her voices told her. *Not like that! Not like that!* they whispered, agitated. Despite her loathing of

Virgin – in particular because she had stolen Mick Delaney and absorbed his attention at her expense – she felt a smidgeon of pity for the man. The drive from a nearby town, not Dublin as she suggested, had been at breakneck speed. She was stopped once, warned by a stern young Garda who looked to be just out of short pants, but was then allowed to drive on for Malla by using the excuse that her daughter had been at that concert.

This was not what was intended. There'd be ructions at headquarters the following day because someone had got carried away by what was to have been a simple enough procedure. Just enough to scare the whore, to threaten her pert little bum with hell's brimstone; moreover, a message to her acolytes to stay away from sin. Fire, real fire, had not been planned, just smoke. But the birdbrain who'd put it together was a complete moron who didn't know where to draw the line, she concluded.

Hilary calmed herself and began to reason again. That was her special quality nowadays – absolute, chilly calm when the whole world lay in fragments. Nothing could touch her. She was powerful, in control, even of her feelings for Mick Delaney. Now and again, she stroked his unkempt hair, but her eyes were distant. As she looked up at the sky in which her God dwelt so thunderously, she knew in her heart of hearts that He had spoken this very night, that His voice which normally trembled in trees and branches throughout the seasons had breathed fire on earth, that he had sent His inept agent forth because perhaps this, after all, was what He had designed. And she was His helper, His gracious and willing hand-maiden. Praise be, she thought, her face transformed to the dolorousness of a Madonna, one hand on Mick's shoulder as he talked to himself and to her about the burden of responsibility which he now carried on account of this; how he was finished, how he could never work again because of what he owed in terms of human life. *Amen,* she whispered inaudibly, *Amen!*

Mitzi Kilgallen had just packed Leo's away bag when she caught the bulletin. The television set flickered in the bedroom, and as Leo emerged, a towel around his waist, clean-shaven and scented from the bathroom, he too heard the tail-end of the news report.

"What was that?" He headed absently towards the bed, a copy of *Esquire* under his arm.

"Some fire down in the sticks. At a concert."

Mitzi's mind was elsewhere, trying to concentrate on what the TV man had said while calculating whether or not to book a holiday in the Maldives for the autumn, when they would both need a break before the onset of the hunting season.

"Fire?"

Leo sounded casual, uninterested, yet turned pages without seeing what was printed on them. Mitzi looked up and thought hard.

"Mmmm. That singer – you know, the weirdo who behaves like a cat in heat," she snickered across the room, "Virgin. Yes, her, so kitsch, you know? There was a big fire – caused by an explosion I think – wherever she was singing. Some kids died. Desperate, isn't it? *Die Armen!*"

*The poor things!* Even Mitzi's way of sympathising could sound appealing, Leo thought, even bringing bad news she could be sexy, with her perfect English and just a hint of Germany lurking in the throaty vowels. Nonetheless, his heart lurched when he heard the news. Mitzi's jibe about the cat in heat had not gone unnoticed by her husband, who squirmed inwardly at such mockery.

But, Jesus Christ, an explosion at Malla! He tightened the fist of his right hand and pressed it gently against his ribs. This would be tricky. The place was under-insured even at the very beginning. The question of reinsuring it had more or less slipped his mind. Anyone could have overlooked it. Now he'd have to pick up the tab. Like hell he would, he glowered. Someone was to blame for the explosion, or the fire, or whatever happened down there, and that someone was going to pay. He'd get his secretary onto it in the morning. One thing was certain. Heads would roll.

He hoped Ginnie wasn't injured. She was – well, she was a lovely girl. They'd had great times. Different, intoxicating at first. Recently, she'd grown thorny, but then that was women for you. It was as if she expected him to jump ship – a ship which was navigating a perfectly good course as marriages went – and for the umpteenth time he wondered why he allowed such problems into his life. Why was his cock so often the factor on which an afternoon, an evening, a night, hinged? He did not know the answer, only that he had to have women, could not resist them, had to woo them and bed them. Never more than one at a time, of course, excluding Mitzi. The truth was, he had to have Ginny too, because she was exciting, energetic, damn sexy. And available.

Mitzi opened a wardrobe, then tutted to herself.

"God, Liebling, but you're so damn tidy! Oma Deutschland would love it!"

"Are you serious about a fire? At Malla?" he said, ignoring the last comment. He tried to control his tone of voice, to moderate the sense of horror and disguise it as concern for the injured.

"Yes Schatz. Why? Not one of your places, is it? Be back in a tick, Lindsay's crying."

117

He lay back and closed his eyes as another, more awful thought, pounced. What if Ginnie had been injured, or worse, what if that adorable, wild-flower woman had been incinerated down in the backwoods? But no, such things didn't happen. They simply didn't. Not to him, not to people he knew.

Anyway, there was nothing he could do. He would fly to Brussels at eight-thirty in the morning. The best he could do was try her apartment on the car phone, but even that would have to wait. Ginnie would be fine, he persuaded himself. She was a survivor, no point worrying about it too much. Wherever she was, Ginnie would make out.

Even then, his mind lingered on those hours together, on thoughts of her. The sheer smoothness of her skin, her appetites, the way she could look at him. There were minutes when the scents and sweats of the pair of them mattered, perhaps deeply. Pity about what she did though. All the same, she seemed determined to stick the pace. Maybe this incident would take the edge off her bravura. Such attitude, such open liberalism, and the brand of explicit sexuality which her lyrics promoted did not sit comfortably with his way of doing things. One had to be so careful. People could have all the freedoms they wanted if they had the guile to play the system properly. But she didn't understand that. She was on a bit of a crusade.

But it would never affect him personally. He could afford to relax and recognise that he was the man who had, literally – everything – the superb Mitzi von Heining, two energetic children, Franz and Lindsay, at pre-school and junior boarding-school. And for the past year he'd had the attention of Ginnie.

Mitzi padded lightly into the bedroom and sighed. Her blonde hair was tousled and she wore the top of Leo's pyjamas.

"At last!" She switched off the main light and slid in beside him.

"I won't see you in the morning, you'll manage breakfast yourself, won't you," she said in what was a statement rather than a question.

"Sure. Don't get up, darling, you've a hard day ahead of you. The Yearling Sales, isn't it? I'll grab a quick cuppa before I leave," he murmured.

Mitzi was his kind, his friend, his own sort. A smashing woman really, statuesque in that broad-shouldered German way. Privately he'd often observed that a few centimetres more in any direction would have created a formidable-looking Brunhilde, a sort of Teutonic discus-thrower. Still, Mitzi knew the ropes better than any woman he could think of. Mentally he ticked off the spouses of colleagues and acquaintances, a rum mixture of unoccupied alcoholics and fashion-fiends, plus a sprinkling of belligerent feminists. None of them had earned their spurs as Mitzi had done, one night years ago when he was trying to persuade a business colleague to restructure a contract. He'd brought the chap home, absolutely sozzled, pickled, the guy could hardly stand, never mind hold a pen. Good old Mitzi had kept the black coffee coming for hours on end, filled him with mugfuls of Douwe Egberts and big, sensible sandwiches until, between them, they'd got him sobered up enough to sign the document. Netted him a cool £750,000 at the stroke of a pen!

Sometimes, Ginnie seemed light years distant, a shadowy pleasure.

Leo smiled, kissed his wife on the cheek and turned

over. He enjoyed making a kill under such circumstances. Again, he considered the permutations and possibilities regarding the fire. His conclusions were threefold: it was unlikely that she'd been directly involved; he would ring her the following am; she'd be pleased that he'd taken the trouble to check up on her at all.

An impulse made him turn back towards his wife again. Her green eyes were open and she smiled, inviting him. Again, he kissed her cheek, then her eyes, and finally her mouth. He ignored what might have been construed as the mildest resistance on her part, and continued to kiss, stroke and caress. Her resistance grew. The bitch, up to her tricks again.

"OK Mitzi, you want it rough?"

Her knees were closed although her tongue darted into his mouth, urged him on. He found a route in, moved his hand to the top of her thighs and began to force his way gently, and deeper until she sighed, whispered, as if he was not really there, then rolled onto her knees. He threw back the duvet and dragged her by the legs further down the bed, until he stood on the floor. Then he raised her buttocks high in the air.

"Talk to me, Leo!" Mitzi hissed.

He ran his hands up along her back, caught her hair in his fist. It was ropey and abundant, grey mixed with tinted blonde. The words came easily, it was all so familiar, something they played out every few months, roughness and readiness, words that in everyday speech would have seemed wrong, not of their world. They became strangers to one another and the viciousness of it, as they spun and wrestled like starving cats, drove them mad.

He whispered to her, his voice suggested shapes, activities, gestures. It aroused them further. The more she begged, the greater his excitement.

"I'm going to give you a taste of something *special,* the best ever, yet I'm not sure you really want it! How much do you want it, Liebling?" he enquired, his hands working on her. It was still so bloody good, Mitzi was still the most fuckable woman he'd ever known.

"I want it! I want you, hard as you can manage it – I want you to give it to me! *Deinen Schwantz, gib mir deinen Schwanz!*" she cried in desperation.

He knew by the way she tensed that she was ready. At first he teased her, but then as his own excitement increased again, he slid inside. His hand continued to work her until they could no longer bear it, until he felt as if he would explode.

He was, he knew, a one-woman man, and that woman was Mitzi.

# Nine

## To the Edge of the Earth

During the night, Luke woke sprawled in an armchair in a strange room, a blanket around him. He knew where he was straight away. There was no sense of having dreamed it all, no unreality. He started in alarm and, still drunk, made his way through the open doorway of Ginnie's room.

She was asleep, the quilt thrown to one side, body draped in a long T-shirt that made her look boyish in the dawn light. Having observed that much, he lowered himself onto the bed, tugged at the quilt, muttered to himself and promptly fell asleep again.

When Ginnie stirred an hour and a half later, Luke's head was by her shoulder, the kimono had fallen open and she watched guardedly as his chest rose and fell, following the contours of his body, a soft tracking of hair which began at his stomach and led down to a thickening in the groin. She smiled at what she guessed would be his embarrassment later on, but did nothing. As she watched and waited, her well-being surged.

His skin reminded her of a Caravaggio print she had

once seen – it must have been in Mick's place – the skin of the boy portrayed, warm and tawny with the blood beneath. She raised one of her arms and scrutinised it. When she clenched her fist the veins on the underside of her forearm jutted darkly. That made the blood pound in her head and she touched the bruise. It was hot and swollen.

She didn't remember much about the night before. An explosion, then nothing. A journey with Luke, who had brought her home, who seemed gentle and kind. Young though, too young for her. The thought was dismissed as quickly as it had presented itself. So what the hell was she doing in the sack with young Adonis? Why didn't she boot him out there and then? She rolled over, then cautiously prodded one of his shoulders. Slow to wake, he snored quietly on until she whispered in his ear that he was in bed with a strange, older woman and would he ever get up out of that this instant.

He shot to life, then quickly covered himself. She laughed.

"Relax, you've plenty of time. I didn't rape you – you wandered in here yourself."

As he turned, she noticed his eyes, flecked, green eyes. Even then, barely awake, they seemed full of light and dark moods.

"Sorry about that."

"Is your head sore?"

"Like a hell-hole!" he groaned.

She hopped out and peered through the bedroom window, then blinked as the light hit her eyes. The sun shone and the roofs of the houses that led down towards the shoreline were washed in a golden downpouring. She examined the view, taking in the coast, the estuary banking down to a smooth green channel, ships docked like great floating towns.

"So's mine," she said. "I'll fix us some aspirin."

She remembered little. Oblivious to his scrutiny, she moved lithely around the apartment, as if it was the most normal thing in the world to have him there. Every so often she stretched, turned and grinned, before filling two glasses. He noticed how unsteady her hands were, how the water in the glasses slopped and spattered all over the floor as she came back into the bedroom.

"Tell me everything." She handed him a glass and some aspirins.

"What do you remember?"

She went back to the kitchen, opened and shut drawers and cupboards, searched for cutlery, plates, then finally arranged the lot untidily on the table. He stood in the doorway and watched as she spilled a variety of vitamin pills into an egg-cup. Her hands still shook.

"The explosion and getting knocked out. Bits about the trip here." Her voice petered out. She sat down, leant one elbow on the table and supported her jaw with her fist.

"It was a bad scene, right?"

"Yes."

He couldn't bring himself to go into details. She looked scared, like someone putting on a brave face who's scared shitless. Her eyes lost their warmth and her lips tightened.

"Go on."

Yet as he recounted what had happened, she knew that nothing could have prepared her. She began to rush around, plugged in the telephone, then turned the radio up loud. The morning news programme was being broadcast. She listened, her mouth falling open.

A woman caller alleged that the Guardians of Christian

Destiny were responsible for the attack on what she had described as "the female consort of the Antichrist".

Almost immediately, the telephone rang. It cut into the silent attention they'd given to the words of the speaker on the radio. Dimly, Luke began to see what could happen, and although they never discussed it afterwards, Ginnie felt the same. Even then, a plan was forming. A seed was planted. By then, they just sat and stared at one another. The room was flooded with sunlight. Silence ticked between them. Their minds began to race ahead. Luke's was full of wild, impossible thoughts. It struck him that already the course of his life had changed completely and he hadn't a clue how that had happened.

"Jesus." She began to chant to herself as if to soothe away the insistent ring of the telephone. She wondered if this was how Nero fiddled while Rome burned.

"Away, away, go away. Don't answer. Let it ring, ring, ring, let it damn well ring."

Luke looked on. He couldn't figure her out. It was too much, her getting her knickers in a twist over the *phone*, for God's sake. Her breath came in little gasps, she stood there and stuffed her fist against her mouth, mumbled gibberish. To his relief, the tears which brimmed her eyes didn't spill over. The phone stopped ringing, then began again. This time, she rushed forward and lifted the receiver.

"Yes?" she barked in a voice that alarmed him.

"No comment."

But she listened as the speaker badgered. It was Bonnie Macbeth.

"Like I said, no comment. I'll be making a statement within the next few hours. 'Bye." Fuck you, she thought to herself.

She hung up, cutting Macbeth off mid-sentence. Blazing Bonnie and her column. The woman on the ball. First into any scrum, the filthier the better.

"Gutter press. A right bitch too! Do you know what she asked? She asked me if this wasn't something we'd set up ourselves to create publicity! Can you believe it? Imagine somebody even *thinking* we could stoop so low!"

She gave a strange, bitter little laugh, then shook her head and sat down, cold with nerves though the room was flooded with sunlight. Luke took the phone off the hook.

"Thanks, but there's no need. They'll be around here soon. Best let it ring out, Luke."

He replaced the receiver again.

"Look, Ginnie – "

It sounded funny, using her name like that. You'd swear he'd known her all his life. She could be his sister, or his cousin. A friend, even! Well maybe not.

"I'd better be on my way. When I get some clothes on." He cleared his throat.

The things people say, she thought, even when the die is cast.

"You don't sound too sure about that."

Luke did some quick thinking, saw his life like a bundle of loose ends that needed to be pulled together again. A sequence rushed through his mind. He should get the hell out. Home seemed the obvious destination. He'd return to real life, to farming, to his mother, to Tod and the lads. He might get to shift Kathleen Quinlan. He'd never see Virgin, or only from a safe distance, and the whole thing would make a great yarn. Anything else was lunatic. Get real. CYO.

Ginnie caught him by the wrist and held fast.

126

"Come with me. You have to come!"

With or without him, she was leaving. It was the only solution. There'd be no compromise this time, no shilly-shallying. Right and wrong could go out the window, into the blue for all she cared. She had to go off, felt the need for open spaces, for fun and rest; it hit her like an intense thirst. She'd languished too long in the glare. Time to go, baby, time to hit the road. Ain't nevah comin' home no more . . .

"Come with me!" she insisted. "We can have a great time – "

Her voice faded and she sounded uncertain. She didn't want to see the pictures of charred bodies which would be plastered across the pages of every newspaper in the country. She could imagine the photographers competing for the sexiest shot, the most shocking view. Well, she wasn't going to be around as the preparations for an inquest got under way. Escape. Flight. An exodus of some sort. She wouldn't even deal with Mick Delaney, he'd be into desperate stunts to get her back on the road, anything to start her up, the right publicity to put her career together again as if she were a mechanical doll that could be wound up and set off. Best walk away from it all, best go as far as possible for as long as she needed. And there was this boy. This Luke. What heaven did he fall out of?

Perhaps her enemies were right after all. Even Leo. Enemy no. 1. Trust her to stick her neck out, believing she was better than the rest of the song-merchants. She'd always believed it. That she was more courageous, a risk-taker. Never be an also-ran. Feel the fear and do it anyway. Come in first.

Again, the phone rang. Again, they ignored it.

Mary O'Donnell

"Well?" She waited for him to speak. He rolled his eyes and looked past her, not meeting her gaze.

"I'm up to my neck in shit anyway, no matter where I go."

"You're coming?" She took a step towards him.

"Yip."

Was he fucking mad? He'd have to ring home to let the mother know he was alive. He lifted the phone, which was still ringing, pressed the button to cut the caller off, and dialled home.

"Bloody hell, what're you at?" Ginnie hissed.

He didn't answer, then straightened up at the sound of his mother's voice.

"It's me. Yes. Fine, no trouble. I can't tell you that. I'm going away for – a while – I can't say – I'll be in touch. Look, don't worry. Honest. Bye."

He'd blundered through his mother's persistent interruptions, and answered all the important questions without allowing her to force elaborations. He could be tight as a clam when he liked. Now, it was time to go. Now that they'd decided to run like hell, the whole thing seemed easy. The phone began to ring again. They ignored it.

"Swivel on this!" Ginnie butted her middle finger in the air. "Get dressed," she ordered, "oh Buddha-Buddha-Buddha! There are some things in that press over there. We gotta move fast, before Mick or the reporters come around."

For a moment, Luke couldn't remember who Mick was.

"My manager. He'll be like a blue-arsed fly, mad to console but mad to get me saying all the right things to the press. Come on!"

Her voice was anxious, but a calculating mood

descended on them. She pulled down a holdall and tore through some drawers, flung the contents into the bag, then repeated this activity in the bathroom. She gathered bottles, shampoos, then threw them on top of the heap of clothes.

He pulled on his jeans and T-shirt, and although the bitter smell of smoke clung to them and called up the sickening memory of the night before, he'd gone beyond that kind of feeling. There was no going back. They had transport, they had a map, they could go where they damn well liked.

"I'm ready."

She waited for him to pull on his canvas shoes. She stood quite still and watched. This was it, a turning away, an attempt at salvage; the freedom to think perhaps, maybe more. This time she'd do it herself, away from lyrics and performance and image.

The apartment door clicked shut. They took the elevator. In the jeep, waves of hot air smothered them and as he pulled onto the main road she rolled down her window. He drove out of the city, down the Naas Road, southbound. The speedometer touched eighty once the suburbs fell behind. She felt exhilarated, safe, the wind sheared through what remained of her hair. She rummaged in her holdall for a scarf, in case the police stopped them. Luke glanced at her and smiled as she bound a purple twist of cotton around her head. She returned the smile, and her eye paused on the suggestion of muscle and sinew beneath his forearms, a light dusting of golden-brown hair.

"We'll have to get a pair of scissors," she said.

He nodded.

"Can you cut the bits at the back?" she asked.

129

He was so excited he gripped the steering-wheel even harder. For Christ's sake, if she kept looking at him that way, under her eyebrows, he'd crash the bloody jeep. The question of where they were headed hadn't even been discussed. It looked as if they might end up in the southwest. He waited until they'd left the motorway before he pulled in, then leant across and removed a map from beneath the dash.

"Where to?"

He spread it across the steering-wheel. The whole of Ireland lay before them, an undiscovered country, like an ancient map with codes that led to hidden treasure; every contour seemed important now, patches of green or brown became enticing hints and clues. They pored over the map, their fingers traced the different routes. Vagabonds, conspirators, suddenly courageous.

"Let's go south. To the sea. To the mountains – the lot!" she urged.

"Kerry here we come!" he shouted, gripping the steering-wheel again.

The further south, the better. The more remote the spot, the safer they'd be. He geared up again. Occasionally, during the journey, they stole looks at one another. Conversation was scant at first. Gradually, she told him more. Not everything, but nearly everything. Anyway, she scarcely knew him. Why divulge all just to impress someone with her frankness? She'd done with that. Impressing. Pleasing. Trying to be an original of the species. Who needed it?

Late that afternoon they parked in Caherciveen and bought a pair of scissors, salmon rolls, bottles of lemonade. A few miles outside the town they stopped over the bay. Deep, intense, it was scattered with sun-fragments, and in the distance on the Dingle side, a long lip of yellow sand.

Around them, gulls wheeled. It was warm. Luke began to cut Ginnie's hair. She sat patiently, ate the sandwiches, took massive swigs of lemonade from the bottle as he snipped and reduced, and let the dark pink clumps fall to her shoulders, from where the wind whisked them away in tufts over the cliffs. He took his time, every cut measured, precise. There would never be a moment like it again. He knew that instinctively, felt its intimacy close in on them and, because he couldn't help himself, quickly secreted a lock of her hair in his pocket. Once he stopped, to ask if she was sure.

"What about?"

"Your hair."

"It's too late now anyway," she laughed.

The result was a very short cut, and she brushed her fingers through the fine cap of hair, satisfied. She looked gamin, her neck was exposed like a pale stem on which was balanced a well-shaped head, a smiling face, a virtually unrecognisable Virgin. Her lapis lazuli earrings flicked to and fro in the breeze, and Luke counted the turquoise studs along the rims of her ears. For all that, she could have been somebody's sister, he thought.

Afterwards, they sat into the jeep and stared out to sea.

"We've escaped," Ginnie sighed.

"Opportunity of a lifetime," he replied.

"My big break. Oh Buddha – " She laughed softly.

"Some things are too much." He reached out, then timidly laid his arm around her shoulder. It was as if she was somebody else, not the woman he'd watched singing, dancing, so often before, the woman he'd lusted after, whom he'd wanted to fuck to Kingdom Come. She didn't shrink from his touch either. He'd half expected her to tell him to keep his hands to himself. To hit him. Well, it wasn't as if he was trying to rape her.

She'd be careful, she promised herself that, she'd be careful where this Luke was concerned. She drank in the warmth of his eyes as he studied her quietly.

Twenty miles on, they found a cottage, followed a For Rent sign and after some enquiries agreed on a price for a week's stay. The middle-aged owner appraised them swiftly. At least they weren't Dutch, she remarked; very serious the Dutch were, always bothering her with questions about the environment, water purity and the savage landscape. It was a scourge, she said; all she wanted was a quiet life, clean tenants, preferably without children. She handed over the keys of the house after Ginnie had taken a quick look through the rooms.

They went out again straight away and bought fish – plump, fresh, sea-trout, potatoes and wine, then staggered in with a box loaded with loaves of bread, butter, jam and cheese. Luke grew more nervous by the minute. What happened now? To give himself something to do, he washed the potatoes and set them to boil. Ginnie gutted the fish, cleaned out the chill, raw insides with indifferent fingers.

"Yuk. Oh Buddha. Yuk-yuk-yuk."

Then Luke asked her what he'd been dying to know all day.

"Tell me about – what I want to say is – have you got a, I mean, well whoever it is – you're seeing?"

"It's like this." She sighed. "Sure, I'll tell you."

She threw the fish to one side and rinsed her fingers, pushed in beside him at the sink.

"The human being I've been seeing – if you could call him that – it's a long story, not a very unusual one, but – "

132

He would have been fairly dim not to have put two and two together after she'd shown him where to find spare clothes back at the apartment. But she told him everything and he took it well.

"It's finished."

"Really?"

"Does it matter?"

She knew she was fishing for affection and approval. He said nothing at first, dropped his head, stuck his hands in his pockets. The cut lock of her hair brushed the middle finger of his left hand. He had part of her, right there, close to his skin. Like an electric shock up the finger.

"I've followed you everywhere in the past six months. But it's more than that."

His voice shook. He hadn't the words, he hadn't the daring, to speak freely. But she stepped close, took his head in her two hands and kissed him on the lips. At first he was so surprised that he didn't respond, but suddenly he kissed her back, grabbed her arms so hard that it hurt. She struggled back from him.

"Easy. Take it easy. I'm not a shagging horse!"

He laughed to hide his embarrassment.

"Sorry," he said. "Kiss me again. See if I can do better."

He closed his eyes in anticipation and held his lips close to her face. This was it, he thought, the real thing. No more practising against the bathroom mirror, no more wondering if his lips were the right shape, or if his teeth would get in the way. Or if he'd make smacking sounds the way the filmstars did. She drew his head down and kissed each eyelid, then his nose, then each cheek, got the feel of each part before she settled on the mouth and pressed closed lips to it. This time, he yielded.

She drew him to the bedroom. In the kitchen, potatoes

bubbled in a saucepan, flies lit on the trout that lay uncovered on the worktop, and outside, roof-tiles cracked in the afternoon heat. A spider crossed the red linoleum floor close to the bed.

They undressed rapidly, kicked off their shoes. Slowly, she unpeeled his shirt, placed his hands on her shirt so that he could lift it, on her waist so that he could undo her jeans, all the time working her own hands along his body. He sat beside her on the bed, shirtless, as she began to open his jeans. He caught her hand.

"Wait."

"OK. No problem."

"Fine." He was terrified.

He watched her, his face deadly serious. He felt as if he'd been dropped from a great height and had landed, stunned, on the ground. All that registered, apart from lust, was the fact that her underwear was blue, and that a little blue feather hung from a silver clasp on a chain between her breasts. Again, she reached towards him.

"My freedom feather," she whispered between kisses, running the feather along his jaw, "it's supposed to be a Native American symbol but it's really tourist rubbish. Oh God." She stopped and regarded him. "Are we mad, or what?" she asked.

"Yes," he replied, then brushed her shoulders with his fingertips. She shivered.

"Too late to turn back," she whispered.

Her breathing was audible. This time he kissed her, and his tongue played more patiently with hers. He thought he'd devour her, he'd no idea that people's mouths could be sweet, and he almost cried out as she opened his jeans and slipped them over his hips. Again he stopped. She'd consider him oafish, horrible, an ugly animal!

When she pushed him back on the bed her hand was light and slow. She undid her blue bra, threw it to one side and placed his hands to her breasts. He moaned as she removed his underpants, then silenced him by closing her lips over his open mouth.

He was eager, his skin smooth, warm and muscular beneath her hands, his smell dizzied as it rose to her nostrils. Now he kissed her freely, her throat and ears, then her breasts. She stopped to remove her jeans, and lay in a blue g-string as he pulled her towards him.

"Now touch me," she said again, and placed his hands on her breasts, "touch me everywhere. If you're ready. Wherever you like, only if you're ready."

He felt his way along her body, and as his mouth fastened to each nipple he could hardly believe the way she responded, it was enough to frighten the hell out of him. Finally, his hands touched the elastic thong which held her g-string in place. He hesitated, then pulled. She lifted her buttocks so that he could remove it, lay back as he stared. He lay against her, kissed her, then slid his hand between her thighs, realised what was about to happen, and tried to stop himself. It was too late.

She pulled him towards her. When was the last time she'd been the cause of such a naive eruption? It had never happened with Leo. With him, everything was controlled, each move timed to perfection for the achievement of maximum satisfaction on both sides. Not that she'd ever complained. But this was different.

Luke groaned beside her, turned his face into the mattress, mortified. What kind of a stupid lug was he! What a bloody fool, imbecile! Idiot, that he couldn't hang on for even five minutes! Yet she held him, touched him again, kissed him slowly, whispered that it was all right,

135

it didn't matter, that he'd paid her the best compliment ever.

He recovered, absorbed and re-aroused. Aware of nothing beyond that moment, his life seemed brightly revealed to him as she guided him, told him what to do, then held him back until she sensed he couldn't stand it, finally lifting herself and manoeuvring him inside her. It was, he knew, the difference between night and day, and to think that all his life until now, it had been darkest night. Three a.m. She watched him in flight, a magnificent bird-man soaring in the light as he raised himself on his hands and looked into her face. She moved her pelvis slowly, he was deep within her, his eyes widened in pleasure and she moved again, finding a rhythm and keeping him with her until he had to stop himself from shouting his way through the burst of pleasure that swept him. She continued to hold him, her legs wrapped around him, hands pressed to his buttocks, closed her eyes and tilted herself up, floated out of her own narrow existence, subsumed in an ocean of imaginings.

Immediately afterwards, he told her that he loved her. He moved again against her, ran his hands across her forehead, down her nose, traced the outline of her lips. She smiled. The declaration made her uneasy, though now she wanted to believe it. Typical, perhaps inevitable, not to be taken seriously. But he read her thoughts, clasped her by the wrists, made her look directly at him.

"You don't believe me, do you? You think I'm too young."

"No. Honeybun, I don't think you're too young. If you can make love like that you're not too young. It's just that people say things they think they mean, and then – "

"I mean it, Ginnie!"

"So do I," she whispered. "So do I."

It was out. At her words, he whooped into the air before falling on her again, hugged her tightly, rolled her over on her stomach.

"Let me see you. I have to see you. I've never seen anything so beautiful – Jesus, I can't believe this!"

He bent, then bit one of her buttocks gently.

"Ahhh, stoppit sweetnuts!" she murmured. She caressed him again. Neither of them noticed the smell which wafted in from the kitchen. Only later did it register that the saucepan had burnt dry. Ginnie ran out, screamed for cold water, turned off the electric cooker, and using a thick towel removed the heat-mangled saucepan from the hob.

"I'm starving! Can you cook?"

"Sort of," he said. "You wouldn't like it. Let's go back into town, find someplace."

They pulled on some clothes and hopped into the jeep. As they drove away, they showered one another with tenderness, with playful tugs, pulls and punches. No other woman could have thought up the words she had for him. *Sweetnuts. Tightbuns. Honeybun. Kiwis. Oh sweet kiwis!* In the restaurant they could scarcely keep their hands off one another. Other holiday-makers eyed them with curiosity, looked away, then back again as they drew attention to themselves by staring into one another's eyes, bestowed unnecessary touches on hands, arms and knees as they studied the menu. Eating, when the food arrived, was nothing more than a business. It might as well have been cardboard.

"Do you think we smell?" she asked suddenly.

"Of what?"

"Sex."

"I don't know. Do we?"

He shifted uncomfortably at the thought.

"Probably. Oh Buddha, we should have bathed."

They ate hurriedly, paid up, bought a litre of red wine and drove off again.

At the cottage, Ginnie filled a bath with hot water, undressed him again, and made him stand stock-still as she oiled his body with one of her lotions. Her fingers worked on every part of him until his flesh felt as sensitive as if he'd never made love. The insides of his wrists, thighs, his lower back stung with desire, teemed with renewed needs. She brushed against him with her breasts, tipped his arms, his chest, as she worked.

When, finally, he could no longer endure it, they made love again in the bathroom. She took his penis in her mouth and with her tongue, her lips, gave him another sensation he couldn't have imagined. Later, he lay on the floor, and she sat astride his hips, moved carefully forwards and back, watching his face, his soft mouth, how his eyes closed and opened, the pupils huge and dark. She sang one of her own songs,

*Ridin' to the edge of the earth with you,*
*Ah'm ridin' to the edge of the earth!*
*We are strong, we are free,*
*That's the way it's meant to be,*
*Just ridin', ridin' to the edge of the earth . . .*

But the urgency of coming made her break off to a high-pitched hum, a cry, as she was gripped again and drew him to his own release.

They lay on the floor. Soft shawls of darkness fell. Night sounds penetrated, bats pipped around the eaves of the cottage, shore-birds called across the bay, a car droned on the shore road above. Exhausted, they climbed into the bath, slid down opposite one another and let warm water lap around their necks. Luke sat with his legs around Ginnie's hips. They washed in silence, soaped one another slowly, scooped the water across one another's skin. Later still, they dried off with harsh-textured towels, grey ones which had once been white.

"Are there any sheets?" Ginnie called from the bathroom.

"I'm putting them on."

She listened to the cottony sound of fresh sheets being thrown open in the bedroom, watched from the doorway as he pulled them on, carelessly, then plumped up a couple of pillows. She found a quilt in the wardrobe, threw it on the bed, over Luke, already curled beneath the sheet.

In the days that followed, Ginnie ate little, shocked by an adventure which she'd have scoffed at even days before. Now it swept cleanly through her, rich and knowable. They walked miles along the beaches, collected shells and stones, limbs of bleached driftwood; sometimes they lay in the dunes, made one or two abortive attempts at love-making in the coarse grass. They avoided radio and newspapers, would stroll half a mile from the cottage to the small shop which sold everything from buttons to spanners, to stock up on food.

She wanted to forget, and at first she succeeded. Obsessed with pleasure, they made gifts of unexpected, useless things – a cloth which Luke bought for her in the shop, a basic cotton weave, bright red, criss-crossed with yellow; the T- shirt she picked up for him, pale blue to replace the black one she'd asked him not to wear any more, because it was a reminder.

Some days they drove to the village and wandered around the pier to watch the fishermen unloading crates of fish. They crossed the bridge to Valentia Island, and turned right at the top of the hill, bore on and up through the ferny road, intoxicated by the view and by one another's attentions. The place was wild, and led them high above the world where they looked down on a scattering of dreaming headlands and coves, searing blue overladen by hints of the earth-world in scraps of islands and fingers of land that suggested a practical existence elsewhere; they ascended, existed on a plane beneath clouds that gleamed in cool quiffs above the ocean, casting inky shadows as they drifted in over the peninsula.

The bruising on Ginnie's head subsided, the swelling went down, but still shadowed her eyes with bands of yellow and purple. Luke coaxed her to eat more, insisted that she rest in the mornings, what was the hurry, they'd all day and all night to do whatever they wanted. Mostly fucking.

She gave in. He made a good breakfast, knew how to whip up an omelette and toast and strong tea, would squeeze two oranges for her and watch as she drank the juice, supervised the eating of the omelette with a care and attention typical of someone much older.

"I feel as if someone really cares about me," she remarked one morning, "apart from family, I mean. They always care in a way you could do without. They say they love you and care about you, but really they're controlling you, they don't want you to change. Or grow up."

She sighed happily. "It seems to matter to you that I'm all right."

"Nothing matters more. They're probably going ape-shit at home. None of that matters now."

He watched as she ate, admired her helplessly, smiled as a slice of toast fell from her fingers and onto her stomach.

"Here. Let me."

He bent to remove it, licked the butter from the arch of her abdomen. She shivered at his touch.

"It wasn't like that before. With anybody else. Leo wasn't like that, you know."

"Like what?"

"Sensitive."

But he felt wistful, out of his depth.

She'd finally told him all about Leo, took the risk of his being shocked, which he was. He should know everything, she thought. Concealment would only patronise him.

"Will you always sing?" he asked, more to bridge the discomfort of that feeling than anything else. Before she could answer, he slipped between the sheets, taking a mouthful of her tea.

"Suppose so. But right now – who can tell?"

His first doubts set in. But he wouldn't mention them. He had no right. The future could damn well wait. It would happen, no matter what they did. He bent over and pulled at one of her nipples with his lips. She laid the tray to one side. His tongue worked steadily, licking, warm.

# ten

## The Lone Crusader

Hilary stayed with Mick through the night, close to him in case she was needed. Later, towards dawn, she dropped him home and drove erratically through the cobbled maze of Temple Bar. Towards nine o'clock she phoned Mrs Kavanagh at the shop, told her that she had a migraine and not to expect her for some days. She settled into a late morning breakfast in the peace of her kitchen. Except it wasn't peaceful. There was much to think about. And her voices were back. She couldn't silence the whispers that pursued her, that pressed close to her ears.

Mick – although vague and distracted, although he'd left her in a hurry to clean himself up and get a bite to eat before meeting the police again – had been grateful. This was as she had hoped. What her voices hoped too.

Arms crossed, she stood at the kitchen window and admired her back garden. *Not bad, Hilary, not bad at all,* one of her voices whispered. Except for a small corner at the far end, reserved for Devotions (weather permitting), the entire surface was concreted. A shrine had been erected at great expense, the workmen had grumbled a

142

lot, cracked unnecessary jokes as they hauled the seven foot blue and white Virgin Mary around the side entrance and across the garden.

Now it was an open-air sanctuary. The time would come, she was sure, when she would be joined by others, when yellow wax candles would flicker above their fingers, when eyes would be raised in adoration. The whispers grew louder as the thought struck her.

Last night was a mistake. She'd have to consult with her brothers and sisters in Christ in order to find out what went wrong. The deaths of young people, whom they had merely intended to warn, had never been part of the plan. Smoke, yes, but an explosion? True, there was rarely smoke without fire, but that was a figure of speech, and some lone Guardian had allowed his feelings to get out of hand. The organisation couldn't afford negative publicity, not now when the forces of liberalism were growing in popularity among people who might have resisted them before. They could not afford to have accidents, moments of over-zealousness. Perhaps a phonecall across the water might be in order, a chat with someone from the west-London cell, for example, the ones who patrolled the clinics. They understood the importance of patience, how to wear through the hardest rock, like drops of water falling on the same spot until the surface gives. They understood patience. Theirs was a vigil of silence, especially on Saturdays, a busy day for the clinics when many of the weekending Irish girls checked out. But patience was of the essence. There was no need to frighten people. Posters and placards perhaps, a few well-chosen prayers. Photographs. But nothing violent.

Ten years ago that woman would not have been tolerated, ten years ago, the Antichrist's consort would have been spurned by right-thinking people. That was then. Now was now. The final years of the millennium belonged to people like her. The Guardians had to block the holes which threatened to open all along that high, moral wall which was their only buffer against the demonic corruption of the modern world. Block them they would, armed and resistant they would fight for what was just, for what their parents fought for throughout the dark forties and fifties. The Guardians would take up that battle, by God they would – she blessed herself and asked forgiveness for using the Holy Name in a blasphemous context – would fight to the death to keep artists and their filthy abominations under heel.

Artists! She smiled cruelly as she poured some tea, popped an artificial sweetener into the cup, no milk, then began to sip, gazing into the distance as she surveyed the cesspit which her country had become. The dam wall had weakened. The tides of evil rose with force, threatening to overspill, burst through, destroy the world.

Had Mick Delaney ever for one minute considered that he was party to such potential disaster, he would not have followed that path. He was a good man, but misguided, under the spell cast by that cavorting, howling bitch.

Oh beware the acolytes of Mammon! Beware Sodom and Gomorrah! Beware the fate of Job, who doubted God and ran with open sores until he was a putrid sack of human flesh, reviled by all, his stink carrying on the desert wind, punished for his lack of faith! Beware! Beware! Sure weren't millions of people suffering the fate of Job nowadays, punished for their fornications?

Mick was the only man she had ever met who came remotely close to resembling Tomas, her beloved brother a year her senior, her ally in childhood and beyond it. A pity he let himself fall under another woman's spell, had married her and emigrated.

Her eyes misted and her mouth wobbled in disappointment as she thought of Tomas. She took a hasty sip of tea, ordered herself to swallow, swallow hard in order to quell the pain of a throat that wants to open and vomit. For a moment, her breast felt heavy, full of loss. Tomas! What would he not have done for her, what had he not done for his sister! Slices of toast lay buttered on the plate. She opened a jar of Marmite and layered them with generous dollops. Tomas had loved Marmite on his toast, first thing every morning. It hadn't been to her taste then, but since his departure for Adelaide, she had taken over certain of his habits as a testimony to his former existence.

Now all she had were letters, long, long letters written in his firm hand, which arrived once a month and described his new life with enthusiasm. They were full of all kinds of trivia, about dreamtime, and the law faculty where he lectured, and how his wife got bitten by a poisonous spider when she put her hand into the mailbox outside their house. A pity it didn't kill her, Hilary had thought miserably.

The one o'clock news began with a flourish of majestic music, then a sour-puss newsreader opened with what was still the day's top story – the fire at Malla. Hilary gritted her teeth at the phrase. *Top story*. Did that mean they considered it to be a piece of fiction, the invention of a group of hallucinating people in a hall down the country, who had created smoke by force of will?

Of course that was more of it. The media could always suggest that things were less than they were, they would naturally be in cahoots with that whore, on Mick Delaney's side, would accept his near tearful apologies and entreaties for calm.

She was on to them. She would handle the media some day – if not she personally, then the Guardians would sort them out; they would expose them for what they were, out there at the broadcasting centre – a crowd of homosexuals and lesbians, a group of twisted, perverted lefties and libbers, swingers, bed-hoppers the lot of them, infidels and deviants interested in using the arts and traditional culture as a front for the promotion of obscene behaviour and moral turpitude! Them and their *cúpla focail*!

Tomas would have had none of it. Even her parents, when alive, had no suspicion that a living saint occupied the house, no notion of the lengths to which Tomas would go in order to chastise himself. And for what? She almost laughed out loud. He was virtue itself, a walking, living saint who knew what love was, like no other man she had known.

Strange, how Mick Delaney resembled him so closely. It was what had first drawn her to him. The idea of looking in on his mother was a mere excuse. She'd spotted him weeks before on the North Circular Road, had noticed his build, his face, his smile, and for a time thought that this was a message from Above, permission that she could love someone else. Even her voices concurred; it was perhaps Tomas's way of contacting her from the other side of the globe, his sign to her to carry on the good work, to pray and to love, to turn the world to their way of thinking, to show what the spirit of love meant, the fiery, hurting, angry spirit of true love, even if he himself had – once and fatally – weakened in resolve.

As time passed, she realised that Mick was not The

One. He sometimes stood her up, forgot to phone her, could not understand her disapproval of Virgin and some of his other clients. Her disapproval was always mild, tinged with kindness and concern. There would have been no point in dismaying him. But she would show him. In time, she would lead him along the path of light, and the day would come when he might – inadequately – take Tomas's place. It was a long way off, but gradually, slowly, she might guide him, teach him.

As she listened to various reports on the fire, she was struck by the fact that the little Jezebel herself did not come forward to make a statement. Unavailable for comment, if you don't mind. Mick Delaney claimed on radio that she had disappeared, that he was quite concerned as to her whereabouts and her condition as she had, he said, received a severe knock to the head.

It was all a front! That one was probably sitting it out right in this very city, laughing at the fuss, knowing she couldn't be held responsible for what had happened. How she could play the innocent! But it would not fool her. She'd beat her to ground, come hell or high water, Hilary Dunne would find that over-sexed vixen. She even knew where she lived. Ruskin Way, no less! Hilary sniffed, tilting her head to one side as a plan began to form.

She washed up carefully, wiped dry her bits of china, replaced the cutlery in a drawer, fork to the left, knife to the right, teaspoon in between, the order of goodness, otherwise she would be smote by the Lord. The news was over and it was time to pray. The finer points of her plan could be worked out later.

She wandered through the house, whispered her orisons, whispered to those who whispered at her. Room by room she went, rearranged ornaments, adjusted things

147

so that they were just so – bone china ballerinas, rustic fishermen, quaint children on fences. Herself and Tomas, years ago, in a photograph, arm in arm, smiling, their eyes focused just beyond the photographer's shoulder, as if something had even then been calling them to seek further, to look past the immediate towards the light of greatness.

Her own bedroom was painted pink, with a floral border just below the ceiling, and pink and green curtains on which huge blowsy roses waved in an imaginary wind. The carpet was powder-pink and her quilt-cover a deeper pink. Damask rose, she called it. She slept on one side of the double bed, as if waiting for the other half to be filled, a copy of the Bible where the torso of the absent male would have lain.

At night, she read Victorian writings – Wilkie Collins, Sir Arthur Conan Doyle – gratified by the moral code of George Eliot's Silas Marner, mentally wrestling with John Henry Cardinal Newman's *Apologia Pro Vita Sua* and John Stuart Mill's *On Liberty*. She often enjoyed a finale of Matthew Arnold's poem, *Dover Beach,* then fretted about the Sea of Faith which had, in the twentieth century, been transformed into a Sea of Faithlessness and Evil, heard in her mind *its melancholy, long, withdrawing roar.*

Finally, the door to Tomas's room, which she unlocked, then entered. Inside, she lit three white candles to disperse the gloom. She kept it just as he had left it. The floor was stripped bare, boards varnished to a yellow waxy sheen. His single bed lay like a monk's, with white sheets and one coarse blanket, a low, firm pillow which Tomas had used only on occasion. Sure he was like the ancient Irish bards, heads on pillows of stone as they composed verses of explicit metrical rhythm. Tomas had composed prayers, not poems.

The windows were completely shuttered off since his wedding and departure, to prevent prying eyes seeing what occupied her at night, or during the day, whenever she chose. She regarded the bed with fondness. *Ah, love, let us be true to one another!*

The walls on three sides were completely covered with images of the kind of corruption which they had challenged: Marilyn Monroe, crossed out when they were very young indeed, in red ink, as soon as news of her death broke; Jane Russell, her smiling teeth filled in with black marker, making her look like a hag, also crossed out in their youth; icons of the 1960s – Shrimpton, Twiggy, David Bailey, Marianne Faithfull, Veruschka, Eartha Kitt, Frank Sinatra, Brigitte Bardot, Sacha Distel, Juliette Greco; later, Elvis Presley (crossed out by Hilary); Jimi Hendrix; Jim Morrison (Tomas), *For the world, which seems/ To lie before us like a land of dreams./So various, so beautiful, so new/ . . .*

Those people had the wrong dreams, and now some of them were dead, drugged-out by their own propensity for evil; those that still survived were burnt-out has-beens who had done their worst to turn the Sea of Faith into the filthy swamp it now was. Swamp, swamp, swamp! the voices hissed in her ear.

Tomas and Hilary had hidden the pictures from their parents, a vast collection, under carefully lifted floorboards, or cut back the wallpaper at strategic points, slipping their hoard to a place of concealment. Only after their deaths was it possible to remove the stuff and mount it, trophies on display, as the battle went on. *Hath really neither joy, nor love, nor light./Nor Certitude, nor peace, nor help for pain;/ . . .*

But they had joy. And love. And light. Certitude, peace

and ease from pain, they'd had it all, Tomas and her, in one another's arms like the young lovers that some poet had written about, who was he anyway, she used to teach his stuff, Yeats, wasn't it? She shook her head. That was all a long time ago, but they'd had it nonetheless, joy and love and light and certitude.

It surprised her as a child. She remembered him visiting her room one night to play draughts, how one of the pieces fell down the neck of her pyjamas; a struggle ensued, shrieks and laughter, their mother shouted up the stairs at them to go to sleep this instant. His hand suddenly halted, long after he'd found the little flat playing-piece. It felt warm and comforting, her brother's hand. That was how it began. Theirs had been the purest, most natural love, for what could be more natural than that blood would enjoy blood, father with daughter, mother with son, brother with sister, what love was more natural! To deny this would have been an abomination, and as they grew older their secret remained undiscovered.

Their parents would tell them to get out and about, to meet other young people, which they did. There were discos and parties at which they went their separate ways, put on a bit of a performance in order to convince their closest friends that they were "going" with somebody. It worked, nobody suspected.

How superior they'd felt at those house-parties in the neighbourhood! As teenagers they'd been above it all, even if they'd joined in for the sake of peace. There'd be an hour or so of stiffness as most of those present waited for somebody else to make a move and ask one of the girls to dance. The lights would be dimmed, so that it was difficult to see the pimples and eruptions on the face of the average boy, the ugly wisps of boyish hair sticking out of a bony chin.

Tomas had never been like that, his skin was smooth, supple, his face blemish-free, the goodness of his being shielding him from such common failings. How jealous she used to feel as he danced with certain girls, oh, they fancied him, they used to pester her about him, try to get her to set things up just for them. As ever, she pretended to collude in the fun, giggled and sniggered with the other girls as they listed the top five favourite and most detested boys in their area.

Things could get out of hand when people would smuggle in beers, or arrive tanked up on vodka. She recalled the smells of such occasions, hints of alcohol, the abundance of youthful sweat, the sense of wet mouths and saliva as the smooching and petting began – in corners, or on the floor, even in some of the bedrooms, usually on top of a heap of coats.

But Tomas and Hilary always left together. Never the first to depart, they waited until things began to break up, would slag one another off, tease and mock one another to throw the others off the scent. Not that those young fools would have had the foggiest notion of what was going on.

She threw her head back and laughed, facing the wall. In the centre hung a massive wooden crucifix, its dead Christ with his lolling head and upturned, frozen eyes, the slack narrow pelvis, chastely girded in a loincloth, bony legs and feet, ribs like girders beneath the waxy skin. All around the crucifix, Hilary had draped rosaries, smaller crucifixes, pictures cut from religious magazines and reproductions of the Renaissance masters.

Madonnas with Child stared solemnly back at her; the

Russian Madonna; beside her, the Infant of Prague with his little fur-lined cloak; then Our Lady of Krakow and the Black Madonna. In an outer ring she had hung framed photographs of her brother. Tomas as a baby, as an infant, his first day at school, various standard school snaps, Tomas at sixteen, Tomas when he did his Leaving, Tomas in Maynooth, Tomas in Spain; finally, Tomas and Hilary, together as brother and sister after he had realised that the priesthood was not for him, that his place was in the world, by her side. Until he fell. Until that tramp bewitched him with her perfumes and her smiles and took him away for good.

She undressed slowly, unbuttoned her blouse, eyes cast down in humility, whispered prayers of praise and submission. Her voices answered. When she was naked, she went to Tomas's bed, lifted the pillow and removed a long, leather flagellum.

Again, she turned to face the crucifix, to face Tomas as he gazed on her from the wall, his face loving, urging her on as she began to whip. She almost cried out as she lashed her own back, as the scourge licked its way into the nerve-ends of her flesh. Her skin was marked from frequent lashings, her back covered in half-healed, horizontal weals.

*That's it!* they cried out in unison, her voices, *That's it! Harder!*

She lashed again, this time to a count of thirty, hitting, hitting, changing hands lest she had missed parts of her most tender mortal flesh, her love of Tomas, and her lust, rising like the Sea of Faith must rise, higher, higher; her face broke into sweat, it ran between her breasts, down her stomach, till her skin shone in the darkened room, and still holding the flagellum her free hand dropped lower,

lower, and slid into her crotch, down the shaven length of her most holy cross, in the candle-lit gloom that threw shadows on the walls, close to Christ crucified, and she was dancing, dancing with Christ, her wild man come, her Tomas!

She cried out his name at the top of her voice, and in that long spasm of pleasure and pain heard the words of truth somewhere in her head, *And we are here as on a darkling plain/Swept with confused alarms of struggle and flight/Where ignorant armies clash by night/*

# Eleven

## A Kerry Beach

Ginnie flipped over onto her back and floated. It was a still day, the water pearly-calm, the sky rippled with fleece. To the south, the sun glimmered through cirrus.

Luke had driven to the town for groceries, warning her to be careful in the water, like someone twice his age.

So life had changed. She'd allowed it to change, had fallen for a nineteen-year-old who showered her with tenderness. She felt herself open like a bud in sunshine. Funny how everything came back to images of nature, she thought, especially when you were happy. She remembered a botany lesson in her schooldays, when the nun got everybody in the class to examine a piece of onion skin beneath the microscope.

"Now, Virginia Maloney, describe to the class what you see in there!" The sight of the activity churning around each cell, like green suns invisible to the naked eye, had fascinated her.

"Chloroplasts – " she muttered, "Nucleus, cell membrane – chlorophyll – " So there was coherence after all! Not that she saw much of *that* at home. Oh, there was organisation all right, but not the sane kind. You'd swear, from Dad's humour, that the end of the world was about to happen, that every step had to be watched for fear life's delicate mesh would explode in their faces. Dad, unemployed since the day he'd lost his job in middle-management at the pharmaceuticals factory just outside the town, permanently unemployed and permanently depressed, couldn't have cared less. His day fell into segments. First breakfast, cornflakes and branflakes mixed, with a banana cut through the cereal, then boiled egg and wholemeal bread. Strong coffee. Off to the bathroom where he shaved. Later, an hour of exercises. Push-ups and sit-ups in the bedroom.

During the afternoons the house was filled with the voice of Jim Reeves and *Put Your Sweet Lips A Little Closer to the Phone*. "Ah, poor Jim!" he'd sigh, reminding them that the singer had died in a plane crash, while Mum told him not to be a damn fool.

Mum struggled, making ends meet, doing supply work in the local school. It was always supply work because she'd never qualified as a teacher, dropped out in second year to marry Dad. And if she wasn't teaching, then she was making up wreaths and bouquets of flowers in the garage they'd had no use for since the car was sold. The local shop which supplied her with native seasonal blooms, or forced exotic things from Holland and South Africa, paid her to make sprays and shapes and mounds. Heart-shaped funeral wreaths, courtesy of *Fenella's Flowers* for a certain *type* of person, so Fenella said, or buoyant, wedding arrangements, like floral explosions.

The memory of her mother, always tired, still galled her. It was no way for a woman with five children to have to live. Some part of every woman was a queen. You started off as a young queen when you were very young.

But things happened along the way and the dethroning was hard. Someday. Someday, she still hoped, she'd make it big enough to hand her mother a cheque, something to free her from the spacious but ordinary house just outside Braymore. What some people would call luxury. Private. A renovated stone cottage, it had been extended and modernised, the long L-shape prodding well into the side of the hill, so that the back was always in shade while the front baked in sunshine and light. But she didn't know if her mother could ever be freed, especially not from herself and her disappointments. Ginnie remembered walks home from school, then the final stretch when she'd cross the stream at the bottom of the field after watching pinkeens for a while. She'd climb the steep shortcut up to the house. At least getting Jack into university had cheered Mum up no end. Even Dad had to admit that it was something to be happy about, a sign of changing times. They were so unsure about what *she* did though. It never seemed up to scratch, or smart enough; it was as if they thought her just a step above some kind of hustler, selling her wares in the street. She felt sorry for anyone who thought like that. The problem was, some people lived in a place for so long that something went very still within their hearts. Arctic winters grew into their souls. It was as if the streams and currents of life blasted by on either side of them or very deep within them and the pace of habit, which was no pace at all, left people like Mum and Dad floundering on the surface. If they were certain of anything, it was in a cut-and-dried way, with no mercy in it.

But today she felt like a pod, a bud, bursting out of a sheath, a world where she did not approve of herself at all.

Virgin and the Boy

She glided into a lazy backstroke, closed her eyes and
began to speculate. Life was good. How could this have
happened? What had she done to deserve it? She
continued to float, enjoyed the cool air on her face,
listened to the glubbing water, until the pleasure of
allowing the body to be pulled hither and thither on gentle
currents wiped out the compulsion to think. There was
little to think about, except how they'd live from then on,
and perhaps where they would live. Herself and Luke,
imagine. What other people thought could be dealt with.
She'd handle it. She could do it. She could always get what
she wanted. Everybody could, if they went about it the
right way. The thing was to know when to fight and when
to lie fallow. She'd had struggles before, had been strong
in solitude, all, all overcome.

She rolled over and immersed her face in the water.
*Glub–glub–glub–whirtle–whirtle–glub*. She blew out
through her mouth, and listened as a white spiral of
bubbles flew past her eyes. The water tasted foul, but it
was good for the skin, she thought, cleansing and toning,
keeping her smooth and supple. Which she would have to
be, wouldn't she?

That was the nub of the question. What others thought
wouldn't matter so much as what Luke might think.
Fourteen years' difference. Things would be said. She
recalled her aunt Anita's tone of voice a few years before,
as she recounted a morsel of gossip after a middle-aged
woman they knew left her husband and children for a man
of thirty.

"How could she do such a thing?" Anita had said, "How
could she be so so selfish!"

But the woman was having the time of her life. Her
aunt was jealous.

She might as well brace herself for a similar response, for sidelong, curious glances. At the very least. It wouldn't bother her, not so long as Luke loved her. She stood up in the water, and stretched her arms in a gesture of pure adoration. Of the sky. Of the water. Of her own heart and longing. The water dripped in silver rivulets along her skin as she waded ashore.

He was young. Now it seemed as if all those lyrics she'd written in such a fever were inspired more by wishful thinking than anything else.

There'd been other men, brief episodes, a few flings in the early eighties, before Leo Kilgallen. Once, she'd hit it off with an environmentalist from Sheffield, a man her own age who gradually but gently bored her with his descriptions of the anti-cruise missile rallies he'd been on. An all-or-nothing man. In the end, she was found wanting, wasn't prepared to join him and lay her body down on the roads before the advancing trucks. Not but that they had plenty to agree on. That, common wisdom indicated, was what life was about. You made out as best you could, in the company of people the same age. You convinced yourself that just because you could talk about the same things, because you and some man thought The Dubliners sounded like drowning bullfrogs, or some New Man agreed that women were still dominated by the Patriarchy, or because the pair of you managed simultaneous orgasm, that what you were feeling was love. It was the mildest rebellion, Ginnie thought. Finally, you got to do what your parents had been doing, finally you got a crack at all the secrets. Above all, you believed that you fell in love *better* than they ever did. You certainly believed you *made* love better than they did. And all the time, most people were doing nothing different at all. That was what it was all about. Following convention. And that was the tragedy in most people's lives. They believed in the illusion of originality. Swallowed it hook, line and sinker.

Of course, she smiled, Leo Kilgallen could hardly be described as belonging to her age-group, but then it was different for men. Nobody blinked if an eighty-year-old man married a woman in her thirties. If anything he was congratulated. But men like that were often rich. Death was just around the bend, if the women weren't driven around it first.

But Luke had confronted her with the contradiction between her attitude towards such women and the fact that Leo Kilgallen had paid towards the cost of her apartment. Not that he needed to point it out, bloody know-all that he was, or that the contradiction was unusual. But being with him meant that certain things had to be owned up to. He was wise, that boy. So how long would it be before his sense of responsibility and commitment to his own family reasserted itself? How long before he began to feel guilty?

Her eyes followed the jeep as it came into sight and jolted out along the coast road, the hum of the engine carried on the wind.

It wouldn't be easy for either of them, she thought. There'd be no whoops of approval. No point imagining they were different from the millions who fell in love every day.

Already she felt it, sensed resistance on the horizon. But for now, they could bide their time. She had no desire to sing or write. Perhaps that had something to do with being out of her head with joy, joy, joy.

She brushed the wet sand from her feet, watched as the jeep disappeared into a hollow in the road, then reappeared again. Most artists she knew produced work when at their lowest ebb, she reasoned; few needed to create if they were getting enough of the right kind of loving. Heaven knows it was rare enough. Sure the whole world was collapsing in on itself like a human black hole for want of affection, adoration. Even a good ride.

The jeep jolted slowly down the path towards the cottage. She stirred again. It was like a scene from a picture, another world, savage but gentle, its people cut off like a deserted race on the long, misted peninsula. Perhaps they were fortunate. Perhaps because of isolation they retained powers long ago stripped from the huge, restless world communities that jostled in towns and cities; from people with regular jobs who'd visit the south once every few years and admire the way the people lived, their quaintness and their colour.

She pulled on her espadrilles and ran towards the cottage as Luke stepped from the jeep, a box in his arms. When he saw her he laid it on the bonnet and they embraced. She held his head and looked into his eyes. They didn't speak. He ran his finger along her browbone. The cut had almost healed, a clean scar. As she helped him carry the groceries in, he looked at her again and felt himself grow weak with love. She wore an old-fashioned swimsuit bought in the town – pink, with blue seagulls down the front, and sensible shoulder-straps which would not slip.

"Here, catch!"

He tossed a newspaper in her direction.

"What's this?" she frowned.

"Time we started to read what's happening out in the real world."

She didn't meet his eye. Even now, it was beginning.

"Oh," she said in a light voice.

Six days had passed. Neither of them had bought a newspaper or switched on the radio. That other, real world could still go to hell for all she cared. She unpacked what he'd bought. He told her the woman in the shop had asked a lot of questions. Where did he come from? What did he do? She made him think of buying a newspaper again – accidentally according to Luke, though Ginnie had her doubts. She'd remarked on the affair up at Malla. The funerals. Wasn't it today they were?

"It's hard to believe," he said.

"It is. Do you think we should be there?"

Give him a chance, at least give him a chance to think too. He hesitated.

"I don't know. Oh, Ginnie. Of course we – well – you – should be there. Not that you could be present at all of them – " he blundered. "Maybe you should be in Dublin, or something."

"Luke!"

She began to rant, stung by guilt as much as by his caution, which to her seemed a reproach. Good God, did she always have to face things? How dare he suggest what she should be doing, where she should be!

Her sigh was pronounced, her face red with disapproval.

"They're looking for you, Ginnie," Luke pressed on quietly, rattling the newspaper to cover his fear of her anger.

"Who?" There was ice in her voice.

"The cops. Mick Delaney."

"Fuck them," she said sourly.

"They're going frantic. And my mother."

She turned away, then flung the fish into the sink, where it splattered heavily.

"Of course. Your *mother*."

She laughed nervously. "The only time I disappear without trace, as they say."

"Come on, it's not funny!"

"I know!" she snapped, her voice rising. "How come you're suddenly so responsible? It was a different story a few days ago, Luke."

Immediately he backed off, intimidated by her rage, but also by the germ of truth. He said nothing, but went to the sink and began to wash the fish while she stood watching, hands on hips.

Now she felt horrible. She'd seen his reaction, how he almost curled up, too sensitive to her anger. Suddenly she felt responsible for him too.

"I'm sorry," she said, after what seemed like a respectable gap and they'd partly recovered their equilibrium.

"It's been too much, Luke, the whole thing. I know I've run away and I know I made you – well, sort of made you – run away with me. That's true. And I know I'm not as brave as I thought I was. I'm a coward, I'm yellow, whatever you want to call it. Leaving Mick to deal with all the shit. You're right, sweetheart. Sweetnuts?"

He turned and decapitated a trout on the draining-board.

"You weren't responsible," he said, anxious for peace.

He detested even the hint of a row, dreaded the thought of falling out with her.

"I wasn't responsible. I know that. But I could have hung around. Made an effort or something."

She went on about all she should have done, then talked about acting her age.

"God knows I'm old enough to know better. I was tired

162

of work, not that I expect anybody to understand that. It's no excuse. The thing is, I had to run off with my lover, my toy-boy. That's what they'll call you, sweet. I couldn't even wait long enough to make a statement of condolence. And that's the least I owe them. Pathetic, right?"

He put his arms around her.

"Can't touch you properly with fishy hands." He nuzzled her with his cheek, used his forearms to caress her.

"Sometimes I hate myself."

"Don't!" he whispered.

But they argued throughout dinner. Luke wanted to return. She didn't. Not just yet. No matter that the world was made up of other people.

The real fear was that everything between them would change. Sometimes when he thought about the future he felt defeated. She'd always have people running after her. She could have anyone she liked, and that other man she dismissed so easily, that Leo Kilgallen. They'd all be waiting. Jealously, he imagined a succession of men drawn to her, phoning her, wanting her. Then Mick Delaney. He'd have plans. Everybody and anybody, it seemed, could claim her.

"You won't go away from me, will you?" He picked through his meal.

"Of course I won't. What kind of a question is that?"

"Obvious, I think."

"But – "

Here it came, as he knew it would.

"But what?"

"There are no guarantees about anything. You know that."

Inwardly, she cursed the contrariness that made her

163

suggest doubts to him. But maybe she was being sensible too. He wanted to throw the plate at her just then, but instead stood up by way of concealing the sense of violence that welled up in him.

"I get the picture. Back to Dublin, we say our goodbyes, go our separate ways as if this was a *fling*." He spat the words.

"You might be used to that sort of thing in your life, but I'm not!"

His eyes were angry and a vein throbbed down the centre of his forehead.

"Don't be such a fucking prig!" she retorted. "I didn't mean what I said about guarantees, stupid I know, but I'm confused."

Before leaving, they made love, took their time in the small bedroom with the red linoleumed floor, left the windows open. As they explored one another's bodies again, with hands, mouths and tongues, shore sounds washed in – gulls, the steady crush of an incoming tide, children's voices, high and light in the distance. Again, as he caught her feet and stroked them, kissed each in turn, it seemed that there was nothing at all to worry about, that nothing could destroy the wonder that filled him.

Afterwards, Ginnie held him in her arms as he slept, his breath warm against her collarbone, his hand twitching against her waist every so often. She wished time would stop, that these summer moments could be held onto. Yet their beauty was sharpened by the prospect of loss. Typical. A bit like the old Romantic poets. Keats and Shelley and the boys. Scribbling about love after the main event was over.

Later, she paid the owner of the cottage. The woman expressed surprise at their sudden departure, a day early, said it wasn't every day she had such quiet people in there. Then she scrutinised Ginnie.

"That was a bad knock ye had, my dear."

Ginnie brushed her hand over the bruise, as if to hide it. Her hair had begun to grow, brown roots were clearly visible beneath the outer puce fuzz that remained after Luke had tidied off the burnt ends.

"It was."

"See a doctor, did ye?"

"No. It's getting better."

"Mind yerselves, now, as ye go." The woman smiled slowly. "Yeer all clear about the way back?"

"Yes. We might see you again," Ginnie said, not knowing whether that was a conversational ploy by which she could halt the woman's questioning gaze, or whether she meant it.

They spoke little on the journey back. Once, she looked back at the peninsula. The cliffs, the yellow strand and ferny mountains, ribbons of cottages and bungalows were fixed in the sunshine, as if cut there for eternity. The sea was choppy but blue. They'd OD'd on beauty. Time out from life, she thought.

They passed through towns and villages, all quiet in the mid-afternoon lull, by-passed Limerick and cut up through Tipperary. It reminded her of holiday trips years back, when she was a child, wonderful holidays by beaches in the south, before Dad's redundancy, when the days stretched ahead forever and she could forget what day of the week it was. Those had been good times, years before she became aware of the seeping boredom which flourished between her parents for a time; she remembered one holiday when her mother's frustration and contempt was restrained by the tiniest threads of

165

patience, as her father slowly pulled the car in on a headland, parked and settled to enjoy a long read of the newspaper while they all gazed out to sea.

There'd been no boredom with Luke. It was too soon for that. Monotony had no place when people were busily lusting after one another.

Her eyes lingered on him, on the way the afternoon fell like gold-dust on his skin, his set expression as he watched the road ahead. His hair was glossy, its brownness lightened now by wind and sun; on impulse, she reached over, ran her fingers through it, and fingered the nape of his neck. He dropped his head back in response, shuddering with quiet pleasure.

As they approached Dublin, the silence between them deepened. Real dread descended. Despite its familiarity the city looked alien. They drove through an outer suburban clot of industrial development, then the roundabouts, watched the mile-by-mile change from brick-fronted terrace, small summer gardens, to the wider spaces of old suburban homes, Victorian and Edwardian housing interspersed at discreet intervals by tasteful apartment blocks. Some places always held on to the flavour of the past, Ginnie thought. Traditional and mature, much like the trees, cut with big, generous footpaths, fine granite steps and moulded chimney-pots.

He refused to come into the apartment.

"Not now. I can't stand it," he said.

She made him promise to phone her the minute he got home.

"I will, I will!" He shut his eyes tightly.

"It's only for a few days, darling. And you were right about us coming back. Luke? You were right to light a fire under me," she whispered. "I'll have to talk with

Mick, the police too. And the press. It won't come between us."

He said nothing. He couldn't speak the question that tormented him.

"And don't be worrying about – about Leo. That's over."

They embraced, their hands holding and smoothing. His mouth sought hers again. Finally, she pulled away.

"Remember. Together we're strong. We're strong, Luke!" She pressed her fingers to his lips. He sucked one of them in and held it. She gasped, said nothing, withdrew it.

"Jesus Christ, where were you?" Mick demanded as Ginnie let him in. He bustled past, stopped suddenly and gaped at her.

"Christ Almighty, why didn't you ring me? We thought you were dead! The police have a missing person alert out on you. Didn't you hear the radio announcements?"

He ran his hands through his hair, paced up and down the sitting-room, a big man in a cream linen suit. He opened the collar of his white shirt and blew out as if exhausted.

"Virginia . . . *Virginia,* we're in trouble and your running off like that has done nothing to help matters!"

She listened and endured as he lectured her on what the fans would think, why hadn't she at least made an effort to sympathise with the bereaved, for Christ's sake didn't she know that fifteen kids had died, that Pete was still in the burns unit, couldn't she have made some effort to appear to be fucking sympathetic?

She muttered something about being rescued by Luke O'Regan.

"What's that?" he turned quickly.

"I don't know what to say. I couldn't face people. I'd had enough. That explosion was the last straw. Then I met this boy. Luke. He rescued me, took me away when I asked him."

"Like *hell* he rescued you. *I* rescued you if anyone did, I did it, good old Mick here, runnin' in and out of that hall like a baluba half the night, what do I do except pop around to the front of the place to deal with the news people. When I come back you're gone, the bus is fucking gone, you've vanished into thin air. Rescued you! Jesus Almighty that's rich, have you lost your reason altogether, woman?"

She shrugged, ineffective and guilty. That night seemed too distant, its harshness blurred by the past week, its injustices remote. She wished Mick would just disappear. She wished the whole episode had never occurred. She almost wished she hadn't met Luke. It would have been simpler, so much simpler.

"I got mixed up," she said lamely, "I remember now. You pulled me out. I was lying beside the bus when he came over, that's all, and – I asked him to get me out of the place. Something like that."

"Well he was seen *helping* you, as you put it," said Mick, "And he was seen *carrying* you from the fucking bus across the churchyard after he left the bus in the *middle* of the fucking street where it could block *ambulances* and *fire-brigades*! You didn't know that, didja, didja?"

Ginnie shook her head, leant against the wall and shut her eyes. What had she done? What mania had seized her that she could have asked a fan at the concert to whisk her away? That was how it looked.

"Luke's not just a fan," she muttered.

"Ahh, for Christ's sake would you cop yourself on, doll! He's a fan, he's another mooning fan who watched you strut your stuff on every platform from hell to Connaught and he had the hots for you. Fair enough – " Mick made a cutting gesture through the air with his hands, "but there was no need to *encourage* him, there was no need for that, none at all! I mean, what do you think this is? Beverly fucking Hills or something? Gone with the fucking Wind? Fucking Romeo and Juliet?'

"Gimme a minute. Want a drink?"

She turned to the fridge in search of fruit-juice. Empty. Stinking of rotten vegetables and stale milk. One mouldy cheese.

"Try the drinks cabinet," Mick suggested forcefully, "you're going to need a few stiff ones before the day's out."

She poured two liberal gins with tonic, handed Mick a glass and sat down. The apartment was stuffy, full of city air and city smells. She looked around critically. Most of the pictures had been chosen by Leo, corporate purchases. She'd have to get rid of them, tell him to get them out, along with his clothes.

Mick filled her in on the police angle, on the outcry which had developed in response to the fire. It was not based on a concern for better emergency exits in buildings the size of the hall in Malla, nor outrage at the rusted state of the security bars on the two chained exit doors which had failed to open; nor was it based entirely on a feeling of outraged sympathy for those fifteen who had died and the thirty-two seriously injured; but on a backlash against Virgin, intense anger that her performance had created a place for such an atrocity, who cared why it happened, it did, it did, while she was screaming her head off about freedom. Some people called it a punishment.

There'd been letters, he said, abusive rants. Then half the country had a go at her on one of the morning radio chat shows. Most of the callers were disgusted at her refusal to face the situation squarely.

"You're joking! I'm being blamed?" She took a swig of gin, then swallowed quickly.

"You don't know the half of it, doll. So whatever you say to the press had better be bloody good, because we're up to our eyes in shit, I don't know if we can carry on at the moment, you're too big a liability."

"But it wasn't my fault! I didn't plant that bomb, if that's what it was!"

Mick began to wave his hands, dismissed her with a shake of his head.

"You've been in this business long enough to know that these things happen. OK, so the public's fickle, they're a crowd of wankers. They love you one week, they hate you the next, you have to know when to move. And don't forget, questions are being asked. There's a top-level investigation underway now, and if you ask me the Guardians are finished."

She slammed her glass on the coffee-table.

"I didn't ask to be fucking bombed out of business! It's not my fault!"

"For Christ's sake wouldja grow up, doll! You can't just say that, you depend on them, Ginnie, whether you like it or not . . . "

"You don't understand, do you? I'm not going to sit here being told who made me and what I owe. The public? I'm the one who goes up there every night, I'm the one who weight-trains and dances and jogs, I'm the one who writes the songs. Don't talk to me about the public. I've taken risks!"

She stopped, tried to temper her outburst.

"And so have you," she added quietly.

"Well?" He stood, hands in his pockets, jingling loose change. His eyes looked tired.

"Well what?"

"I'm thinking. You'll have to make a statement tomorrow, first thing, an apology. How about it? I'll set things up in one of the hotels. No smiles, remember, doll. Keep it very humble. No make-up either. And a few tears, a bit of crying wouldn't harm you!"

He smiled grudgingly. "And I'll be in touch with the cops, pet. They'll want to see you for sure, out of curiosity if nothing else. They'll want to take a look at the woman who ran off with lover boy."

"Will there be charges?" she asked.

He ran his hands through his hair as his mood dived again.

"Jeesus Almighty I must be mad, I must be fucking crazy! If it wasn't for the fact that you're bloody good, I'd be on a slow boat to China, and that's the truth! All you lot are the bloody same – singers!! Think the whole world's a mirror you can admire yourselves in!"

Ginnie told him that she'd handle it, but she couldn't promise tears. "You know me. Not that. Not now. But I – I'll make some kind of reparation. I don't know how, or with what. Or when." She stopped for a moment, as if unsure whether to continue. "The thing with Luke – it's serious."

He stood there, his stare one of amazement. For a moment she felt sorry for him. Harassed, tired and worried, he'd had little sleep in the past week, had taken the brunt of the hysteria. She was fond of him. A man with whom she could have an argument and no grudges held.

That, at least, was understood. It was rare. He was one of the best.

Two hours after leaving Ginnie, Luke pulled into the yard, exhausted after the long drive. He'd driven slowly all the way from the city, oblivious to everything but his thoughts.

His mother strode towards him, saw the jeep turn into the drive. The first thing she did as soon as he stepped out was to clap him with the palm of her hand around the ear, then burst into tears. Speechless with shock, his mouth opened and closed as he tried to form words. But sensible words escaped him, and he couldn't speak, defeated with every attempt by his mother's onslaught. His ear stung.

"Do you realise I've been worried *sick* about you? Up all night, every night! Mary was in a state – the children were frantic – at first we thought you were dead. Until you phoned – "

He murmured an apology. She'd probably be in a more reasonable mood after a while, he thought, trying to hold himself back, to be firm when the subject of Ginnie was discussed. She should be relieved he was home but you'd never know it.

"You might be sorry. I don't know what got into you, I really don't. You've never – ever – given me the slightest cause for worry, God knows, I thought you were dead, I really did."

Her voice broke again and she began to sob. Luke put his arm around her shoulders as they walked towards the house. Nothing had changed. The place was as before – a spacious bungalow with creepers growing around the side, a deep front porch and a yellow door with opaque-glass panels.

172

Mary was out, but Tom and Ferdia stared at him as if he'd just landed from outer space.

"How's it going?" Ferdia said.

"Grand. How're you?"

Luke slapped him on the shoulder, his eyes met his younger brother's penetrating gaze, the awed expression which suggested so much that hadn't yet been answered.

"Is it – is it true that you drove off with that one in the bus? That's what they're sayin' at school!" Tom interrupted.

"Eh, more or less. But it wasn't like that."

Tom and Ferdia exchanged furtive, smiling looks.

"And it wasn't funny either." Luke scowled.

His mother rattled the kettle on the draining-board in the kitchen, and made a great fuss of filling it.

"That's enough now. Tom! Ferdia! I want to speak with Luke."

They left the room, both sniggering as they closed the door. At the last moment Tom turned back, made a cutting gesture across his throat with his forefinger, and grinned at Luke.

*"Tom!"*

She might as well have mopped the floor with him. She was gabbier than he'd ever known her to be before. By the time she'd finished ranting and raving, she'd nearly convinced him that he'd done something dog-awful, that this was the worst ever. Perhaps he'd lost his grip on reality, she said, but by God she wouldn't stand by and watch him throw himself away, and on a woman like that.

He stood suddenly, and the chair fell back.

"She is not 'a woman like that'!" he interrupted.

Mrs O'Regan ignored him, lowered her head doggedly as if addressing the table, hands spread flat before her.

"Don't argue with me, son, I know what I'm talking

about. You know a lot about some things but you know nothing about women. Believe me, there's something distinctly odd going on when a woman her age is interested in a boy – that's what you are, a boy – your age, there's something peculiar there. Is there some want in her, or what? It's not money she's after, so what's wrong with her? Why isn't she married already?"

He picked up his chair, sat down again and clasped the back of his neck with both hands. He groaned, his stomach responding to the smell of bacon and sausages on the grill, his mind in turmoil.

Where should he begin? His mother kept calling him "son". She considered him a mere boy, she spoke of Ginnie as if she was crazy, a nutty old windbag, a neurotic slag.

"There's nothing wrong with her," he said. He'd be patient, he'd prove his maturity. "She's the most wonderful person I've ever met. I love her."

His mother snorted. She cracked an egg onto a pan and stood back while it spattered and sizzled.

"Of course. And I suppose she loves you?" she replied tartly, scooping hot fat around the egg with deft movements.

"Yes. And – she's just thirty. Thirty-three," he amended. "She was very shocked after the fire. I – we – didn't think this would happen. I mean, you don't think things through like that. Not in a real way. You don't plan them."

"Is that right? My, my!"

Her tone reduced him. A livid hatred quickened in his soul.

"Mother!"

"But you're only a boy! Does she know the kind of life we lead here in the sticks? Has she any notion at all of the way you work? How we have to survive?" Panic crept into her voice.

"Not really. I've told her all about it. She knows what we do – what I do. She understands that, but I don't know whether that matters."

"Of course it matters! You're my eldest boy and you know nothing."

"Stop calling me a boy. You always found me man enough to keep this place going, after Daddy died, so stop it! I'm not a boy – "

"You're still a boy in my eyes. And that woman's only seven years younger than I am!"

"I'm not a boy, I may be your son but I'm a man, I'm a man! I can work like a man and she thought me man enough to – "

He stopped abruptly and they glared at one another. Seven years younger, was that what she said? He blushed and looked away. His mother scooped the egg off the pan and slammed it summarily onto a plate. It burst. He watched as the yolk spread in a yellow pool, leaving the egg-white flat and limp.

"Did she now!" his mother sniffed in defeat. "I don't want to hear any more. Just remember that you're too young and that you were reared to behave yourself with women. I don't want any trouble on account of your antics, especially today. There are so many – *diseases* . . . "

He ate. There was no point rising her further, no need to shove her nose in it. She'd prayed it was a fling, that he'd grow out of it and recover with a few weeks' hard work.

"That Delaney man. The manager. When he rang to tell me what had happened, honest to God I thought somebody was having me on. I still can't believe that you would do such a thing. You! Of all people!"

He ate on in silence, reluctant to upset her further.

"Do the police know I'm home?"

"They do. Mick Delaney rang a while back. It must have been after you left herself off. That poor man is hopping mad!"

That night, Luke bathed before going to bed. Being back in that bath again was unreal; his mind revved over every detail of the first night, only a week before, when he'd got ready for the concert. If only he'd known what lay ahead, if he'd had the faintest notion of how things could change! Not that knowing would have made the slightest difference. The thing about being able to see into the future, his mother once said, was that if we knew what was ahead we'd lose all hope. But if he'd been able to see this great love! If he'd only seen that! There'd have been nothing *but* hope.

He didn't belong here, he'd grown up and cast off the place as if it were an old skin. If he returned he'd had it for good. His hands closed tightly in the water as he thought about Ginnie, he went over her pleasure in his imagination, heard her sighs, remembered the hours of attention she'd given him.

After, he breathed out and and his body grew calm again. For some reason he remembered Kathleen Quinlan, and the walk home from Westross Castle, her damp hand as they trailed through the dark, grief for a dead sister like a load on her shoulders. She was the only other girl who'd ever made an impression on him, the only one who hadn't played games. Unlike Ginnie.

Ginnie's games were different. They were her livelihood, and because of that they were more than games. Her life wasn't as cut and dried as other people's. Things worked differently for her. They had to. Yet behind all the professional antics, weird clothes and wild dances, he'd found a different woman from the one he'd imagined he loved, a woman he loved now above everything else. Nothing was going to separate them. Not ever. Not if he had any say in the matter.

In bed, he studied the cracks on the ceiling, his mind idling on river journeys down the Nile and the Mississippi. He might as well be dead, there in the quiet divan, with its cool white quilt and uncrumpled blue sheets. Then Ginnie rose before him in the dark and he smiled. He was an ear of corn, green turning to tawny yellow, firming, a tight toss, seed in a new sun. His hand clutched his penis.

He felt different. He *was* different. For the first time, he knew who he was.

# Twelve

## The ~~Hostage~~

The following day, Hilary called at Mick's house. She had spent hours on her appearance, and arrived shortly before noon, straight from the hairdresser.

Her dense black curls confronted him when he finally opened up. She was dressed in pale pink; suit, shoes, handbag; even her fingernails were painted and pointed into short little hooks. His face dropped.

"Ah. It's you."

She hesitated, waiting for him to invite her in.

"You'd better come in."

"I was just passing," she said in a husky voice. "Wondered how you were."

He jerked his thumb in the direction of a chair by way of telling her to sit down. This was all he needed. Just when he was up to his eyes. He hoped that the mess of the place would put her off, happily conscious of the mounting debris in his new kitchen.

"I'm fine," he replied vaguely. "Not a bad day either," he added by way of fixing the conversation on a neutral course. She gazed up at him with intense blue eyes that bored into his face, her mouth curled in a smile which made him want to run like the clappers.

Jaysus, he groaned privately, when would it dawn on that woman that he was not available?

Before she knocked, he'd been on the phone and was in that state of elation which preceded the signing of a contract and – at last – the prospect of a European tour. It was a move which he would hug secretively to himself until the offer was firm. Only then, within the next week he hoped, would he go over to Ginnie and present her with the fait accompli. It would give her a lift, even if he still felt like giving her a toe up the backside. He imagined her expression when he told her, how her eyes would light up, how excited she'd be. A European tour. Just in the nick of time to get her away from Ireland and the dog's dinner her career had become. Allow time for things to cool off. Maybe too, it would take her away from Loverboy Luke. She needed him like she needed a hole drilled in her head.

"I suppose you've sorted things out with that girl," Hilary interrupted his train of thought. "Terrible, terrible. It must have been shocking."

He filled the kettle, knowing Hilary was settling to roost.

"Yeah. But Ginnie'll be all right. She's that kind of girl."

Hilary said nothing, her eyes fixed on the black and white tiles that framed the kitchen doorway.

Five minutes later she sipped her coffee at a stained table, cradled the mug with her hands, warming them although it was a warm day. Already, the air in the kitchen hinted of mould and decay. A small bin overflowed with faxes and orange-peel, a spider was busy in the corner of the window, parcelling up a buzzing fly.

"This is a nice place you've got, Mick," she said, looking around. "You should keep it better. I've told you that before."

*Fly, fly, oh to fly,* her voices chorused.

He said nothing, looking over her head to the skyline outside. His mind was elsewhere, and he loosened his tie. Hilary made him feel as if he was choking. They sat in silence. It ticked between them, a cord which strained tighter with every second. Hilary feared she might scream, if only to silence the voices within.

"Of course, you could always get help, someone to tidy up."

His eyes travelled over her face. Christ, but she looked dotty. He wondered why he'd ever allowed her to help with his mother. But back then he'd been grateful. She'd seemed nice, old-fashioned and uncomplicated. Kept her distance too. You'd never have guessed she was looking for a man. Gave him the heeby-jeebies, she did. Women like her belonged to a non-sex. To think of how he'd wasted his teenage years and early twenties, wondering what in hell was wrong with him, going around with his head up his arse when things could have been so different.

"Hilary," he began nervously.

She sat back, expectant.

"Hilary. I don't want anybody in here tidying up. I have a system – "

"We all have systems. I just thought that maybe if you got a woman in – or indeed – " She sounded surprised, as if the thought had just occurred to her, "I could come in myself occasionally, I'd be delighted to help."

Mick's face was a mask.

"No, no. I wouldn't hear of it. Anyway, what I'm saying is that I like it this way – "

As he spoke her expression hardened.

"But I thought – "

"Don't think, Hilary, don't think."

"You like it this way? Heavens, what's got into you? You can't live in a pigsty forever! You're being influenced, you realise that, don't you?"

He scratched his eyebrow and stared at her.

"By that one. By *her*. It's your way of life Mick. She's at the bottom of it – this – disintegration."

He stood up abruptly and opened the kitchen door.

"Conversation's at an end, Hilary. Look – I'm busy now, I'm expecting an important call."

He realised he was trembling and his normally benign temper flared at the mad insinuation. No matter how he admired Ginnie, he did not desire her, not in *that* way. He couldn't; it was beyond him, and nobody except Ginnie sussed it.

"You could regret this. Mark my words, she'll drag you down with her."

She spoke mournfully, and stood up, handbag swinging from one arm.

"Cop yourself on, Hilary. Come on. Out."

She glared at him.

"That's the way you'd talk to an animal!" She grabbed her handbag and rushed from the kitchen.

He sighed as she slammed the hall door. Then relief flooded in. He turned again to the phone, grumbling about women.

Outside, Hilary hurried to the car. She knew exactly where she must go, geared up steadily and tore down the road, just within the speed limit. If at that moment, anyone had chanced to overtake her, they would have seen a face contorted with screaming, the mouth wide open as she roared obscenities in the safe vacuum of her car. She roared and roared until her throat gave out and she was hoarse from invoking her worst on Mick Delaney's life.

It was perfectly clear. He had abandoned her. There was not the slightest chance that he would recognise what was happening. It was too late, just as it was too late to guide him into the safe harbour of her life. There remained only one choice. It beckoned, a sign in the sky, glory in the noon sun, benign, helped by the love of her Tomas. She must cut the rot at the root, scour it with the sabre of righteousness till the wound was clean and the blood of pure passion flowed freely again. It was what Tomas would want, she was sure of that.

The buzzer sounded. Ginnie threw down the pen and went to the intercom.

"Whozat?" she called. Silence. Static hiss, then a woman's voice. A delivery for Miss Maloney.

"What kind of delivery?"

Damn. She'd just begun a new song, had set up the synthesiser, even if more out of habit than desire. A batch of unfilled music sheets lay stacked on the desk. She'd tried out a few bars, played them, then wrote, played again, re-wrote, improvised the original line until it scarcely resembled itself.

"Flowers," the voice replied.

At first she hesitated. Flowers were the last thing she needed. But perhaps she had a sympathiser. Curiosity got the better of her and finally she pressed the downstairs release catch, waited, then undid the locks on her own door. It slammed back with such force that she fell to the ground. A female figure with black hair stood over her, curls tumbled and bounced around a small, heart-shaped face.

"Flowers!" Hilary sneered, tossing a bouquet into the apartment.

Ginnie attempted to stand but the other woman beat her back, battering her around the head with her handbag with such ferocity that the newly healed wound on her forehead split open. She rolled to one side, hands to her head as blood coursed down her face and over her eyes. Hilary struck again, but this time Ginnie fought back, caught the other woman by the lapels of her suit and tried to force her to the ground.

They struggled, Ginnie gradually edged Hilary back until she threw her down and straddled her. Hilary was silent, her eyes furious. Her hands clawed up at the other woman's bleeding face. But Ginnie worked rapidly, caught both hands and used them as a lever with which to bang the intruder's small, stiff body as brutally as possible against the wooden floor. She released one hand to slap Hilary across the face.

"No point yowling! The place is empty as a tomb during the day – full of working people!" she gasped, struggling to throw Hilary over the threshold, " – who leave at eight and don't get back – till six!"

But Hilary suddenly bent forward and sank her teeth into Ginnie's hand. She broke the skin, her incisors sank in. Ginnie screamed in pain, let go, and Hilary was on her feet again. She slammed the door and lifted the first object to hand, a small bronze sculpture. She advanced on Ginnie.

Ginnie's right hand bled, the skin was lacerated. She could scarcely see through one of her eyes, began to shake, stared at the madwoman who moved towards her wielding the heavy lump of metal.

"Who are you?" she whispered at last.

"Now, dear. Which is it to be – another knock on that pretty head of yours or do you do what you're told?"

Hilary stood, tense as a cat waiting to spring on its prey, every gesture, every expression, threatened.

"What do you want?"

Ginnie tried to keep her voice steady. The other woman did not relax, and held the sculpture before her body as if it were a flaming brand. She breathed heavily, her hair stood out in an even wilder frizz after the struggle, and the buttons of her pink suit hung loose.

"Into the bedroom," she ordered.

Ginnie backed towards the room, kept her eyes on Hilary. She'd play along, she'd catch her out, overpower her. She couldn't risk getting clobbered, not now. The effect of being struck had shocked her. Her legs began to tremble and she felt sick. On some level it registered that this was how half the world lived and died. In humiliation. By blows to the flesh. She stumbled against the unmade bed and Hilary laughed softly.

"Get me scarves. Or tights. Tights will do!"

Ginnie opened drawers, searched through them; scarcely in control of her body, she forced her fingers to close on the light garments.

"Who are you?" she asked, as she threw a bundle in Hilary's direction. The woman smiled slyly.

"A friend of a friend," she drawled, kneeling to unravel a pair of black stockings from the mess.

"Very nice. Very nice. Only the best for Virgin," she said to herself. She lifted the stockings and inhaled, then threw them back.

"Good. Nice, clean tights. Now sit on the bed and tie your feet together." For a split second Ginnie considered making a jump at the woman.

"A friend of a friend?" she asked.

"A friend of Mick Delaney."

Ginnie laughed outright in disbelief. That was a mistake. The woman moved in and raised the sculpture over her head.

"Don't! I'll tie them, I'll tie them – "

She bent and tied her feet together, too tight for comfort, obeying the madwoman's instructions. There wasn't the slightest chance of easing her feet from the knots.

When she had done this, Hilary placed her weapon beside a terracotta nude in one of the wall alcoves. She eyed the little figure speculatively, then lit a cigarette; she inhaled and exhaled, turned again. The cigarette was clamped between her lips as she moved forward and punched Ginnie in the solar plexus, caught her hands and tied them. Ginnie cried out. Her stomach heaved with the shock of the blow. She was going to be sick, she was, she was. She groaned.

"Shut your gob!" Hilary whispered between clenched teeth. Cigarette smoke wavered from her mouth. She stood back and regarded her handiwork. She saw that it was good. Tomas would be pleased at this, her first offensive against the Sea of Faithlessness.

On the bed, blood seeped into the coverlet from Ginnie's forehead. A friend of Mick Delaney. That meant nothing whatsoever. The woman was crazy. Mick had never mentioned any woman. He never mentioned women in a romantic context. She couldn't imagine him befriending anyone who was so out of their tree. Even disarmed and bound, she found something ludicrous in the spectacle, couldn't take seriously the possibility that Mick might have had dealings with her.

"Did Mick send you?" she enquired.

"Tomas sent me."

"Tomas?"

"If you knew him, my dear, you wouldn't be lying here now with your hands and feet bound. Knowing Tomas would have sent you along a different path in life."

"I like the path I'm on, thanks all the same, Missus," Ginnie muttered.

Hilary jerked forward and caught her by the head, interrupted her scream by pulling a thick wool scarf across Ginnie's open mouth. She knotted the scarf tightly. To the madwoman's satisfaction, there were tears in Ginnie's eyes.

"Now listen to me." She shook her by the shoulders. "If you'd known Tomas there would be no such thing as the Virgin Tour, there would be no such thing as the filth which has infested this country!"

Hilary paused to gather her thoughts, placed her fingers in little steeples.

"Do you realise – *whore* – that your work is evil, controlled by evil forces? That you are an implement in the hands of a dark power greater than you – a pawn, a pawn? You and your so-called music," she jeered, "you and your secret messages! Don't think we're not on to you, you fool nobody."

Ginnie tried to scream, bucked and struggled on the bed. In one swift movement Hilary pulled the pillow from beneath her head and held it over her.

"If I choose I can press this to your scalped little head and suffocate you!" She watched Ginnie's face, fascinated, amazed at how level her gaze was, even now. How defiant.

"Listen now," she spoke softly, "Bide with me. I have

186

instructions. I can bring you forward, I can guide you towards light. Bear with me. Bear with me."

Her voice dropped to a whisper. Ginnie closed her eyes. Hilary left the bedroom and immediately bolted the front door, considered ripping out the telephones but decided against it. She would not answer callers. She returned to her victim again, lit another cigarette and considered what was being asked of her, the luminary.

The phone rang. Ginnie threw her body around the bed and attempted to roll onto the floor. In an instant, she was blocked by Hilary's body. Hilary smiled until the ringing ceased, her eyes glittered with triumph. *Yes, yes,* came the whisperers in her head. They laughed and snickered.

"That's how it's going to be, dear, until I've completed my work. Let them think you're out gallivanting, not available. We have a long, long night ahead of us."

She wandered again into the sitting-room. Before long she assessed many details of Ginnie's life. She drew back in admiration and wonder from the small cupboard in the other room, eyed the selection of men's clothing, the two ties, the trousers and the shirt, even a pair of shoes. It was worse than she thought.

But first, the creature must be weakened, starved for as long as necessary. Weaken the flesh to sustain the spirit, what all the mystics would have urged. She rummaged through the dressing-room just off the bathroom, examining bathrobes, tunics and trousers, jewellery, oil, body-stockings, gaudy, sparkling high-heeled shoes and soft, suede mules.

"Manolo Blahnik!" she read aloud slowly, peering into a shoe, flexing the supple sole.

She carried her booty out and flung it on the sofa. It

was one of the worst cases she had had to confront, exactly the type of thing which the Guardians would eradicate, wherever it was found, in whatever form. The signs of fornication and seduction were everywhere.

Hilary's voices slept. She looked out over the city. It was illuminated and quiet, a place for floundering human souls. How deceptive those still yellow lights when twilight fell; lights in the rooms of sleeping children, in the rooms of lovers, street-lights, car headlights, mizen lights in the harbour; even the broad suffused glow of the dying day, frail attempts to ward off darkness. Salt air from the incoming tide wafted through the open window. She sniffed, then rolled her shoulders slowly as she contemplated what lay ahead, what the flowing, dark peace of night held, when Tomas would guide her, tonight and for the following two nights, until it was complete. Abruptly, she closed the window and turned again to the Jezebel who writhed on a bed in the next room.

For the next two days, Hilary kept Ginnie bound and gagged, led her hopping and stooped to the bathroom whenever she indicated a need to relieve herself, would watch, taking sadistic delight in her victim's struggles to remove her own garments – the effort of raising a tight, red dress, the equally laborious one at forcing down her pants. She was cold and she was hungry.

Mick flew to Berlin on the afternoon of Hilary's visit, and tried to ring Ginnie the following day, to pass on news of tentative developments. He was not surprised when there was no reply.

The phone rang frequently. It was Luke. He believed she'd deserted him already. Yet he lived hour by hour in hope. He watched and waited as his mother casually went about her day's work, as she watched and waited, pitied him, convinced that she'd been right. He couldn't even contact Mick Delaney.

After that first meal at home, Luke ate little. In the days that followed, the silence from Dublin grew like a poison in his mind. Maybe he was going mad. He didn't know how to put one foot in front of the other, how to do the ordinary things. His body just didn't do the things he wanted it to. He'd gone bonkers. He lost his appetite. He couldn't sleep, and sat all night before the telly, staring at the flickering screen, his misery eased by late-night satellite news from America. Certain stories caught his attention, made him forget. A tale of survival from Idaho; the dog that walked from Iowa to South Carolina in search of its owner. The owner was a wanker who didn't deserve such a good dog, Luke thought; a black New York grandmother who gave birth to her own daughter's child; a Florida-based campaign against ageism, led by a multi-orgasmic eighty-year-old couple. Well *that* was good news anyway. Nice to know the jingle-jangle was in the old triangle even at eighty.

He was looking out. He was always on the look-out.

Then one night he flicked on the telly again and found himself in the middle of a documentary about Malla. His forehead began to perspire and he breathed a puff of relief as he realised that his mother was out. He wouldn't have a leg to stand on if she was watching.

It was an RTE inquiry into the Guardians of Christian Destiny and the abortion business. Leo Kilgallen was mentioned, although he was not interviewed, but other men spoke to the reporter about him. They gave the impression, although Luke couldn't grasp exactly what they meant, that Kilgallen had bought all kinds of property during the late seventies, that there were deals and double-deals. But that was only a small part of the report. The main thing was to examine how public disagreement over certain women's subjects had led to the explosion at Malla. The pro and anti people couldn't stand the sight of one another. Anyone could see that. Both sides pretending to be so reasonable. It made him sick.

The programme closed with a couple of minutes of the funerals of the victims. It was almost more than he could bear to watch, but he sat it out. He had to. If he didn't see this now, he'd never know certain things. At this point the reporter just stopped talking, so that the camera panned along the proceedings at the funerals. There were just hundreds and hundreds of people present, probably thousands, he thought. They'd swarmed down the streets of Dublin city and streets in other places too. Malla. Dundalk. Cork. They'd followed coffins, mountains of flowers. The camera stopped and closed in on the face of one man. He was out of his mind with grief. His eyes rolled and searched the air in front of him, without really seeing anything, the tears poured down his cheeks as he yelled about his little girl, the best lassie ever, the best ever. Luke's eyes filled as he watched, as the camera froze on the man's face and the credits began to roll. Jesus Christ, Jesus Christ. He wanted to hide. Anywhere. For as long as it took. In the end he went to bed.

The next morning he got up and behaved as usual. His mother ignored him at first. He hadn't slept for thinking about the programme and how he might be blamed for keeping Ginnie away from the funerals. He knew he'd been right, down there in Kerry, when he'd said they should have come back sooner. Well, if Ginnie saw the programme last night, she'd know what to do. She'd probably phone him that very day, upset of course.

"I believe there was a programme about Malla last night," his mother said casually.

"I saw it."

"Is that a fact? Was it any good?"

"It was terrible," he snapped.

He realised she'd trapped him. She'd known it would be on, had probably left the house on purpose. For all he knew, she'd watched it someplace else.

But the day went as usual. They had a row every time they tried to talk. He'd never seen his mother so mad before, hadn't a clue that she ever possessed such inexhaustible emotions.

In desperation that afternoon, she brought in various relatives to back her up; then her own sister, Aunt Joan. At first, they were kind and more or less right-on, but then they began to whinge and give out. Luke switched off when he heard things like "for your mother's sake" and "remember your poor father, God rest him." Finally, in a last pitch to restore him to his former sanity, Mrs O'Regan faced him by herself again. But he was damned if he'd open his mouth, sulked through her halting arguments, knowing full well that she felt herself to be on dangerous ground, out of her depth.

They needed to hire someone to take over the business.

"Are you aware what this carry-on is costing us?" his mother fumed. "We lost four contracts within two weeks because you weren't here. It's not fair, Luke. You can't go on like this. The rest of us have to live even if you've decided to live on fresh air. And by the way – " she paused, "the farm account is in my name now. I closed the joint one this morning. So you'd better think about what you're going to live on. See how far that carries you in a chill wind."

Her words washed over him. Deaf in one ear, hard of hearing in the other. He refused to go out in case Ginnie phoned. She'd promised to keep in touch, just as he had. But his confidence was eaten away; he imagined parasites gnawing within his head, keeping him in pain. He couldn't stand the possibility that his mother might be right when she said that Ginnie had forgotten him.

The days were mild and windless. All around, fields of potatoes had ripened, early silage was cut. People were busy. Luke sat and brooded, his mother was in and out, while Ferdia, Mary and Tom regarded their elder brother with renewed interest, as if the Luke they once knew had been replaced by a stranger.

"It'll work out. You'll see," Mary said once. Her sympathy surprised him. In the past, he'd been too busy to take her seriously, or even to acknowledge the signs of her maturity.

"Don't encourage him, he's bad enough!" Mrs O'Regan snapped. In a flash, he saw his mother's view of the men who ran the world. Strange, physical creatures who had to be handled, who mustn't be encouraged in wild ways in case they went out of control, who must be prepared to take over – without question – the business of overseeing the lives of dependants, usually wives, mothers or children.

On the third morning after his return, as he pushed a piece of bacon around the plate, she sat down opposite him. Her expression was sympathetic, she seemed ready to hear him out. But he had nothing to say, turned away from her as if she wasn't there.

"Just because I've said all I've said doesn't mean I'm not – sorry – for the way things have turned out," she began uneasily.

It was an attempt to recover lost ground, to re-establish a sense of filial affection and respect. He scowled at her under his eyebrows. It was too late for that. None of them understood, none cared, not one of them was capable of understanding how he felt about Ginnie. He loved her, with all that that involved in the fields of lust, tenderness, mad feelings, affection and wordless things that filled him.

"You'd be happy if it worked out like this, wouldn't you?" He couldn't keep the spite out of his voice. She said nothing at first.

"I would like you to get back to work, Luke. Not for the money and not for the business either. I know I've said plenty about both. But it would occupy your mind. The regularity of it. Take your mind off things."

"My mind doesn't need to be taken off Ginnie."

"You must try to let go."

"But I don't want anything else to think about. I can't!"

"Not now. But that will change. I know it will. Trust me, I've done a bit of living too."

She stopped and thought, bit down on her lip. "You know – perhaps I shouldn't tell you this – your father wasn't the first man I loved, but he was the one my parents approved of."

"That was then."

The same old drivel. What it boiled down to was that she thought she knew best, and that she did not give tuppence for his feelings, insisted by her words and actions that he was no more than a great lump. Well, he'd be twenty in December. He could hardly wait.

"If your father was still alive none of this might have happened. I know it." She sighed with a trace of bitterness, gazed at her knees, ran her wedding ring up and over her knuckle, then back down again.

193

"Well, he's not and it has happened and you can't turn the clock back!"

He left the room to try the phone once more. She followed on his heels, stung by the remark.

"You – are – not – " she faltered, " – to use that – phone again! Is that understood? Not in my house and not – if you're trying to get through to her!"

Quietly, he replaced the receiver, went to his room and packed a rucksack. She stood by, knew she'd pushed him past some limit, that without meaning to she had driven him out.

"I've taken the keys of the jeep," she said as a last resort.

"I've a spare set," he answered quietly, confidently. He rushed from the hallway and out through the garden, across the gravel path, aware of warm flashes of colour, the bloom of Devil's Pokers, butterflies quivering on the buddleia.

"What'll you do for money?" she shouted.

"I'll manage," he muttered to himself. Even then, he had no idea where he was going. He drove unevenly, forgot to depress the clutch, scraped at the gears as he accelerated down the road.

Some time later, he pulled up outside Kathleen Quinlan's flat on the other side of the town. There had been traffic-jams all the way, mid-morning shoppers, hawkers on the street selling fresh fish, clothes, sturdy boots.

To his relief, she was there. As she opened the door, she exclaimed in surprise and pleasure when she saw him. She was a small-boned young woman with pale red hair and grey eyes. Her skin was pale, slightly freckled, and she wore a denim skirt, a white blouse and white espadrilles.

"Lucky for you I've a day off!" She laughed and stood back to let him in. He was relieved. For one awful moment before she opened the door he thought she might stare at him blankly, or at best vaguely, but she hadn't forgotten their walk home the previous summer.

Her flat was small, pretty and cared-for. When he admired it she told him that she'd done everything herself – wallpapering, painting, the lot.

"See? I've even got a spare bedroom if anyone stays over. You're staying the night, I take it?" she said, nodding at his rucksack.

She showed him into a box room papered in small red and white hearts which reminded her of one of the rooms in Mary's old dolls' house.

"If you'll have me. Let me explain."

He rolled his eyes in frustration. "Oh *shite!* I don't know where to begin."

"It can't be that awful," she said. "Throw your things on the bed. Let's have some tea. I don't know what you must have thought of me that time last summer. I suppose I seemed a right eejit. I was still upset, and I always meant to phone, but I hadn't the nerve. I was a bit embarrassed."

"I thought nothing of it. You just sort of acted out the way I was feeling," he answered.

She watched him as he told the story. Every so often she nodded, lifted her eyebrows as she absorbed the details, her lips turning down at the corners as she considered his words. Instinctively cautious, she decided not to betray her astonishment.

"Use the phone when you want," she said. "And stay as long as you need. I'll be out anyway. Just leave a note if you have to go."

After a while, she left to meet a friend. Although she didn't go into details, it crossed his mind that she probably had a boyfriend, and that he'd probably be a major inconvenience in her life. Arriving just like that on her doorstep. Still, she'd asked him to stay, hadn't she? And Kathleen was a straight talker.

He phoned and phoned Ginnie's apartment, waiting each time as it rang out unanswered until the call was automatically cut off. Forty rings before a high-pitched whine interrupted the rhythmic sound of an unanswered telephone. He talked to himself, shocked that it had happened, that she could do such a thing, drank cup after cup of tea or coffee, whatever came to hand, ate nothing but the occasional slice of bread, or an apple.

Already, she'd shagged off and left him. The bitch. That Leo cunt had been waiting all along. He should have gone into the apartment with her, he might have had a chance then, he should have gone right in and laid his cards on the table. But Leo had come back, they'd made up and he'd whisked her away, that was the truth of it.

The nights passed. Luke lay sleepless and fidgeting. His eyes traced the rows of hearts on the wallpaper. Every so often, a car roared down the street, braked hard, took off again. Voices rose in the dark as people passed beneath his window; he listened to the curses and swears, a girl's high-pitched scream, laughter, then a succession of vehicles. There must have been a party, people were on their way home, or out the road for a courting session in the peace of the night.

He rose and went into the hall quietly, then dialled Ginnie's number again. At first, when he heard the strange voice that answered, he thought he'd dialled the wrong number. Then as he listened it dawned on him. His heart pounded in his ears and he tried to guess what had happened. He had not mis-dialled. It wasn't possible after the number of times he'd tried to make contact. As the voice at the other end sneered and giggled hysterically, his mouth went dry. Ginnie! He cried out loud, then stuck his fist between his teeth as the sheer dim-wittedness of it struck home, his own self-absorption and lack of trust.

At the apartment on Ruskin Way, Hilary ate her way through the contents of the freezer, taunted Ginnie with lewd remarks, and every few hours undid the gag to check for signs of conversion, or even the mildest consensus with her and Tomas.

"Do you believe?"

Ginnie shook her head.

"No, of course you don't. Nice cheese this, didn't know you could freeze it. Ah well, so much work, so much work. Just you and me together, dear. What could be nicer!"

Ginnie was silent. Pinioned with a rope ladder which Hilary discovered beneath the bed, she couldn't even roll around as on the first night, because Hilary had decided that mobility was dangerous.

It was the third night, when change would either occur, a circle of light closed, or nothing at all would happen, which meant that she would take matters into her own hands. Her head throbbed with voices. They refused to be quiet, gabbled among themselves, then urged her on, *Do it! Do it!* they cried.

The first step towards redemption was the humiliation of the victim so that she could witness the impoverishment of her own frail life. Without undoing the bonds, Hilary pulled at Ginnie's feet, removed her canvas shoes and threw them to one corner of the room. Ginnie did not move. Her eyes followed the woman. She no longer felt fear, but the weakened, light-headed resignation which results from hunger.

Next, she pulled up Ginnie's dress until it was bunched beneath the rope ladder, then, using a pair of scissors cut hurriedly until her entire back was exposed.

"Snip-snip!" She bent over and laughed, prodding Ginnie's buttocks with the scissors, her voice mocking.

"Oh my heavens, heavens! Is this what it's all about then, is this what makes them follow you so avidly, my dear?"

She pointed and laughed again. Ginnie whimpered. They'd deserted her. Three days. Not one person had come. Even the phonecalls – which she guessed to be from Luke – were lessening in frequency. She tried not to weep for fear of smothering, had controlled her terror of suffocation from the gag for almost three days. Crying would make things worse.

Hilary removed from her pink bag a bundle of candles and the flagellum. *Light! Light! More light! More illumination!* the voices called.

Slowly, carefully, she placed the candles in vases and bowls throughout the apartment, one on either side of the bed, then lit them and switched off the electric lights. It was eleven-fifty. It would be a white night. Even then, the horizon to the northwest was aglow with midsummer twilight, the promise of new light in the coming hours.

She blessed herself, then stood in front of Ginnie and slowly stripped, mimicked the movements studied on a video she'd once borrowed from Mick. Her body, which was pale and slender, belied her enormous strength. Her shoulders were narrow, her pudendum shaven into a cruciform. Her voices sang themselves to a frenzy. She saw herself as a snowdrop, humility of growth amidst harsh frosts and the biting gales of a secular world. In the long mirror opposite the bed she beheld herself, listened to the throng of wisdom in her own head, listened hard and long to her advisers.

Clad in Ginnie's toga and thonged gold sandals, a golden torc resting on her slight collar-bones, Hilary began to dance and sway, moving her hips provocatively. She stopped then, bent suddenly and cut through the gag with the scissors.

"Snip-snip! This is how you do it, dear, isn't it?" she whispered gently, finding her own rhythm, "this is how you seduce them, how you plant iniquity in their minds, take them away from their own blood and draw them towards the flesh of strangers, of people who belong not to their flesh!"

Her voice rose to a shriek, then broke. Ginnie shut her eyes and tried to forget. She was not here. This was not happening. The centre of her ears, deep in her head, burst like little pods with the sound as the woman lurched around the apartment, her voice violent, her body unquiet.

*Virginia Maloney,* she incanted mentally, *born Tipperary 1960, school St Agnes's, interests music, maths, the square on the hypotenuse is equal to the sum of the square of the other two sides, fashion, life. Single, female. I will get out alive. This woman is mad and I am sane. I am quite sane.*

So it was true, what they'd said about her career. The comments and cautions which flooded back were all true; that she'd regret it in years to come, what use would it be, why take such risks and work so hard when she could have an easier life?

"Fairy!" She gasped in surprise. The word burst out of her, escaped from the well of silence.

So they'd been right. This was what it came to, it had to happen sooner or later. Fly too high and you'll tumble to earth, turn your face to the sun and you melt! She thought of Icarus spinning, falling into that drop of ocean he thought he'd mastered through distance and height, felt herself tumble, every ambition crumbling before Hilary's performance.

"Fairy! Fairy!" She said it again.

Hilary froze.

"What's that? Fairy? Fairy *what?*"

"He's a fairy!"

"Who? *Who?*" She shook Ginnie as if to throttle her. Ginnie laughed, in spite of the pain, she laughed and laughed and felt she would never stop.

"Mick Delaney's a fairy and you can't see it!"

There was a brief, shocked silence, then Hilary's voice shrieked once again, loud enough to match the voices in her head.

"You're lying! Liar!" she screamed, and ran from the bedroom, out to the CD unit, where she turned up the volume of Ginnie's latest hit as if to obliterate the truth. In she pranced again, emulated Ginnie's movements, bawling over the deep bass sound. She bent over and pushed her victim's head to one side.

"You lying bitch. You can scream as loud as you like. Nobody will hear!"

Her lips were drawn back in manic laughter. Ginnie did not respond. The music was loud enough to cause a disturbance throughout the entire building. Hilary kept on, threw her arms out at an imaginary audience, thrust her hips and swung her legs. *Dance,* her voices told her, *dance the evil out of this place, dance for the truth!*

It burst from her then again, uncontrollable and

raucous. Before she knew it Ginnie had laughed, try as she would she couldn't hold back, it floated up through her throat as she beheld the spectacle. Her ribcage shuddered, convulsions seized her body and she roared with hysterical laughter, even when Hilary suddenly turned and disappeared outside.

The music ceased.

"What's so funny?"

"I – I was thinking – "

"Indeed. You were thinking about me, about how stupid anybody could be not to notice when a man's not interested, not to notice when a man is a *pervert!*" Her voice broke off in a crescendo.

The lingering, secretive smile on Ginnie's face taunted her even more.

"I'll give you something to think about, shall I?"

Hilary had soured again. Ginnie said nothing, lay quite still, her eyes widened in fear as again she felt herself at the mercy of the panting lunatic.

Candles shimmered all around, churned light and shadow, transformed Hilary's face into a grim and flickering mask. She released the rope ladder which bound Ginnie's torso, then rolled her from the bed onto the floor. Ginnie gasped at the madwoman's strength, felt herself gripped by the bound feet and dragged from the bedroom into the sitting-room.

The telephone rang out. They listened, the drag between them tightening by a notch. Ginnie willed whoever it was to sense something amiss. But that would have been telepathy, something which other people experienced, never at one's disposal when it was needed. She'd managed to hold her face clear of the floor while she was being dragged. The wound above her eyebrow had half-healed, though her face was streaked with crisp residues of blood. The telephone went silent.

Her breath came in shudders, her lips slid back and she wailed. Hilary Dunne stood over her and stroked the leather flagellum, hummed to herself, absorbed by its softness and flexibility. *Do it!* the voices shrieked, *show her!*

"I told you I'd give you something to think about, my dear! You've certainly given me *lots* to think about. So Mick Delaney is a sodomist, is he?" she whispered, raised the flagellum high and laid it in one swift lash across Ginnie's bare flesh. The woman beneath her screamed as the pain tore in, she screamed again and again as it bore down and gathered momentum, as her back, buttocks and legs were assaulted. Just as nausea threatened to overwhelm her, she passed out.

Every so often, she regained consciousness, was aware of flickering darkness, of Hilary Dunne close by, ranting and singing. She needed to cough. *Oh, Buddha-Buddha.* The air was dim, fuzzy. Sensations were of hot, stinging pain, the smell of burned skin when the cigarette came down. That reminded her, called her back to that first night. Fire. Malla.

Hilary regarded the shivering form with distaste. The Jezebel lay covered in lacerations. Now she had something to think about, now there would be an end to her nonsense.

"Oh God," the voices intoned and she repeated, "I take on myself the sins of this woman and ask you to absolve us of the blemish of her life, to liberate us from the pain she causes Your Holy Eyes as the roots of her evil sink deeper and deeper into the body of your community. I thank you Lord for granting me strength to scour out this cancer from the company of Saints, to uproot sedition before it infects your universe. For your sake Lord, I *am* Virgin, I take on myself the mantle of responsibility for her living and her dying, I am Virgin, I am Virgin most immaculate, I am Virgin unsullied, I am Virgin most pure."

She stood with the flagellum poised between her praying hands. The leather thongs drooped over her wrists. She raised her eyes to the powers in the ceiling. Above her, already, the clouds of heaven swirled. She would be elevated, she would! It was a vision, surely a vision, heralded by frankincense.

"Save us from perdition, save us from corruption, save us from frailty. Save us! Save us! Save us! For they know not what they do, they are carriers of destruction, they are the faithless ones in your Sea of Faith, O Lord, deliver us from this woman and all her pomps and glories. A-men!"

When the telephone rang again, Hilary-Virgin checked her watch. It was three-thirty in the morning. Virgin would have to answer it this time, she would, she would. Virgin would answer the telephone. How strange to be Virgin! How good for Virgin to be Hilary! Without hesitation, she lifted the receiver and answered in a light voice.

*"Hello?*

"Ginnie! Where have you been? For God's sake, Ginnie, I've been ringing and ringing, why didn't you answer?"

It was the voice of a man, he sobbed with relief. Eejit.

*"Oh darling!"* she breathed down the phone, *"I couldn't answer, I was terribly . . . preoccupied . . . tied-up, you know?"*

She laughed and laughed, stopped once to draw breath, turned away and coughed, then smacked a loud kiss at the caller before she laughed hysterically again. The line went dead.

"My heavens!" said Hilary. "An irate caller who wouldn't even speak to his Ginnie! *Ginnie!*' she simpered, "And why not? Because he is wanting in love, because he is a young man, a very young man by the sounds of it, who inhabits the territories of pure *lust* and little else!"

She went to the window. Behind her, the woman lay unconscious. Saliva trickled from her open mouth and onto the carpet. It would soon be dawn. Even now, a roseate sheen churned to the northeast. It was over. No more could she do. She slipped the black toga from her shoulders, undid the sandals, then removed the jewellery and lay prone and naked on the sofa. The mark of the Lord was upon her, even there, in her crotch, down there, sanctifying and purifying. The Lord's work was exhausting. Tomorrow she would leave, she would begin afresh, setting her sights on new, fresh targets. She would reassess her objectives, consult with Tomas, blessed Paraclete, her wise, white dove! He was in her head. It was nearly too much. The noise, oh, the noisy chorus!

But her work was complete.

Within half an hour they'd broken into the apartment, just after Hilary had dozed off. A woman wrapped only in a blanket, who struggled, who told them all about about Tomas, was led to a waiting vehicle; another, a shivering figure, was carried out on a stretcher and slid into an ambulance.

At the hospital, Luke watched the woman on the stretcher in casualty, not sure if he really knew her. In some way – he was not certain exactly how – he felt completely responsible, saw himself as the link which had precipitated the attack. How could he have been so stupid not to know something was wrong, not to trust her! He chewed on his fists as he raged and wept.

The nursing staff allowed him to stay all through the first morning. They checked on Ginnie every half hour, and he watched as the monitoring continued. Blood-pressure, respiration, pulse, temperature.

Her back, buttocks and legs had been scarred by the flagellum. Conscious but sedated, she watched Luke, her attention never waned as she lay on her stomach.

He came back. He finally got through. He alerted the police. In her entire life she had never been more vulnerable, more lost to herself. Her thoughts were reduced to a sense of wonder that she'd ever faced an audience at all. What was she, in the end? As Hilary Dunne had said, often and with ferocity, she was worthless. Quite worthless. But Luke was there, with her. They could get together, go away together, live as they pleased. Between them, they'd manage. The crazywoman was correct. She was a nothing, an absolute nothing, a minus infinity, wasn't that what she'd said?

"Mr Maloney? Mr Maloney?"

Luke looked up, puzzled.

"Your sister needs rest. Perhaps if you went to the canteen and got yourself a spot of lunch?" the nurse suggested.

"She's not my sister," Luke answered.

The nurse looked at him, sized up the situation. "I see."

"Do you? What do you see?" he said.

"Well, you know, she'll require a lot of rest. Go get yourself a bite to eat. You look as if you could do with it –" she urged again, her voice kind.

"I'm not hungry. But thanks."

She sat down with him. He leant forward on his knees, his head in his hands, his expression dejected.

"You need to keep yourself strong too," she said in a matter-of-fact voice. "It'll be a while before she's better."

He sat there, his face white, knuckles clenched so that the silvery gristle showed through stretched skin.

"How is she? Really?" he said then. The nurse lowered her eyes evasively. "Critical. Critical but stable."

"That's it? That's all you know?"

"That's all we can tell you at the moment, I'm afraid. You'll just have to be patient. The first forty-eight hours are the most important. She's still in shock. You must understand that these things take time – "

# Thirteen

## Bodies

It was a nightmare broken by seedlings of daylight. Ginnie thrashed about on an unfocussed plane between sleep and lucidity, sensed people near her, voices above her head. She dreamt of doves, remembered Hilary Dunne's Paraclete, saw white light, heard whirring sounds, then the flapping of wings.

She wondered if she'd died. Was this death? Hell? All that pain, burning, burning. The nurses dressed and re-dressed the lesions, then covered her with the metal cage through which the bedclothes were prevented from making contact with her flesh.

Back to square one, as if she'd never grown up and escaped her parents' over-careful existence. She wanted none of it, pushed them away when they bent close, reviled them for their approaches.

"Just leave me be," she said in a slurred voice, temper frayed by the stinging nerve-ends which flared along her back and legs.

How bright it was, how bright! Her head hurt. She viewed herself from above, a grotesque white beetle beneath a cage, her arms moved slowly on either side of her trap. Hatred poured into her, resentment and loathing. She was marooned. Terrifying, moreover, to lie in the same position in which Hilary Dunne had imprisoned her. Binds and gags replaced by bandages, stiffness and further torment, malice by care and kindness, but still the pain, still a cage, rigidity, and all the time her skin roared.

Each day, Luke drove to the hospital in Dublin from Kathleen Quinlan's flat. Sometimes he sat by the bed. Often, he waited outside in the corridor, or walked through the hospital grounds. It was enough to be there. He stopped buying chocolates and flowers, books and magazines. She was too ill to notice, reaching towards him once or twice, tugged at his hand but did not smile, her eyelids sliding open and shut.

To pass the time between visiting hours, he wandered around the city, his hands in his pockets, or he'd stroll through the parks, then sit on sun-warmed benches and admire gardens and borders and ponds. He became a watcher, glad of distraction, as flocks of marsh-birds flew overhead – ducks, a solitary shag, kittywakes. In a month of hospital visits, he lost weight, forced himself to eat a burger in the middle of the day, followed sometimes by an apple, then later at night, a sandwich at Kathleen's, too exhausted to enjoy food.

One night when he arrived back, she was waiting up, still dressed, sitting by the electric stove. She looked up, pleased to see him, then insisted that he join her. More out of politeness than anything else, he accepted tea, biscuits, and finally, a glass of white wine.

"I know you're not sleeping," she said. "This'll do the trick."

"How do you know? I just lie there!"

She laughed, then tossed her head knowingly.

"I just know when someone's awake, even if they're in another room. Maybe I hear their eyelids opening and shutting, or their thoughts jerking up and down, sort of creaking."

"Like garage doors?" he grinned.

She giggled. "Something like that. An uneasy soul twisting all night long. A bit like living in a haunted house."

She sat quietly and watched him from across the room. He began to relax, remembered the ease of her company, how untroubled a conversation with some people could be, like stepping into tepid water after a hot summer's day.

"By the way," she began casually, "your sister called by today."

"Mary did?"

"Just to see how you're getting on."

"I suppose she was sent," Luke grumbled, inwardly calling himself a pig-headed bastard.

"Probably," Kathleen agreed, "well, what do you expect? It's a bit much, Luke. I mean, maybe you should call home or something."

He said nothing. He couldn't very well tell Kathleen to mind her own business. As if reading his thoughts, she swiftly changed the subject.

"So how's your girl?"

"Coming along. So the nurses say. But I dunno. She's messed up. In really shit form. The pain's driving her mad."

Luke looked away. His lip began to tremble.

"Do you know something?" she said calmly, "You'll drive yourself crazy if you don't ease up. You'll have to think about other things, if that's possible. But stop being silly about this. You'll make yourself ill."

"I suppose you're right. I'm so tired."

"'Course you are. Dead beat. Here. Fill up?"

She passed him the wine bottle, began to talk about a forthcoming holiday to Thailand which she and a girlfriend had saved for.

"Right in the middle of the monsoon season too. Have you ever travelled?"

"Nope. Haven't been any place. Not yet," he replied.

"Well, you should. Maybe when Ginnie gets better, something like that might happen."

Her voice trailed away as his expression changed again. She went over and took his hands in hers.

"She *will* recover, Luke."

"Yeah. But I think she's changed. It might have ruined her." He had to change the subject. Otherwise, he would have wept.

"I used to dream of going places. Up rivers, across the Great Lakes, fishing off Alaska, or on the Black Sea. I like the idea of catching Pacific salmon, all that – have you read *Sea Wolf* or *The Call of the Wild?* – now all I do is drive up and down to Dublin like a yo-yo, put one foot in front of the other and know I'm just fucking myself!"

"You're not fucking yourself. You're doing fine. Give it time, you'll see. Things will improve and then you'll know how the future's going to shape up. And Tod says to say he was asking for you."

"Tod?"

"Tod Grimley. We go out every so often."

"You're joking!"

It seemed unlikely, Tod and Kathleen, Kathleen and that baluba. He chuckled.

"Well," she said, "he makes me laugh. I like that."

"That's important. Having someone to make you laugh," he conceded, his amusement unabated.

They sat there, locked in thought. Luke was confused. He couldn't speak of the changes he felt were coming. The truth, he thought, was never where you thought it would be. It was never neat and simple, and words could never describe it. But there were moments in his life when he'd sensed something happening, taking root, when he knew that events had burst beyond his control in a great untidy splodge.

"Maybe I should clear out of this country right now," he took up morosely, feeling the need to break the silence which fell between them. "It's too small, everybody's leaving."

Kathleen told him a story and it pacified him.

"An uncle of mine did just that. Left home, sailed to the States and ended up piloting the riverboats along the Mississippi."

"Really?"

"He headed for the South. Something about it had always attracted him. I think he read Mark Twain and never looked back. He used to write home, send us local newspapers – I remember one called *The Patriot* – just like some of our own local rags!"

She stopped and took a sip from her glass, her eyes bright.

"Go on," Luke urged, "tell me more."

"Well. He started out as a deck-hand on this riverboat which carried crude oil from New Orleans to Memphis. It was rough work. It took the other men a while to accept him. They couldn't understand his accent, they thought he looked funny – he had red hair, not like mine, but blazing bright red carrotty hair – and then I think they wanted to sort out whether or not he was gay."

Luke's face became dreamy as he listened to her soft voice. She was so lively, so funny as she told the tale.

"What made them think that? Was he gay?"

He leant forward, closer to her, hanging on every word.

"Not as far as I know. But they used to ask him –"

She stopped and drew herself up to imitate a Southern American accent.

"They used to ask him 'Hey yew, yew bin gedin' any? Say, when yew last ged any?' I think they felt better when they saw him disappear into a brothel in Memphis. Then they knew he was into women and straight sex, stuff like that."

New Orleans! Memphis! The Mississippi! He thought again of the y-crack on the ceiling of his room at home, remembered he'd wanted to sail the rivers of the world, something he'd nearly forgotten recently, as if it was a sign of his younger, childish imagination.

"Anyway," she went on, "eventually he was promoted and became responsible for piloting a riverboat. He had to operate by radio, taking instructions about where to land the cargo. The trouble was, he couldn't understand the accent of some of the men in the ports and they couldn't understand his either. I think my uncle cost that shipping company hundreds of thousands of dollars by the time they let him go for being so – incomprehensible! And he just couldn't understand a word some of the blokes said! It was garble."

"Must have been some man, your uncle. It takes guts to cut loose like that. On your own. Where is he now?"

"Last heard of living with some rich woman in Texas. Nobody knows for sure, but we know he has a daughter by her and they say he breeds horses. But you know how it is. These stories get bigger and bigger and the truth is somewhere deep inside. He'll never come home, wise man. You know what families are like when it comes to –"

"Black sheep?"

"Yeah, black sheep, exactly. Or to put it another way, the ones who know what they want."

"He had guts."

"He had to go. If it's in you, then you have to go. Our family's always been full of wanderlust. Clare and I – that's Clare who died – we planned working our way across America, going on to Hawaii, on to the Fiji Islands, New Zealand, right around the world, the Philippines, China, India. There's so much we don't know, right?"

Suddenly they were singing the same song, the words came from one person, one voice, one powerful strand of longing and dreaming.

"About ourselves?"

"That we can discover only through seeing how the world works beyond this little island – "

"You could still go!" he interrupted.

"I probably will, though I don't know when. But so could you for that matter. Well, maybe not. But if you wanted to badly enough, you would. God, this holiday to Thailand is costing a bomb, I've been living on next to nothing for the past year in order to afford it!"

They sat up until three in the morning, when the wine bottle was empty. He did not feel it wrong when they touched hands and he kissed her on the lips. They said goodnight slowly.

Kathleen, he thought, was one of the shrewdest people he'd ever known. But sweet, kind, easy-going. Ready to take on the world regardless of terms, to go out there and make something of her life. He fell into bed, felt stronger and calmer. He'd carry on and he'd manage. The past weeks had changed him in ways he could never have imagined, and although he was in bits, his nerves stretched like thin wires about to snap, there could be no going back to his old, dogged way of living.

But, he realised, there was his mother to consider, and in the coming days he'd have to go over to the house to make peace with her, to apologise. While making it clear that he'd already made his move.

After that night, Kathleen left him to himself. One night he woke, heard whispers, then recognised Tod Grimley's familiar laugh. He turned over again, and slept. During the days, Kathleen would breeze in and out of the flat without talking very much, but sometimes when he got up in the morning, she'd have left a glass of orange juice and a bowl of cereal on the table, with a slip of paper attached: *Eat!* So he forced himself to swallow the mixture of nuts, fruit and cereal, reluctant to spend so much time chewing, his mind already in Dublin, hopeful that perhaps that day, Ginnie would have improved.

Her parents didn't dismiss him outright. At first, the reception was cool. Both of them shook hands with him in the hospital corridor, sounding too vague to convince him that they didn't really know who he was. He sensed they'd hoped he might visit once or twice and then disappear from their daughter's life, that if they denied him acknowledgement, he might dissolve like a bad storm from the edge of their existence.

By the end of the second week, when it was clear that Luke knew more about Ginnie's condition than they did themselves, they thawed considerably, to the extent of inviting him to lunch one day. He agreed, though the thoughts of a full lunch made his stomach heave.

Ginnie's mother was an organising woman.

"You must eat something," she insisted. "You can't sit there all day and starve!"

He looked up at her, caught her eye, and saw at once how much she resented his presence. Her face was still attractive, though finely-lined. She was carefully dressed and made-up. There was no sign, as far as Luke could see, of hardship and struggles. Maybe Ginnie exaggerated. Maybe Mrs Maloney was one of those types who felt she'd come down a step.

Ginnie looked like her. They shared fine skin and thick hair, her eyes discomfitingly like Ginnie's in expression.

In the hospital canteen they queued for lunch. Just as Senan Maloney had ordered minute steak and chips, his wife cut in.

"Think of your cholesterol level! Salads, Senan, salads!" she hissed. He pretended not to hear and accepted a plate piled with glistening, hot food from the man on the other side of the stainless steel food basins. Luke took soup and a cheese sandwich, while Mrs Maloney picked her way through a Hawaiian salad. They talked about the weather, how dry it had been, and Mrs Maloney complained that they could do with a good wetting, it was so airless. Luke said nothing.

"Ah well, that's the way." Senan Maloney stared at nothing in particular. Luke felt he wanted to talk about Ginnie.

"She's getting better anyhow," he said non-committally and felt himself blush.

"When I think what that girl could have been!" Mrs Maloney said. "She had the world at her feet when she left school. Could have gone on to do anything."

"Even got a place in science. Wanted to do pharmacy," Mr Maloney took up, gazing mournfully at Luke.

"You needed very high points for that. Even back then, you needed them," his wife went on. "Or accountancy. She could have done accountancy," she added quickly.

215

Luke looked from one to the other.

"But no, our one had to go off with a crowd of hippies and weirdos. Off to England to protest at Sellafield." Senan Maloney shrugged his shoulders helplessly. "That put a kybosh in the works!" He attempted to laugh.

"No doubt she's told you about all that," said Mrs Maloney.

"She never said," Luke remarked.

"Oh, that finished her all right," Mrs Maloney went on, "drifting around with these hippy types. Trying this and trying that. Then coming back to live in a commune in Sneem, God knows what went on there, not one of them was married, and three little children in the house as well. Then the rock singing began. She's not a girl to stay still for very long, you should know that. Thinks she's made her mind up, then changes it at the drop of a hat. It's only fair that you should know that."

Luke ate as they talked. He nodded when it seemed appropriate, or put in an "Is that so?" or an "I see" and "Mmm" every so often.

"Well now, I'd better go up to see her again." He sat back, uncertain as to how they would respond.

"As you wish. But there's not much point hanging around the hospital, Luke. She's in no mood to see anybody. "

"It doesn't matter. I'll stay. I won't bother anybody," he replied sullenly.

"If you're sure." Mr Maloney put down his knife and fork, placing them precisely down the centre of his empty plate. He sighed. "Pity she ever got caught up in this business," he grumbled to himself, as if hoping someone would agree with him.

Luke nodded as he stood up. "It could have happened to anybody – the business in her apartment, I mean."

"Well, hardly," said Mrs Maloney. "Not if that bomb hadn't gone off, because if there'd been no fire, the chances are she wouldn't have – have met you either."

Luke struggled to stay calm.

"Are you saying it's my fault?"

The bitch got his dander up.

"No, no, not at all son," Mr Maloney cut in, only to be interrupted by his wife.

"Hold on a minute here, Senan. Let's not beat about the bush. The fact is that she and Luke ran away after the fire, and – " she jammed her fork into a piece of tomato on her plate, " – he actually drove off in a bus with her!"

"All right, all right." Her husband was clearly annoyed, unwilling to open up a full-scale disagreement in the hospital canteen. His forehead was beaded with sweat. Around them, groups of nurses sat and smoked, or drank coffee, talking and laughing.

"But look at the state she's in! Look what's happened to her!" In a flash, Luke understood the axis of power in the Moloney household. The husband sat back while his wife ran their lives, even their conversations. He'd been fool enough to lose his job, the poor bastard. Now, years later, he'd got used to apologising.

"Mrs Maloney, if you don't mind – " Luke gripped the back of his chair, then forgot what he meant to say. He was flustered, a bit like a kid being rapped over the knuckles by a teacher.

"I do mind. I mind very much!" she snapped, then searched her bag for a tissue.

"Then listen, willya!"

Her mouth fell open. She fixed him with a look of unconcealed dislike.

He opened his mouth, then shut it again. The bitch unnerved him. He glared down at her and tried again.

"What happened after. That's different. I didn't take her away against her will. I didn't force her, and I'm fed up feeling like Jack the Ripper.'"

The woman stared him down.

"There's no need to raise your voice like that," she said.

"And I'm staying here until I hear her say that she doesn't want to see me. I have to hear it from her!" he went on.

For whatever reason, he was unable to say aloud just how weighed down with guilt he felt, and most of all, how he despised himself for not being at the funerals of the kids who died at Malla.

Mrs Maloney took a glittery compact out of her bag and examined her face in the mirror.

"That's as may be. But I hope you realise it's over now. It has to be. Ginnie will think differently after this spell. I'm sure of it. She might even – come home for a while. Or she could go to university as a mature student. Even at her age. Anything she wants. She's been through a lot and if you care for her as much as you say you do, then you'll stay away from her."

Her husband nodded in agreement.

"I'm sorry, son," he said in a defeated voice. His wife threw her eyes up.

Luke turned and strode down between the crowded tables and out the canteen doors, a slim boy in black denim jeans and a blue T-shirt, his hair now long and unkempt.

"Why, he – he looks like a wild *dog*!" Mrs Maloney murmured in a puzzled voice.

Weeks passed. The pain lessened. One morning, Ginnie

woke up. She'd slept through a whole night without an analgesic. Her skin was knitting, flesh grafted, weals thickened and closed. The physiotherapists had her up and walking, using a frame.

Three days later, it was like reaching the shores of that peaceful haven which she'd longed for. Hilary Dunne's face surfaced with less frequency in her mind. She'd never forget that demonic cackle as the madwoman whipped and lashed, lit and re-lit her deadly cigarettes.

As the physiotherapist helped her from bed and to her feet, Ginnie suppressed a cry, then stood as every muscle, every tendon, every subcutaneous fibre seemed to realign itself, searing her. But walking seemed simple enough, bound and bandaged though she was. It was possible to place one foot in front of the other, to walk a short distance from her room, leaning on the physiotherapist's arm.

Luke sat on a bench on the corridor, stared at the floor as usual. He happened to look up. It was her – thinner, paler – in a loose red gown, with stiff doll's legs. With a gasp, she gripped the physiotherapist's arm as if to pull back. But when he ran towards her, he laughed and cried at once.

He embraced her gently, stroked her head and face with one hand, held her arm with the other in case she should stumble. Instead, she wept, turned her face to the wall.

"Go away, Luke. Go home. Get lost."

But he insisted, and held on, talking to her, walked her back to the room. At the door, he stopped.

"Only if you want me to," he said.

At first she didn't answer, but leaned on his forearm. When she turned, he saw the weariness in her eyes, the dullness of defeat in the face of indignity, a new sadness.

"Come in," she relented.

He drew her thin red robe around her shoulders and helped her to a chair. It was a slow process. Her eyes smarted as she sat gradually onto a ring of soft cushioning.

"Oh, Buddha!"

"You're doing all right," he whispered.

"How am I going to get out of this mess?"

"You will. You're a fighter."

He held her hand, then bent to kiss her cheek. She turned from him.

"Don't. I mean it."

Disappointment stabbed him. "Why not?"

"You're doing this out of duty. And pity," she said in a weary voice. Her face was pale, her hair tousled. It had grown over the weeks, and resembled its old rich thickness again.

His patience snapped. "Ginnie, if you think I've spent every day of the past five weeks in this hospital just for the sake of pity, then you're crazy, you're just crazy!"

She looked puzzled.

"Five weeks? Five weeks?"

"Yeah, five whole weeks, Ginnie. You lay talking gibberish, except you kept saying my name, and that's why I stayed."

Gradually her body relaxed and she rested her head against the back of the chair, her face full of wonder.

"But you're getting better. You'll be out soon. Then we'll see. We'll have plans to make, won't we?"

She sat quite still, but she looked surprised. It didn't dawn on her before how vulnerable he was.

"Your face is bony," she whispered.

He'd grown pale, his eyes seemed huge, full of fear. For the first time, she smiled, tilted her face up and waited to be kissed. It was all he could do to restrain himself. He held back from crushing her, from pressing too hard on her mouth, her cheeks, her eyelids.

But everything had changed. Ginnie saw it quicker than Luke could.

"Some of the scars are disfiguring. I've seen myself from behind." She shuddered. "I got a mirror as soon as I could stand and made one of the nurses hold it for me."

"The only difference it makes to me is that it hurts you. I love you!" Luke said.

She laughed sadly and touched his cheek. But there was no stopping him. "And when you're back on your feet again, we'll – be together?" he said.

She hung her head. "Don't rush me. I don't know." She rested her hand on his neck, enjoying his warmth. They sat in silence as she traced the outline of his shoulder, his upper arm, right down to the light-haired forearm and the long, strong hand. She held it in hers and turned it over, traced the creases in the palms, examined his bitten nails, then lifted each hand and kissed each finger, slowly.

"I wonder what a fortune-teller would say?"

"Whatever you'd want to hear," Luke said. "What do you want to hear, Ginnie. Tell me."

She released his hand. "I've heard it already. The main thing." She broke off. "Don't rush me. It's too much to take in. I don't know."

"All right. We'll see. Just take it easy and get better. Did you see the notebooks I left?"

"What notebooks?"

"I left them with the nurses weeks back. For your lyrics, so that you could start again."

Lyrics. The farthest thing from her mind. She'd told one

221

of the nurses to take them away, that she was finished with singing.

"I remember. Thanks."

Just then, Mick walked in waving a bouquet of red roses at arm's length. At first he ignored Luke.

"These arrived. From Kilgallen," he said, a pained expression on his face. "What'll I do with them?"

"Whatever you like," Ginnie grunted. "Flowers won't bring those kids back."

"Oh, your man's for the high jump," said Mick.

Luke looked on but said nothing. So Kilgallen was in the past, a has-been. The effects of the fiasco with the hall at Malla would go on though, he thought, that business of the two locked exits which stopped the kids escaping. All because of a careless bollocks who knew next to nothing about what he owned but thought he had rights to everything. He was in the hot seat now. The legal enquiry, the group of bereaved relatives who demanded answers and justice, not to mention the Victims at Malla Committee Group howling for compensation, it was like a noose gradually tightening around that cunt's neck. No more than he deserved.

Yet when he'd said as much to Ginnie the day before, she brushed aside his remarks. He looked at her now and she looked back, as if reading his thoughts.

"The whole thing's more complicated than you think, Luke. People get so caught up in the business of making money. Leo forgot that he owned the hall at Malla until I mentioned it to him in June – on the afternoon of the eleventh."

Luke stiffened and pulled a face.

"Yeah, Luke, that's the last time I saw him."

"But if he owned it, then he should be responsible – "

"Should be. Should be. But the place was under-insured to begin with. And I don't think he even knew who was managing the hall. Not then."

"Why are you siding with Kilgallen?" Luke demanded.

"I'm not. I'm just explaining that it's not as cut and dried as it seems. Don't worry, sweetnuts. He'll pick up the tab all right!"

Mick looked on, rolled his eyes and let out a long-suffering groan. Sweetnuts! Jaysus!

"Hey! You haven't called me that since – " Luke stopped himself.

"I know. Not since we were in Kerry." She smoothed the front of her robe and smiled. "But maybe it's time I took up where I left off."

That day Luke left the hospital with Mick, skipped down the front steps in twos and threes, gave one final leap into the air and let out a yelp of joy. It was happening, Ginnie would get better, she would leave that place soon and maybe, just maybe, they'd be together. He thought back to his conversation with John Thornley in June. Something about whether he'd ever thought about marriage. Well, whatever about *that,* here he was on the brink of getting hitched in some style. Only two months later.

It was the time of year when he'd normally be run off his feet, during the corn harvest, when the yellow combines with long funnels droned around the grain fields. But he didn't miss it, sure he hadn't so much as seen his mother since the night they'd argued. Let them at it, he thought, let them thresh the barley and the corn for themselves. But he paused at the jeep in the carpark and thought back, remembering the way gulls and crows would scavenge in the wake of the combine, how wild cats prowled along the edges of the fields waiting for mice and other rodents in flight from the great pentagonal cutter as it spun and rattled, devoured the crop, left coarse stubble behind.

He decided to celebrate by treating himself to a meal and a bottle of beer before going home. He'd forty quid in his pocket. After that he was skint. The jeep was costing him a fortune.

"You coming with me?" he asked Mick.

Mick eyed him. So they'd better make the best of things; he was going to have to put up with Luke. The kid wasn't about to vamoose, worse luck.

"I might as well." He fired the roses, which he'd forgotten to dispose of in the hospital, into a bin in the carpark. Not a word passed between them for some time. Luke didn't care. Very soon, he'd take Ginnie from the hospital, she'd walk down those steps on his arm and they'd drive off together. He loved the idea of driving off, of escape. Together forever. For the rest of their lives. Long, long years stretched ahead, stacked endlessly like chapters in a story which was already written, which they could explore together. The old eternal love-line. When he was thirty, he'd be mature, a mature man, just as Ginnie was now a mature woman. She'd be over forty then. Forty-four. Old. But he couldn't imagine her looking any different, no matter what age she was.

Mick, sunglasses glinting, combed his hair carefully, then chain-smoked in the passenger seat as Luke drove through the city in mid-afternoon traffic. They parked on double-yellow lines in D'Olier Street, then wandered the streets aimlessly. On Westmoreland Street they paused outside Bewley's and watched a protest march make its way across O'Connell Bridge.

"Jaysus!" Mick muttered.

Luke caught a glimpse of the leaders, saw the hoisted crucifixes. Rosaries swung and glittered from the raised arms of placard carriers who bore messages in vermilion and black. They were quiet and organised. A pretty woman with straight brown hair led them, behind her stretched two lines of skin-headed young men. As the traffic came to a halt, car engines hummed in the heat. Shoppers stood and watched and the eerie atmosphere of a city turned almost silent was marked by the tapping of heels over a marching hymn, *Faith of Our Fathers*.

Luke and Mick turned down Fleet Street. Away from the main thoroughfare, the place throbbed with the lazy sounds of late summer in the city; the drinkers and buskers and shoppers; groups of young people sprawled along the pavements, oblivious to the march passing within four hundred yards of them; a traditional Irish group piped beneath the awnings outside a pub. Luke hadn't a clue where he was going, but Mick tagged along regardless, eyed the pints of stout ranged along window-ledges, or on the edges of pavements. From an upstairs studio, a rock group played and re-played the same few phrases.

"Well, head?" Mick said gruffly.

"Well what?"

"She's on the mend anyway."

Luke said nothing.

Posters on hoardings – some torn, others weathered – advertised gigs, carnivals, readings. He smelt hot fat, coffee, the river.

"You driving back to the sticks again tonight?"

"Yes," Luke replied.

"You're welcome to kip at my place," Mick offered, not

looking at Luke, his attention trained just past his head, "self-service and all that. It's just around the corner." He thumbed proudly. "Brand new, the latest everything – design, furnishings. Mind you – " he paused, raising an eyebrow, "I'm not too happy with the fucking futon which came free gratis. Fucking interior designers have a thing against real beds. Don't know how the Nippons manage it."

"Thanks. But no." Luke was too exhausted to concoct a reason for not staying.

Then he saw it. A picture of Virgin used to promote the last concert tour before the fire, defaced. Her teeth had been blacked out, someone had painted red horns on her forehead, and her eyebrows had been smudged into deeply-indented points. Her mouth was drawn in an evil leer. The image was overlaid by graffiti. *Bitch. Cunt. You'll burn in hell. Tracey loves Alfo. Mothersucker abortionist Bitch now the puss is coming out!*

He ripped it from the hoarding, then tore it to shreds.

"Right on!" someone called from across the street.

"You've got it bad, kiddo," Mick grunted.

Eventually, attracted by the violin music which drifted from an overhead speaker, they found their way to a quiet restaurant. They were the only customers, and throughout the meal two waiters hovered at an attentive distance. He scanned the menu for something familiar like steak and chips, or even a bolognese. He was wall-falling with hunger, and finally settled on grilled goat's cheese with a warm salad, then a mixture of seafood, followed by hot, syrupy fritters. Since there was no beer, they consumed most of a bottle of red wine, and left the place half cut.

Out on the street, Mick belched.

"Great food!" He sighed contentedly. He'd wolfed his

way through the meal, spent the time watching the two waiters, but didn't risk passing comments to Luke. Suddenly, he straightened his suede tie and ran his hands through his hair. A sudden need which he had to fulfil now gripped him, so urgent that he had to go off on his own, on the hunt again.

"Listen, head. Gotta go. See ya later."

Mick slapped Luke on the shoulder and hurried off in the direction of the quays.

"See you," Luke whispered.

As he wandered the cobbled streets, hands in his pockets, he heard again the sound of marching feet, a murmur of prayers carried downwind from the river. He looked back the length of the alley and they came suddenly from the direction of Dame Street, down Eustace Street, their voices shrill and violent. Behind, a riot. What was to have been a peaceful demo from Parnell Square to Leinster House had become a hysteria-edged brawl. At the junction of Eustace Street and Temple Bar, the two groups met head on, goaded one another with placards and photographs. Luke dodged into the porch of a pub, then changed his mind and moved out onto the footpath again as the crowds ran towards him, some of them flinging books and candles at passers-by.

"Here! Take this! Read it!" a man screamed, pushing a leaflet into Luke's arms.

"Read the truth, read the whole truth for yourselves!"

"Murderers!"

He was pushed and jostled on all sides as the two groups clashed.

*The new Holocaust is here! Women's bodies are like death-chambers!* he read on a placard which two men hammered up and down rhythmically on the street.

"Abortion out! Abortion out! Abortion out!" the crowd roared to the beat of a bass drum.

*Knowledge is a human right,* Luke read on another placard.

*Our bodies, Ourselves!*

He fumbled with the leaflets, then glanced at one as the crowd shouldered past. There was a colour photograph, an image of a skinless, pink and glistening shape which could have been an unhatched chicken or a frog. Then he spotted the group's young leader, the pretty girl he'd noticed earlier. She held an enormous laminated poster before the other crowd, stood stock-still as if to dare them. She wore a blue veil, like many of her pals. He was struck by the strange, romantic beauty of the women, the way their veils floated softly around their faces and hair. At the same time their eyes frightened him, full of a fierce and angry conviction. They hurled slogans at the opposing group. He sensed the violence which underlay their words. The two groups screamed one another down.

"Keep your rosaries off our ovaries!"

"Murderers!"

"Women's right to choose!"

"The Blessed Virgin weeps for your sins!"

"Freedom to think and read, freedom to meet a need!"

"Babies have rights! Babies have rights!"

"Body fascists!"

In the end, he forced his way through the group which didn't carry gory pictures. They weren't so scary. The drums and tambourines and whistles made him feel panicky. But he took a brisk right turn, elbowed his way through the crowd in Merchants' Arch, then crossed Ha'penny Bridge to walk the quays on the far side of the river until the racket died down.

Nothing, he realised, was so violent as people. Nothing made them so crazy as religion. It made them think they knew all the answers, that they had rights over anybody else who disagreed. My God is better than your God, *nah-nah-nah-nah-nahhhhh!* He sniggered. What really got him was the fact that some religious people made a big deal about sin. Sin was on their minds, big time. And if you believed in sin and things like that, which he wasn't sure he did, then that crowd with their banners and their disgusting words did a hell of a lot of sinning against the people who didn't agree with them.

The wind was mild. He looked back in the direction of Ha'penny Bridge, enjoying the blue lighting which flared up from beneath the railings; it bleached the faces of pedestrians who crossed behind him, also in flight from the protesters. Then he glanced up at the stars, as if he'd find answers to his questions there; startled, he watched the dazzling arc of a falling meteor.

# Fourteen

## Hunter's Gold

After he split with Luke, Mick headed back to the penthouse to freshen up. He climbed the stairway towards the upper gallery, bumped into the fashion designer as he locked up his own apartment, mumbled an apology, and carried on, puffing as he ascended the last eight steps.

For some reason, the designer stayed in his mind. People made out in all kinds of ways. Somehow, they got by. Come to think of it, he noticed some of the garments the last time he peered through his neighbour's apartment window. Colourless was the only word to describe them. The sort of gear that film directors would dress actors in for space movies. Kind of porridgy, anaemic, rough-looking fabric with sleeves long enough to cover a chimpanzee's arms. But people could be persuaded to like anything, he thought, absolutely anything. You could sell shares in shit and make a go of it.

He stopped to catch his breath outside his front door. Now, if Luke were here, he'd have mounted the stairway in a flash, would have arrived at the top of the flight without losing control of his breath. He had to hand it to the young buck, but he'd a lot going for him. He was that bit different. Not your average twit. Perhaps Ginny was right to grab her chance, what she saw as a change, and he hoped she wasn't making a big mistake. Life offered so few breaks. You had to know when to recognise the big one.

Inside, he stripped and showered. His eye lingered on a poster of Caravaggio's *David* which he'd had framed and placed on the wall opposite his bed. As he stared through to the bedroom from the open shower door, he felt suddenly despondent. So. Out on the razzle again. But what hope had he? Who'd want to do more than literally fuck around with him for a couple of hours? Who'd want that something more, more than fellatio or condoms, or admiring one another's members, who the hell would want a second meeting?

Initial encounters were child's play, but tackling a follow-up was a different matter altogether. The fact was, he mused, that the city was teeming with gay men, often too desperate in too many different ways. There were the guys who were desperate not to have the heterosexual cover blown, then the guys who were gay but terrified of so much as taking a late night walk for fear of being bashed to death with baseball bats in some suburban park. Finally, there were men like himself. Real men who longed for love, in the effortless, easy way that Ginnie and Luke had discovered love. He no longer wanted to find himself hunting, always hunting. He'd had enough fellatio to do him till he died, not that his appetite was in any way diminished, but nevertheless, he wanted more than having his organ sucked by some stranger to whom he could not reach out, or who could not reach out to him in a way that was meaningful. But it was the stuff of dreams, pirate's dreams, hunter's gold. He didn't know if he'd ever track it down.

He sighed as he dressed, as he thought of Ginnie and Luke. That was it. They were normal, so normal. He thought back to the scene at the hospital over the past weeks. There they were, together, at ease with one another despite the age difference, convinced of the rightness, the appropriateness of their love and affection. It was how he wanted to be. At ease, sort of elegantly at ease. Certain that something was right in his life. One hundred and ten per cent spot-on.

That night, *Araby* was quieter than usual. Once inside, the regular duty boy gave him a cubicle number. He went there promptly and stripped down again. It was a functional space behind a sliding wooden door, with a narrow bed, a couple of chairs, some ashtrays. Before he entered the sauna, he shook his head as if uncertain of something. What was the point, he wondered again. None, came the reply in his head. With such fatalism he entered the sauna and sat down on a bench. As usual, it took him a while to figure out who was who in the steaming heat, who was familiar and who was new. Most of the regulars were already chatting. It was the usual kind of conversation, found in any pub or overheard at any business lunch throughout the country. Moneytalk. Work. Sport. The occasional mention of "the wife and kids". Mick leaned back and relaxed. As he reclined and looked straight ahead to the opposite bench, he made eye contact with a newcomer. Brown skin. Slightly slanted eyes. Beautiful, Mick thought, then dismissed his admiration. The others would be after this one. Fresh to the scene. A big galoot like him hadn't a chance.

In the sauna, many of the bodies looked alike. Most men when stripped down were, he'd observed, softly contoured, flabby, with drooping minor breasts and small grey dicks. Mick always looked first at the feet, then at the hands. If these measured up, then the crown jewels would too. It was an infallible rule-of-thumb. But the sauna was a place where men could also come to relax, to be at ease with tiredness, tension, with their turmoil and their lust, which, by and large, was insatiable.

The new man was around his own age, possibly younger, with the refined body of Tom Selleck gone oriental. Mick swallowed. OK, so here was a *man*. Maybe that signalled that he should do absolutely nothing; if he was wise, he should lay low and wait.

He waited. Five minutes passed. He made no effort to join in the general conversation, the jokes and the ribaldry. A well-tanned, grey-chested man whom he knew to be a banker suddenly sat forward, slapped his thighs as if to wake them all up.

"Listen to this! The Missus told it to me yesterday. Heard it at work, she did. Coffee-break stuff. Hah, hah, hah." Another voice called out encouragement. At first, Mick couldn't see who it was because he was perched in the corner, concealed by an elderly priest who sat and puffed gently in the heat.

"Two homosexuals are living together. One day, one of the fellas comes home from work and finds his partner with his trousers down and his backside in the fridge. 'What are you doing that for?' asks your man, kinda curious. 'I thought you'd like to slip into something nice and cool,' comes the reply. Can you credit it? Hah, hah, hah! That's my Missus for you."

The others fell around the place laughing, not so much

233

at the joke, but at the thought of the unwitting spouse regaling him with her idea of a bent joke.

Hah, hah, hah. Hah, hah, hah. For some reason, Mick couldn't laugh, not just then. Neither did the man opposite. As if by telepathy, they both sat forward suddenly and began to speak at the same time.

"Excuse me, but – "

"Is this your first – ?"

Apologies, smiles. Mick made his move and crossed the floor to the bench opposite. He caught the man's particular body odour now that he was beside him. A good smelling person, a person with an attractive natural whiff, usually an indication that the person was worthwhile. Healthy. *Mens sana in corpore sano.* Or the other way around. He hoped he smelt well. Either that or not at all.

"Mick Delaney," He offered his hand.

"Trevor. Trevor Hung."

In Dublin for the week at a sales conference, he'd come out for a night on the town. Used to speedy encounters and hastier departures, Mick recounted his history fluently. It was like a convention. He knew it by heart, as if he'd written it. He spilled the lot. His work, where he came from, his mother's death, his excitement about promoting Virgin in Germany, and now, even the fire at Malla. But Trevor didn't respond automatically. He took his time. He listened, his head tilted to one side. Every so often, he asked Mick to repeat something.

"Sorry, mate. Your accent. And me right ear's a gonner. Got kicked in the 'ead last year."

"You mean – ?" What Mick always dreaded. The gay-bashing routine.

"I was identified," Trevor said quietly.

In an instant, Mick lost his heart. The admission of vulnerability, the open sign of frailty in what amounted to a steaming salon of men high on a flow of testosterone, was like a depth charge to the centre of his affections.

"Jaysus! How did they know?"

"They didn't. It was guesswork. Guesswork and ignorance, mate. No shortage of 'em around London. Some folk have nuffing better to do."

To his relief, it didn't end there, although Trevor was booked into a city centre hotel. They dressed quickly and left for the penthouse. As they walked down Grafton Street they cut through the crowds just out from the Duke Street pubs, passed shuttered windows. There was an urgency to their mission which never faltered. Mick ignored the street children, the beggars, the laughing hordes. For once, he had an appointment, perhaps even a destiny.

They puffed their way up the stairway to Mick's apartment, stopped at the top and giggled and gasped in the dark like boys up to mischief, their heels grating on the stone flags of the balcony garden.

"Jaysus, but we're two mad fuckers!" said Mick, sliding the key home.

"Mad fuckas!" Trevor echoed him in a London accent.

Inside, words failed them as suddenly as they had flowed outside. But there was no hesitation about what each wanted. They regarded one another, then embraced. Trevor's lips were warm and sweet. They stood for a long time, holding one another, stroking, nuzzling. There were no words, just sounds of satisfaction, disbelief. They took their time. Mick poured two whiskeys. Trevor lay back on the *le Corbusier* lounger, settled himself into the black leather comfort. They sat and talked for at least an hour, holding one another's gaze as they exchanged the simple facts of living. Life in London. Selling computer software. The gay scene. Soho Square. Putney, where Trevor lived. The Piccadilly Line, his parents and sister, the family home in the East End. All points on the constellation of Trevor's experience. Later, they stroked and caressed with a tenderness and a violence which Mick hadn't known since he was much, much younger. What was sheer magic, he thought later as his eye lingered on the trail of disgarded clothing that led through the living-room area straight to the futon in the bedroom – Trevor's tousled brown head cradled in his arm – was that there was something so marvellously gentle about this man, with his history of a London rearing, an Asian mother and a Moroccan father. He had brown skin and a brown voice, brown eyes and needs just like Mick's. This was something special. A mutual want had for once been satisfied. He'd fucking clicked.

The next morning, the dream didn't evaporate as he'd feared it might. Trevor joined him at breakfast, tolerated the mess of the kitchen, mooched around and made himself at home.

"So. 'ave we got a problem or wot?" Trevor asked circumspectly.

"Not in my book, we haven't!" said Mick, refilling both mugs with real, dark, steaming coffee, a special concession to the morning and to the visitor. Trevor added milk and sugar to his mug, helped himself to another slice of toast, which he buttered heavily, then layered with marmalade. He spoke and munched at the same time.

"OK so. Shall we make anovver arrangement? Soon?"

"Yeah. Soon. I'd like that."

"So would I." Trevor smiled. His eyes still invited attention, intimacy. Again, Mick melted.

It would be easy to maintain a London–Dublin based contact, Mick thought. A short plane-hop away. When he thought about it, the distance was nothing, especially not when you loved someone. They spent the morning in bed, exhausted themselves by noon. Feelings of self-disgust which had always dogged Mick like a dark unwanted twin evaporated in hours. He felt cleansed. No, even better, he felt clean. Even heterosexual people, he guessed, must feel filthy, if they had nobody to love them. But he was normal, lovable, somebody *wanted* him and not just for one night. This could be it, he thought. This man could be the *one*. Before Trevor left the penthouse, they embraced again, met in a deep kiss of such intensity that Mick thought he'd faint. The door closed, Trevor was gone. Mick held a black and gold edged business-card in his palm, studied the phone number and the address again and again. Next week, it was London for him. Putney here we come. He didn't know how he'd pass the time in between, how he'd survive the ordinary details. He'd have to eat. To sleep. Talk to people who bored the fucking pants off him and all the time he'd be fizzing with this new secret. He looked around. That futon would definitely have to go. The time had come to buy a decent bed, king-size. A men's bed. And furniture for real men to sit in for Christ's sake.

Already, his fax machine had unrolled yards of messages, all of which he'd ignored that day. He picked up the end paper and read it. Then he stopped. His heart nearly missed a beat. What he'd been waiting for. Germany. They wanted Virgin. It was all there, a tour, all the best stadiums and halls, a German publicist who actually wanted to work with him.

Jaysus, he breathed, wiping his brow, *Jaysus*. It was all working out.

# Fifteen

## The Last Irish Witch

Mick visited the hospital a day later, bursting with news, plans and the pent-up excitement of thinking too much about his first trip to London. Trevor's place. Sounds so good that does, he thought: tripping with Trevor. Ginnie was expecting him, and sat with a regal air, her ankles crossed casually and her nails painted. Luke had just left. She did not want the two to meet again, uncomfortable at the thoughts of arranging a three-way conversation. From separate worlds, Mick and Luke still suspected one another.

"Jeeeeesus have I got news!" He threw himself into a small wicker chair which creaked beneath his weight. He mopped his brow with a crumpled blue handkerchief. Ginnie watched, waiting for him to get to the point.

"Let me guess. London?"

"Wrong. Try again," he teased, unable to suppress a smirk.

"Further afield. Europe?"

"Be specific."

He rapped his fingers on the arm of the chair, his chin set with the satisfaction of being the herald of good news.

"I give up," she said indifferently.

"Germany," he said triumphantly, "Hamburg, Cologne, Munich and Berlin. The Deutschland Halle! Howsabout it, pet? A tour of the new, united Germany!"

He rubbed his hands in glee. Ginnie stood up. It seemed far too easy. Too much, too soon, before she was ready. Her confidence had vanished like last year's snow. Hilary Dunne had seen to that. There was something she had to get off her chest.

"It's time you and me had a chat. First of all, I don't know what kind of manager is such a *dope* that he strings along the likes of Hilary Dunne. You made it possible for her to do what she did," she accused. "Do you think this Germany thing matters to me right now?" she mocked.

"Big deal, you've got me a tour in Europe. Not before time, Mick, not before time, and remember you're not the only agent in the world. But you were messing Hilary Dunne around! You! A gay man! Didn't you *know* she wasn't normal? Did it not dawn on you that even the Guardians of Christian Destiny would love to get rid of her? Well, they have anyhow, because she's been committed. She's been transferred to Dundrum Central and the psychiatric report states what should have been obvious even to you. Paranoid delusions among other things. One of the doctors here told me, so wipe that innocent look off your face. How could you be so stupid?" she asked bitterly. "Why did you pretend not to notice?"

Embarrassed, Mick closed his eyes. Why couldn't the doctors keep their bloody traps shut?

"Look, Ginnie. Look."

He cleared his throat.

"Careless. That's what you were. Fucking careless."

"I didn't know, I swear I had no idea, I didn't see her that often – "

"You'd no idea," Ginnie said more softly. "You have no idea about a lot of things, Mick, and it's costing me, it's costing me the hard way. You don't live on this planet, do you? Do you? Not one inhabited by men and women, real women. We are the other sex. The sex you can't handle unless they're saints or madwomen!" She bit her lip and paused.

"Ginnie. I wish I could turn the clock back – I'm sorry, there's nothing else I can say. I feel lousy about this, lousy."

"Well you might," she said lamely. He was hardly a central cause, hardly to blame, but she needed to vent her spleen on someone and who better than the gobshite who'd fucked around with Hilary Dunne.

"Is it all set up?" she said, changing the subject.

"What?"

"Germany, Mick, Germany." It was like addressing a slightly stupid child.

"Oh. Yeah. All set," he answered, still troubled.

"Like when? Will I be ready? What about my back? I'm as stiff as a poker!"

"No problem. And you just dress differently from now on. Less exposure. We can make you precious. The cosmetics people can work wonders."

She turned away.

"Is that a fact? I don't want cosmetics people near me."

"Why not?"

"I'm not the same any more. The old Virgin's a thing of the past. Beaten up, a scarred old trouper. I'm so *ugly*, I don't have skin, I have a hide like a – " She spat the word, "rhinoceros!"

241

Rhinoceros, she repeated mentally. She'd be codding herself to imagine that Luke would be able to live with it. He wouldn't. He was too young. She thought of him in years to come, and her jealousy grew at the imagined scenario in which he would eventually tire of her.

"And I don't know about my voice either," she moaned.

Mick slapped his hands against his thighs. The combination of women and tears still unsettled him. Female upsets signalled imbalance, inconsistency, an absence of control which had – occasionally – broken within him too. Look what happened with Hilary, he thought. Now this, though the situation was hardly comparable. Even if he was full of remorse at his own stupidity, his blindness to the signals pouring from Hilary Dunne, the truth was that the doctors were right. Just now, it was all up to Ginnie. She could be as agile and strong as before, even with scars. But skin-grafts would work wonders. One operation a year, the doctor suggested, enough to restore a smooth epidermis.

He wondered about what might be happening in her head. They warned of the depression which might set in, black denials and angers.

"It's up to you," he said, wanting to soften the words as soon as they were spoken, but knowing he could no more put his arms out to hold her than he could have touched Hilary Dunne. In that moment, he knew he was impotent, as scarred in his way as Ginnie or Hilary. Such scary emotions these women had, manageable at times, but scary, weird. Not that Ginnie should be compared to Hilary Dunne, he reminded himself, but nonetheless she had a mountain of heavy-duty problems on her hands now. Plus a complexity which he didn't want to deal with but which, if she didn't sort it out, could screw up her professional life. More important still, unless she got shot of that Luke, she might be screwed up anyway. No matter how normal they were or how *nice* the arrangement was. He couldn't for the life of him get a handle on that buck. Just what did they think they were at, the pair of them? Luke had better not get in the way. Ginnie, he hoped, had sense enough not to let that happen.

"I have contracts. Good ones. The best you've ever had. The woman we're employing for publicity is one of Germany's top people. Just sign and you're a rich woman!" He forced himself to laugh. "They want you to re-record in German and we can get the lyrics translated within a month. You'd just have to OK them. If you don't like the feel of them we get 'em done again. Simple!"

He tried to lighten his tone, rubbing his hands with satisfaction trying to dispel the mood of self-recrimination which she had provoked in him.

"I don't speak German so how would I know? And what about my appearance?"

"That'll sort itself out. Give it time, pet. Wear long dresses, loose trousers, plenty of glitter, new hairstyle, that kind of thing. The music's what matters, not the other stuff. These Krauts want songs, not just the video performance and the stripping and the oil. That kind of thing's old hat over there."

She opened a box of chocolate-covered pecan nuts which Luke had left.

"I'll think about it," she said.

Her head was like a vacant lot. Nothing doing. Nobody at home. Not a note or a word worth writing down. It made her tense as hell. But where did she go from here? She looked Mick straight in the face and decided to lie. It might help.

"As a matter of fact, I've a couple of new ideas. Funny. I thought I'd never write again, but Luke brought in some sheet music. Notebooks and stuff. Yeah, it's starting again, Mick."

Well, good for Luke, Mick thought, good for lucky Luke as long as he doesn't overstep the mark. He made to leave, mopped his forehead again, helped himself to one of the chocolates and hurried off.

"I'll be in touch. Main thing is, take it easy. Just take it easy, pet," he whispered, sticking his head around the door one last time.

In spite of herself Ginnie smiled, then reached over to the bedside table and picked up a novel. But it lay unopened on her lap as the minutes passed and she stared through the window, down at the hospital carpark. A metal tea-trolley clanked against the door of her room, causing her to turn sharply.

"Tea, love?" the blonde middle-aged attendant called in.

"No thanks."

They insisted on asking twice daily even though she'd told them she didn't drink tea or coffee between meals. She listened as the trolley was pushed and banged down the length of the corridor, in and out of rooms, then on to the day-room where the more mobile patients whiled away the time. Funny how they managed to make conversations out of the hospital's ordinary routines. Who was or wasn't on 24-hour collection, who was due to go under the knife the next day, hearsay about this or that doctor or nurse, different interpretations of the blood-pressure readings on the charts at the bottom of every bed. It was a bit like living in a neighbourhood. Despite yourself, you got to know people. The other patients got into a bit of a flap about someone like herself, on crutches, made a great to-do of plumping up cushions and supports on the best chair in the day-room anytime she'd put in an appearance. She turned back to the window and stared down at the carpark again, automatically counted cars in lines across, then lines down. Finally, she counted them in diagonals.

Maybe she could pull it off. Maybe it wasn't over yet. How could it be? And Luke was behind her.

There was the new apartment to look forward to. A new base for when she left hospital. Mick had scouted around and found something smaller, even organised the removal of her things from Ruskin Way. Weeks back, she had written him a shaky note while still lying on her stomach, and begged him to get her out of the contract with Leo Kilgallen. Every hint of his presence was to be removed, from his clothing in her wardrobes, to his aftershaves and his ridiculous spare sets of underpants. Burn the lot, she'd instructed Mick.

For a time, Leo sent baskets of flowers, ornate arrangements of fruit, and one vague, initialled note explaining why he could not come to the hospital. Indifference made her return the fruit, the flowers and the note to his office, instead of his home. She had no axe to grind with Mitzi. She wished Leo no ill. But she sent no explanations either. Not surprisingly, Kilgallen made no further attempt to contact her. Up to his eyes in legal proceedings, questioned about safety regulations and insurance claims, under pressure from the media, Leo was in such a stew that she was the last person he'd want to hear from.

"Get rid of his letters, Mick!" she barked down the phone one morning from her hospital bed.

Mick knew the score, drove around to Ruskin Way and

located a small black cardboard box in the apartment, tucked at the back of a polished walnut wardrobe. It was plump, over-filled and sealed. Whatever its contents, he didn't want to know. Arsebollocks Kilgallen's love-letters, he thought incuriously and with disgruntlement. He smeared the package with mouldy dripping found in the kitchen, then tossed them into the living-room fireplace. The box smouldered at first, but he burst it open with the poker, and the letters suddenly exploded. They burnt beautifully, curled blue, green, yellow and pink as layer after layer of Kilgallen's spiky endearments went up in smoke. Every so often he caught scraps of sentences, Kilgallen's erotic lines, then turned away because it made him feel like a Peeping Tom. Mick watched in satisfaction as the only other threat to Ginnie's peace of mind was removed. It was a good half hour's work.

Leo Kilgallen, thought Ginnie, running her thumbnail along the spine of the unread novel, had been one of those mistakes which everybody makes once in a lifetime. It could have been worse, much worse. The most charitable thing she could say about herself was that she'd lost her courage from the moment she agreed to live in Ruskin Way. It was his apartment, no matter how you twisted the interpretation of the phrase "joint ownership". It was his, not hers. In fact he dominated her. But she'd convinced herself otherwise and it cost her dearly.

So much for her lyrics. So much for what she believed in, so much for the freedoms she used to make so much of, so publicly. Total, absolute personal freedom. Freedom to come and go, to love, freedom for all humans to control their bodies by whatever means possible. Yet Hilary Dunne had punished her. Although the focus of her crusade was ill-judged, mad as that woman had been, some thorn of warped intelligence was alive and sharp, had proved itself more powerful than the language or the silence of freedom.

She understood pain now. She understood the nature of relentless, stinging, unbearable pain. What she'd suffered at Hilary Dunne's hands, so too had thirty-two young people endured as a result of being burned at Malla. Not that she should ever have suffered like them. Sometimes she got to wondering what century she was living in, and in what country. The last Irish witch was burned in the closing years of the 19th century. Millions of women had been burned as witches throughout Europe between the 14th century and then. She wished she'd never met Leo Kilgallen. It was as if the source of all her troubles lay in him, as if he was tainted with bad luck. Gilded though his own life might be, a trail of disaster followed in his wake.

But he was receding; she couldn't seriously blame him. Absence of contact had brought relief. On certain days, when he flitted across her mind like a troublesome, smiling ghost, she wondered about the failure of imagination on her part, and what had led her to settle for less than she deserved or wanted. And as the press continued to pursue him and his business interests, as the debate about safety regulations became heated, she allowed herself some satisfaction that Leo Kilgallen was getting the roasting he deserved.

They owed those young people a debt that was unpayable. They – all of them – herself, Kilgallen, Mick, would have to make reparation. She'd keep in touch with the kids, and more. Their tragedy was also hers. Where money was needed, she'd find it. Hadn't Mick more or less promised the big breakthrough in Germany? Her time was coming. That was Mick's guarantee. She would be wealthy yet.

And Luke? She sighed. The scars. The scars on her body. Wealthy perhaps, but marked by the past, just as Hilary Dunne would have wanted. She remembered reading about people who had been burnt and injured, about physical damage and broken bones, how the shape and state of the body influenced the shape and state of the mind. All her adult life she had felt beautiful, glowing, fit. Now she was defiled. She was pulled down, had tumbled into a mess which some might say was of her own making, even if the Dunne woman was locked up in the Central Mental Hospital. But Hilary was sly. She was intelligent, well able to outwit most of the morons with whom she came in contact. Ginnie pushed to the back of her mind the thought that one day Dunne might be released, that the psychiatrists might consider her fit to live in one of those half-way houses between one crazy world and another. She smiled to herself. Who could say who was crazy and who was sane? Who could say that that blackbird bursting his throat out there on the branch of a beech tree was even real?

She looked down again at the novel and flicked through the pages. She had to recover. She would grow strong again. She would endure an annual visit to the hospital for four or five years, until they'd at least got her legs smoothed out again. One of the doctors, in a lame effort to console, told her she'd never have to worry about hairs on the backs of her legs, that the skin would be grafted from her inner thighs and from her stomach, that it would grow smooth and young and new.

Her head began to throb with rage as she thought again about the Dunne woman. No, she could not forgive, even if she now recognised certain things – the intelligence, the warped anti-poetry of her dancing and singing as she mocked and tormented what she could only hate. She had flung away her fragile hold on reality in the frantic quest to achieve a state of association with her crackpot Australian brother.

Ginnie shivered. Hilary Dunne, and the chance coincidence which attracted her lethal attentions, had almost destroyed her.

She rang for one of the nurses. She needed company, badly. Luke wasn't due back until later in the day. She'd sent him out to buy her new books, a few blank cassettes, some cigarettes. She hadn't smoked since June the eleventh. Time to test the hospital's No Smoking rule. And awaiting her tomorrow, in one of the hospital conference rooms, the little matter of meeting the press. Remorse – extravagant or humble, sorrow fitting to the moment, being sorry or being good – such things did not come easy when most required.

# Sixteen

## Art and Justice

Mick insisted on a wheelchair although Ginnie wanted to walk. "No, doll. You can't afford to look too healthy. You've suffered. Let 'em see it!"

It felt worse than waiting to do a gig. Despite what he said about no make-up, she insisted on looking her best. It was a combination of vanity and the need to put a barrier between herself and the critics. If she looked good, then she automatically felt stronger in herself. So she made up with care, applied fake tan the night before, then touched it up with foundation, made her eyes look sultry and dark, her lips full and plump. When she was ready, dressed in a black and red velvet kaftan, with gold leather pumps on her feet, Luke pushed her into the conference room.

A deep hum curled beneath the door towards them. Inside the beige-coloured rectangular room, the atmosphere fizzed with anticipation. As Luke pushed Ginnie inside, preceded by Mick, they fell silent. Ginnie wanted to run, conscious of the rubbery sound of the wheelchair wheels on the polished floor. They were all there, friends and enemies from the press, faces she recognised, the hacks and photographers who had followed her career over the past years.

As they arranged themselves, the silence intensified, broken only by one of the photographers who moved into action the moment they appeared in the doorway. Ginnie smoothed the front of her kaftan, gazed out at the group and thought, not for the first time, how bizarre and yet how perfectly ordinary it was to have to deal with men, always with men, to justify herself before men, men and more men, as women always had and maybe always would. There were three other women in the room apart from herself.

Then someone hiccupped and everybody laughed, tension broken in a nervous explosion. She reminded herself that she'd had a good working relationship with some of these people, had gone in for plenty of tongue-in-cheek banter which kept both sides happy. They were only doing a job.

"OK people, OK, OK . . . " she began, the laughter not quite gone from her voice. A photographer crouched in front of her, then moved slowly to her left profile. Her expression grew more serious, still and open to their questions.

"Just a few things, Virgin." Bob Farrelly, arts reporter from one of the Sundays. His face was sombre as he flicked over a page of his notebook. A slight dowager's hump on his back made his head hang lower than it should. His shoulders sloped, so that he seemed prematurely tired and old.

"First of all, we're all – " he hesitated and looked even graver, "really sorry about the personal attack which you suffered."

Ginnie nodded. Personal attack. What did that really mean to someone like Bob Farrelly?

"But can you take us back a little before that time? I was thinking of the night of the eleventh of June – ." He drew breath and Ginnie felt herself grow tense. "Isn't it true to say that you left the scene of the tragedy with Luke O'Regan although it was clear that something very very serious indeed had happened?"

"Well yes," Ginnie drawled, raising her eyebrows, "That's true. Everybody knows that by now."

"Virgin! Virgin!" Bonnie Macbeth cut in. Ginnie turned her gaze on the woman and waited.

"You left the scene of the fire, as my colleague here just suggested, without the slightest thought about anybody else's welfare. Doesn't that strike you as unusual? Even criminal?"

"Unusual? Yes, perhaps unusual. Criminal? I suppose no more than the people who managed to get off the Titanic alive were regarded as criminals."

A murmur ran through the room. But Macbeth was not to be dismissed. Her face sharpened and she flicked her glossy red hair back with one hand.

"OK, Virgin. Let's say it was pretty strange that you left the scene of the explosion while *hundreds* of young people were injured, I mean some of these kids *died*. Don't you think you should have stayed on the scene?"

Mick moved forward.

"We're not in a court of law here – "

"No, no, Mick – " Ginnie cut in. Time to head for high moral ground, she thought. She turned again to the journalist. "Forgive me, but Ms Macbeth is quite right. I left and that is inexcusable. I don't expect to be excused either. But I was confused, concussed – whatever – after my manager pulled me out of the auditorium. I was knocked out when the rigging collapsed. Something hit me."

She spoke even more slowly, stared at some mid-point between herself and her audience, as if trying to see again the events of that night.

"I don't remember anything between the explosion and coming to out at the back. And for the record – " she paused, "I *asked* Luke O'Regan to take me away. It was not on his initiative that we went, but mine."

A reporter from RTE News called out from the left. "So what have you to say to the parents of the boys and girls who died or were injured in the fire at Malla?" he asked quietly.

*Oh shit, this is it,* Ginnie thought. She looked down at her knees and pursed her lips. The silence deepened again. She turned to Luke and whispered, "Help me up."

She felt his hands tremble, the clammy touch of his skin, as he lifted her out of the wheelchair and onto her feet. It was the first time he'd faced a public gathering. She held the mike with both hands, spoke quietly but clearly over the rumble of voices which filled the room again as she stood.

"What I have to say," she began, "is obvious. I do not know *what* to say to those parents. No words are adequate, are they?"

Still they waited and she was conscious of their faces as the question hung there. They looked at her, as if to test just how strong or weak she was. What they'd like, she realised, would be to see her wounds, to peer and poke and gape. The only thing that would satisfy them.

"You've a huge following in this country, Virgin. Some people believe you let your followers down. What would you say to that?" Bob Farrelly again.

253

"I'd say I didn't let them down." Her voice was sharp.

"But don't you think justice comes before your, eh, art?" he pressed.

"Art is justice," she answered.

"Oh come on now, Virgin, isn't that a bit unrealistic?"

"Don't push me on that, Bob. In a broad context, art is justice. In a specific context the terms of reference are different. Either way, that's not why we're here," she said quietly.

"Oh, isn't it? Well where do you see your career going from here?" Bonnie Macbeth snapped.

"Down the sewer I'd say, hah-hah-hah!"

Ginnie caught the riposte from the one of the photographers at back of the room.

"Some people say that you're an icon for the younger generation, especially for the younger women," Macbeth pressed on, "but don't you think your brand of – " she chose her word as if it were a weapon, then brandished it with a smirk, "*liberation,* is as dated as it's dangerous?"

Silence.

"I mean, Virgin, all those free-living, easy-ride lyrics – some people would say they're just not on for a generation of sexually-active young people who also face the threat of AIDS. Even if you throw packets of condoms at them. What do you say to that?"

Ginnie felt trapped. She noticed how Macbeth pronounced the word, giving equal weight to both syllables. Con-doms. Her face flushed red with rage. The woman reminded her of a terrier. *Yap-yap-yap-I'm right-I'm right-I'm right-caughtya-caughtya-caughtya!*

"I can't respond to that. It's an unfair question."

"Oh come on, come on! Some people say that you promote a sexual climate which ensures that young women will continue to get pregnant and cross the water to spend a weekend in an English abortion clinic!"

"Oh, for God's sake!" Ginnie replied. Goodbye, Diplomatic Corps, she thought.

*For God's sake!* Bonnie Macbeth noted rapidly in shorthand.

"Look, Bonnie, it doesn't matter what I say. In the end the newspaper you work for will have the last word. So get off my back."

Bonnie Macbeth shrugged. A succession of questions followed from the other journalists.

"What about the parents?"

"Yes! What about the parents?"

"They have rights too!"

"But surely your role was critical?"

The babble grew. She caught phrases, words. A comment about her "swanning off", from a fellow with an amused look on his face, clearly enjoying her dilemma. She shifted her weight slightly.

"Bob Farrelly mentioned justice a while back." She tried to keep her voice even, but wanted to tell the lot of them to shag off home and leave her alone. "There'll never be justice for the people who died at Malla, even less so for the survivors who have to – to carry on."

"Well, what're you going to do about it? Somebody has to do something!" A woman with brown eyes and short brown hair interrupted.

"My name's Delma Finn, I'm a parents' representative on the Victims at Malla Committee. Do you have any idea of the material compensation which we need if the injured are to have any kind of life at all? Do you?"

"Fuck this, it's a set-up," Mick said under his breath. "Excuse me, Madam, but we're not in a position to answer questions regarding compensation – beyond repeating what you already know – that Leo Kilgallen is the owner of the auditorium at Malla, and that the various questions regarding compensation will be dealt with through the courts. You must realise that Virgin is under no obligation to involve herself at this point, if at all."

"It happened at her concert! She's liable!" the woman shouted. "I've a son and a daughter injured. They're still over in the Burns Unit. The daughter's boyfriend was killed in that place. We have rights too, y'know. We have to live. People like us have to pick up the pieces and get on with life!"

But her voice began to break and the man to her right put his arm around her shoulders and kissed the side of her head.

"All right, pet, all right, take it easy now," he murmured, then straightened up. "I agree with my wife." He spoke quietly, but to the others in the room as he gestured towards Ginnie with his free hand. "I want it on record that I object to everything this woman stands for. It's the likes of her that has the youth driven mad. If it wasn't for her none of this would have happened!"

Ginnie straightened to her full height and clasped the mike tightly. "Hold it there. I didn't cause any of this. My gig was sabotaged – "

"Ah, your arse 'n parsley! Give us a break, love!" he scoffed.

" – by people who want to control freedom of information and freedom of movement."

As soon as she'd said it, she knew it wouldn't wash. Bye-bye again, Diplomatic Corps. The man shook his head and smiled as if to indicate how naive she was.

"Wise up, wouldya! How do you explain the words of your songs?"

"What has that to do with anything?"

"Don't get dragged in!" Mick sang at her under his breath.

"I don't explain my lyrics. I write songs. That's the business I'm in. Or the art." She nodded at Bob Farrelly. "I was just a target," she began to plead. "They needed somebody – somebody obvious. They were looking for headlines."

"Some would say they were right to choose you."

Mick turned to Luke and rolled his eyes in exasperation, shaking his head as he moved forward yet again.

"Please don't overlook the facts." He straightened up, his face grim. "The concert at Malla was sabotaged by a group called the Guardians of Christian Destiny. These people planted explosives. Some of their members were interviewed by the Gardai shortly after the incident and they have been charged. Virgin did not cause this explosion. Lyrics did not cause this explosion. But remember – please! – one of the members of this group held Virgin hostage in her own apartment. Caused serious harm."

He lowered his voice. "In case you people don't realise it, this woman has been through *hell*. She could have died."

A murmur went around the room. Ginnie looked at the ground.

"Please hear me out, people."

She looked at the Finns again. They glared at her, arms entwined as if the bond could shield them against the world.

"Nothing I say or do will make the slightest difference to you personally. But I intend to donate fifty per cent of

257

future earnings to the families who have been affected. I will, of course, keep in touch. We have all been injured. We have all been wounded." She stared hard at the ground. "Some part of all of us has died."

Delma Finn stood, furious. "Ah, fuck you and your fifty per cent! You know what you can do with that, don't you, just shove it up your arse as high as it'll go!" Pink in the face, she clenched her fists, then raised her voice over the titters that spread spontaneously among the journalists.

"You people really amuse me! You, Miss Born-Again Goody-Good, make me want to puke, and if you think you can do what you like and get away with it then you're making a big mistake. You'll rue the day you were born, you and the likes of you, running off with your Toy-Boy there while people were being burned alive!"

Luke and Ginnie exchanged looks. He held his elbows, looked sometimes at the ground, sometimes over the heads of the crowd. Delma Finn's outburst had him biting his lower lip with embarrassment. He felt naked. Would he be exposed to the whole country on the evening television news, and then in the following day's newspapers? He imagined the comments from the people who knew him and his family. For the first time, he felt stupid, a right dickhead. Who did he think he was anyway? Even worse, he felt in the wrong.

"It's OK, it's OK," Ginnie mouthed, silently pleading with him to stay calm, before turning again to Delma Finn. The last thing she needed was to have to cope with Luke's feelings.

"Mrs Flynn – Finn. Sorry – Mrs Finn. I didn't come here to defend myself. Don't underestimate how seriously I take the issue. Just remember that I was injured, I nearly lost my life on account of these – loonies."

"Yeah," said Mrs Finn in a voice which made it clear she couldn't care less. She avoided Ginnie's eyes, and her mouth was fixed in a small, bitter smile.

"That's right, Mrs Finn. And if you don't believe me I can show you the evidence. Would that keep you happy? I nearly lost my life – " She stammered and grew breathless as she pulled at the shoulders of her kaftan.

"I know that doesn't matter to you – but it's my life and – and – " One tug and the garment slipped off one of her shoulders, revealing wads of gauze and muslin, an outer exposed web of what looked like scalded flesh. She stood in the weight of a silence that dropped like a slab on them. She remembered how it felt to be beaten to within an inch of her life, how it felt to believe she was going to be killed.

"Instead of blaming me, get your committee to look at the Guardians of Christian Destiny and what they represent. And look. Go on. Have a good gawk. This is what you all wanted to see anyway. Isn't it?"

Mick and Luke rushed to cover her up. But by then the cameras were flashing, and the journalists scribbling. Mick's stomach began to burn. He took an indigestion tablet from inside his jacket, popped it into his mouth. There were times when he wished Ginnie wasn't such a natural exhibitionist, ready to milk critical moments for impact. This was one of them. Luke pulled the kaftan back over her shoulder and gently forced her into the wheelchair. Disgusted, she let him. She reached out for his hand and held on. Now it was she who trembled. There was no way out of this one, she thought. The fire at Malla would dog her forever. Virgin. Oh I remember her, wasn't she the one who – ?

"OK, doll. Easy now. Luke, see to her wouldya?" Mick

tried to gain a few moments advantage from what remained of the interview. Jaysus, what a shambles, he thought. They'd either hate her or love her to bits after that little display.

"That's it, folks. You've seen it all. Heard it all. And if any of you guys print those pictures I'll see you in court," he said grimly.

"One last question, where do you go from here Virgin?" Djonn Monahan from *CyberRock* called out. Hunched in his chair, a thick wedge of blue-black hair hanging across his face, he scratched at a page with a cartographer's pen.

"No comment," said Ginnie.

Quickly, Mick wheeled her out of the conference room, down the corridor towards the elevator.

# Seventeen

## Words

"Well, what's wrong with you?" Ginnie snapped, back in her room. Luke tutted and sighed, paced over and back between the window and the door.

"Everything. The whole thing. I think we've done something terrible."

"Bye kids." Mick pulled the door shut. Let 'em at it, he thought. Let 'em sort it all out once and for all. Maybe the youngster couldn't hack it. Maybe that was all for the best.

Luke felt weak. In his mind, he could hear the voices of all those teachers from his schooldays who used to yak on about "backbone". There were times in life, they used to say, when everybody needed backbone, something that made them stand out from the weaklings who drifted this way and that, like grass in the wind.

He had no backbone. He knew it now. It had all been a terrible mistake. He could see that clearly. All because he'd been so hung-up on Ginnie. Nobody'd ever told him he could get so carried away. But he never had been carried away before, so how could he have known how it would make him feel? What it would make him do? That

261

he wouldn't give a damn about what anybody thought, or about what was right. Shite, but he was stupid, plain stupid. Letting himself do the things he'd done. What was it all about anyway? He'd got himself the ride to Kingdom Come he'd always wanted, so many times he'd lost count. He'd done things Tod Grimley and the lads might never get around to. But who was the better off? Was that what it was all about? Riding? Scoring? For a moment he wondered if he'd had enough of sex, if he'd had it up to here with the whole shebang. But then he thought of Ginnie, saw the ruddy cleft between her legs and he changed his mind.

He thought of Tod again, imagined him doing the ordinary things, coming and going between his home and Kathleen's place, getting ready for college in October. He was going on for veterinary, Kathleen said. In years to come, Tod would come back to Malla and set up a practice. Things would continue, as if a baton was handed on by the older generation, taken up by the younger one. That'd never be his way of doing things. It was too late. He hadn't a fucking clue what his father had handed on to him, and what his mother wanted to hand on he didn't want.

Now that he really thought about it, he didn't know what the hell he was doing. He was stupid, stupid, stupid, no matter what way he looked at it. It was as if he couldn't go forward, but he couldn't go back either.

"Luke."

*"Luke!"* Ginnie said sharply. "We haven't done anything terrible." He turned on his heel and walked across the room again. She kept saying that. She kept saying everything was all right, when it wasn't. It couldn't be. It could never be again. Holy fuck but he was getting mad at her. She really lived in cloud cuckoo land.

"Can't you see that everything has changed?" he said.

"I can see plenty," she muttered. "Like maybe you've had enough."

"Maybe I have." He stopped and crinkled his eyelids against the light as he peered down at the carpark.

"That's it. I've changed, Ginnie. I can't see why you haven't."

"What do you mean?" She turned and stood, quicker than he'd seen her manage it in the past weeks. "Do as I do? Is that what you're telling me?"

"No. Not that. It's just that – back there – in the room with all those people. God, Ginnie, I dunno. And that woman. I mean, I didn't like her or anything. She was a dog. But all the same. All those deaths. And we didn't even get to the funerals."

"I was being attacked back there. Does that mean nothing to you?"

"Of course it does. But – "

"But what? Maybe they were right? That's it, isn't it? In some core cell of your moralistic little mind you think that they were right. But it's not as simple as that, Luke. The world just isn't divided up into nice black and white strips which say Right and Wrong. There's loads of grey. Grow up."

A vein pulsed down the centre of his forehead and he shoved his hands deep into his jeans pockets.

"Fuck you," he said.

"Thanks very much."

"You're welcome. Fuck you again."

"I already thanked you."

"Don't tell me to grow up. Just because you're older doesn't mean you know everything. There's a right and a wrong about this and we were wrong. And to hell with you and your black and white *strips*. You didn't even see the programme on telly."

"What programme? When?"

"The documentary, whatever. It must've been the weekend you were locked up with that psycho. It showed the funerals. All the stuff that happened when we were in Kerry. Other stuff about Kilgallen. You should still see it. Ring up RTE or something. Maybe you'd have said different things today."

"Mick and I agree that I've seen enough grief to last me a lifetime."

"Mick and I," he mimicked jealously, then scowled.

"That's right. Mick and I. We go back a long way, whether you like it or not. Anyway, if you think we got everything so wrong, tell me how. Come on, Luke, tell me if you can," she goaded.

"Do I have to spell it out?"

She turned and sighed, then threw back her head as if she was going to read something about patience off the ceiling. She had wanted to claw Bonnie Macbeth's eyes out, now her hands itched to slap Luke's face.

"OK." She turned again, then smoothed the air in front of her with both hands, as if it too had to be calmed.

"I should have been at the funerals. I admit it. I've always known that. But I've apologised and apologised and there's nothing more I can do about it. I don't intend to spend the rest of my life apologising. It'll change nothing. Do you understand? And in case you haven't noticed, I've had it up to here with people who think I should do time just because I wasn't around immediately after the explosion."

They faced one another, their eyes blazing. She almost hated the sight of him.

"Once things are done you have to live with them," she went on, "they can't be changed, Luke. Oh, people can pretend to change things. They can pretend their feelings have changed. But actions last forever."

He stared back, detested the bossy voice she was using.

"We must have looked a right pair of monkeys in there," he grumbled. "Me standing behind you like an eejit. And you ripping the bloody dress off your shoulder. Why did you have to do that? Why? You made us look like fools."

"You're starting to give me a pain in the backside. I called you a prig before and I'm saying it again. You're a prig but I wish you weren't. The only reason you think we looked like fools is because you're scared of being seen on television. Maybe when you grow up – "

"Don't you ever tell me to grow up again. Not as long as we're together. You're spoiled. That Finn woman was right. And you couldn't even remember her fucking name, you couldn't even get that much right – but she was right. You think you can do what you like and get away with it. Just because you're a rock star. Pathetic!"

"I don't think I can do what I like. I never thought that. But there are times when a woman's gotta do what a woman's gotta do. You did what you had to do. You came away with me. You took your chances."

She sat down on the edge of the bed, then raised her head. "I don't want to fight. Ah, fuck you anyway, maybe you're gutless after all. I wish you weren't. I don't need another gutless wonder hanging out of me."

He grunted. The silence between them was awkward. Things had been so perfect when they were in Kerry. Why couldn't that go on? Ginnie had been so perfect too. It was why he loved her. Now she was becoming almost ordinary. She'd said something about the colour grey a while ago. Loads of grey. A colour he couldn't stand. Irish weather colour, the bog in winter, water swirling in gullys. Porridge and low mountains.

"So nothing's perfect," he whispered, more to himself.

"Nothing. Which is why life is interesting. You'll realise that soon," she whispered back.

"Yeah, yeah, I know, don't say it. When I grow up!"

They did not kiss when he had to leave.

"See you," she said stiffly.

"See you soon," he replied, unable to move towards her to make up.

# Eighteen

## The Freedom Feather

Two days before she was due to be discharged, Ginnie booked a taxi, signed herself out and was driven to Malla.

It was Saturday. At Kathleen's place, Luke's anger had gone and his dreams had taken over again. He took his time over a late breakfast, planning a future in which Ginnie would be with him, spilling into him, over him, full of love for him.

The doorbell rang.

Kathleen was still in bed. He had just brought her a cup of tea, weak and with lemon, as she liked it. He tucked his shirt into his jeans and went to answer.

It was her. He nearly dropped. And after all their arguing the previous week. Well, at least he knew why she had come. This was it. Crunch-point. Break-off time. Well, he'd be ready for her, even if she was still the most beautiful, dignified thing he'd ever seen in his entire life.

She wore dark orange silk, her skirt long, gathered and soft, her feet laced in black boots; clinging to her head was a matching orange beret, the edges of which swirled with blue-green peacock feathers. Her lapis lazuli earrings had been replaced by pearls. Silver rings glinted where there had once been turquoises. When she came into the small hallway she did not walk with ease, there was no trace of her former swinging stride. She had gained weight and it suited her. Each step was measured, her left hand brushed the walls every so often as if to reassure herself that she could still stand.

Kathleen appeared from the bedroom, still in pyjamas. The two women exchanged quick, interested glances. There was a moment's hesitation before Kathleen spoke.

"You must be Ginnie. Hi!" she greeted easily, her hand outstretched.

"Well, well, well. What a charming little scene. So homely," Ginnie shook the proffered hand but couldn't keep the sarcasm from her voice. She looked candidly at Kathleen, searching the younger woman's face.

"Well. I'll leave you to it. I'm off back to bed, can't miss my Saturday morning lie-in," Kathleen said briskly. Too briskly, Luke thought, feeling himself on the sidelines of some strange piece of womanly communication.

She stared briefly at the space Kathleen had occupied. Luke felt sick. Ginnie's arrival was like an omen. He hated it when things happened unexpectedly. It threw everything out of kilter and he didn't know which end of him was up. Some of the worst things in his life had happened too suddenly. But he acted surprised, pleased to see her.

"Cripes. What're you doing here? It was Monday you were supposed to get out. I was going to collect you."

"Saved you the trouble then, didn't I. I wanted to come. Had to see you. Today."

He poured her a cup of tea, placing it before her so hurriedly that the cup clattered in its saucer and the contents slopped over the rim. She removed the cup, lifted the saucer and poured the tea back.

"Honey-bun," she began, not looking at him. "Tell me. Tell me everything. I want to see Malla. I want to see where you live. Meet your mother?"

She spilled her requests as if time were running out, her tone urgent. *Honey-bun.* It was as if the row had never happened. Oh God but she was one cool woman, he marvelled. Could she meet his mother? Might this be the opening for them to make up, a chance to convince her that Ginnie was human, normal, lovely? He sighed.

"We'll take a run out to the house. Why not? Mum'd probably like to meet you."

She gave a little snort. "I doubt it. But perhaps she should meet me. For your sake. Let her see the Incredible Melting Woman, who ruined your life."

"Don't say things like that. Just don't." Her words filled him with softness and pity.

"Like what?"

"Melting Woman stuff."

"Can't help it. Makes me feel better if I can talk tough."

"You've had enough tough things to last a lifetime," he murmured.

She tossed her head as if scorning his words, then smiled. They sipped their tea in silence and Ginnie looked around. The kitchenette was functional, the wooden floor stained and varnished to a honey colour, the walls painted yellow. A mound of used tea-bags filled a brown glass ashtray on the table. To the left of the door a small, block-mounted print of Picasso's *Blue Nude* hung above Rodin's *Praying Hands*. Propped against the wall near the sink, Van Gogh's *Sunflowers*, and four or five Renoir prints. Ginnie was struck by the expression of rapture on the face

269

of the young girl peering over the shoulder of a dark-suited man in *La Danse a la Campagne*. Oh heck, she thought to herself. Oh Buddha. That's how I feel. How Luke makes me feel. In spite of everything. That's my rapture when he's close to me. It's what I feel because he's alive. She smiled to herself. It's enough for me that he's alive. In the world. Part of the place. Even if we were to –

"Kathleen's?"

"Yeah. She's into art. Buys posters and prints every time she takes a holiday. Her bedroom's full of Van Goghs. Amsterdam the Easter before last."

Ginnie wandered around, then pushed open another door. What has gone on here? she wondered. Just the two of them. A very cosy arrangement.

"That's where I sleep."

"It smells of you," she remarked from the threshold.

"You animal!" he guffawed. She smiled, then ran over and sat beside him. They kissed. It was a sharp embrace, and a stillness seemed to fall not only on the room but on the entire building, the street, the town, save for bickering jackdaws on the roof.

Ginnie pulled back.

"Show me around, sweetnuts. I want to see Malla. The town. Where you live. But not the hall . . . "

"OK, but let me kiss you again. I'll do anything, but first let me taste you."

He pulled her towards him again, his lips eager, his hand reaching for the buttons of her jacket. Again, she withdrew, her doubts not completely gone.

"Not yet. Not yet. Take me out, show me around. I've hired a taxi for the whole day!"

"Well, tell the driver to shag off for a few hours. Tell him not to come back until late!" he whispered, caressing her neck. Kathleen wouldn't have approved, Luke thought. Not in her place. Not with Ginnie.

Ten minutes later they sat in the jeep and drove off.

"I'm sorry," he said quickly, not looking at her.

"What for?"

"Y'know. The other day."

"Ah, that. Sure I'm sorry too. Let's forget it."

Then it was like old times, the pair of them rattling along, drunk with freedom. The day was warm and windy, the town busy, cluttered with street-stalls, racks of clothing, wellington boots, duffle-coats; traffic crawled along, tractors, trucks, cars with bales of new straw in the boot. Shoppers crossed the roads laden with baskets, and the smell of fish wafted from one of the stalls.

They drove slowly, windows down, like travellers in a foreign country. That day, it was foreign, it was an open place, a prairie in their minds, an unsheltered sky. Finally, he found a space in the market square.

"Hop out. I want to show you off," he said.

"But what if I'm recognised? People know us."

"There won't be any trouble. You look so different in that get-up. Like a bird, a flamingo."

He could not stop grinning at her, he felt so happy, and his face kept breaking into huge smiles. The giddiness was uncontainable.

They strolled arm-in-arm along the footpaths, pausing to look in shop windows, intrigued by bits of cheap glass, brass ornaments, bizarre garden furniture, gnomes and leprechauns, then beneath the striped awnings pot-plants in earthen urns, river-gods and fish fountains.

She clasped his hand, squeezed it at intervals, would stop to kiss him, unembarrassed. As they passed, people made way, friends and acquaintances of Luke's moved

271

shyly aside, bid a quiet greeting, their eyes curious. He
began to enjoy himself, certain that they were full of envy
for him and Ginnie, that they too thought her beautiful. He
pitied them for having such dull lives. For having to
endure such ordinary girlfriends and boyfriends when he
had the plum of them all. It was important for them to
look, to stare. To see him and Ginnie, to know the
importance of their love.

They walked with the shocked expression of lovers.
Flushed, bright-eyed, speaking little, life seemed to be a
brand-new invention – pavements, the quality of the
stonework in some of the houses, people's faces, the curve
of the streets, the way the main street opened out
gradually into a huge square with a limestone market-
house, which was used as an art-gallery. This time, Ginnie
thought, I am part of it all, this time it's different.

He had lived there all his life, but for Luke the place
was like a new city, untouched by the dirt of living. For a
change, he saw nothing boring in Malla. He was an
explorer, had stumbled at last on his new world, like
Columbus in the Americas with an Indian queen on his
arm. He walked slowly, with pride, never too fast in case
Ginnie got tired. Her boot-heels clicked along and he
enjoyed the pressure of her fingers each time they
tightened on his arm, responding in flashes of delight to
her smell, her smile, the feel of her skin.

They bought pâté and bread, a bottle of wine, fruit
juice, slices of apple tart, then headed back to the jeep.
Beyond the town, the land fell away from undulation to
flat fields as far as the eye could see, rolling acres of uncut
barley and corn, the roadside fringed with beech trees and
ash, abundant with late summer seed.

"That's our house," Luke remarked, pointing off to the
left. Ginnie looked.

"Do you still want to go up?"

She frowned. "I don't know. What do you think?"

"Why spoil a perfect day? It could be tricky."

"Let's leave it then. I wouldn't know what to say anyway," she replied. She pulled a mirror from her bag and adjusted the hat on her head.

He was relieved. The prospect of introducing Ginnie to his mother scared him. He did not want to be undone, to seem childish or silly because of his mother's disapproval which remained fierce and unrelenting. He drove on for a while, then pulled the vehicle off the road and parked in a gateway.

"Let's find someplace to eat," he said.

He jumped down, was round in a flash to the other side of the jeep to help her out. She swore quietly as one of her heels caught on the hem of her long skirt, then clasped him around the neck and kissed him. They picked their way along the edge of a cornfield, looking for a picnic spot.

The land shimmered with the aroma of ripe seed, corn-dust, soil; the air felt like warm breaths, a sweetness exuding from the earth's lungs, filling them with a heat of expectancy, uncertainty, then again, hope. Luke looked up and saw one hundred and eighty degrees of pure sky.

Ginnie tore at the bread. She drank straight from the wine bottle in long, thirsty gulps, then passed it to Luke. The wine dribbled down his chin. She watched as it slid slowly around his jaw, reached out and daubed it with her finger, then leant forward and slowly, carefully, licked his neck and throat.

"I know why you're here," he said abruptly. Senses in uproar, the arch of his cheekbones flamed as his mood veered between lust and angry suspicion.

She said nothing, went on eating. Her face seemed pale.

"And I wish you hadn't bothered."

"Why?" she asked.

"Because you're leaving. I'm right, amn't I?"

She did not answer, but stretched to lift the wine bottle again. He reached forward and caught her wrist, preventing her from drinking.

"Answer me," he said, as evenly as he could.

There was no avoiding him. The moment she looked into his face again she saw that delay was futile. He was crazy about her, insistent, angry.

"I wanted to talk first. See you alone, find out how you'd feel if – " She sighed. "Maybe we can work something out."

She stared at him, hesitant.

"There's something you haven't told me." His words hung between them. She hesitated, reached out and touched his cheek with her hand. He had grown hot and flushed in those few minutes. His eyes glittered. She looked around again as if searching for words.

"Have you told me everything?" she asked in as gentle a voice as she could manage.

"About *what?*" He gaped.

The golden atmosphere of the day, of the place itself, conspired and threatened. Above, the sun beat down, the sky lit with racing clouds while the wind carried the distant drone and clack of combines working fields beyond the main road.

"I've nothing to tell," he grumbled.

She opened her mouth to speak, then shut it abruptly, as if she had changed her mind. Then she said she'd had an offer. Luke had the distinct impression that this was

274

only part of what she'd planned to tell him, but he did not interrupt.

"It's mega-break time. A German tour in eight weeks. It's a chance I should take. At least, I think I should. So does Mick. But – I wanted to know what you thought."

Luke lifted the wine bottle and drank slowly before laying it to one side again.

"Sounds like you've made your mind up."

"I haven't. Not completely. It depends on you too."

His mouth curled in cynicism.

"Come off it! I'm not even in the picture!"

"Darling, let's not fight. Not today. For heaven's sake, of course I want to take the tour and as a matter of fact I've signed – I've signed up already. But – " She bit her lip. "I'd like you to consider something – "

She paused to see how he was reacting. He said nothing, twirled a blade of grass between his fingers until it broke, then began on another, turning and twirling. Again, it snapped cleanly. Coarse, dull green grass, late summer grass, exhausted grass, the kind you could cut your skin on.

She cleared her throat.

"I wondered, I was wondering if you'd – if you'd come with me, you know, come away. For the tour. See how you like the life?"

Still he said nothing, tugging now at clumps of grass and wild corn, ripping and tearing, the sound of it scratching at the spaces between her words.

"You've always said you hadn't the chance to get away. This could be the start and – and we'd see how things will work in the long run."

"Christ, but you're so friggin' cautious now!" he muttered. "A trial arrangement, is that it?"

275

"It's not like that. Oh, it's not in the least like that." She shook her head. "You haven't a bloody clue, have you?"

"I suppose we have to be – lemme see, what's the right word – *realistic?*" he replied slowly. O'Regan, you're a sour bollock when you want, he thought.

Ginnie knew she was right. In spite of everything, in spite of Luke. She was not finished yet, she would grow stronger, the world would be her stage again. Even there, in the heat, she could not forget her concerts, her music, the sense of power, the sense of enjoyment, the thrill of being one of the best.

She unbuttoned her jacket and removed her hat. The hair beneath was glossy and brown, a complete contrast to the long, wild bush she used to braid and coil for her performances. Luke stared at the white bodice beneath the jacket, then looked away furiously, noticing as he did so pink ridges of scars that crept around her shoulders and upper arms.

"But how sure are you, Luke? How sure are you that you want to spend your life shacked up with me? Have you the faintest idea what I'll be like when I'm fifty and menopausal?"

He hung his head. "Don't be a bore, Ginnie. It doesn't matter to me. You'll always be the same."

A lie, and part of him knew it. Looks mattered. Luke didn't want her to change. The thought of change still frightened him. He would always want to be near her. That, at least.

"Think about it, Luke, think about it."

"I'm sure. I'm totally sure. Far surer than you ever seem to have been!" He turned and stared into the hedge. His body was rigid.

"But what is it? – " she faltered, "Won't you come? It

could be fun. New places, new cities, the freedom to move around on your own. Good hotels. It'd be hectic, so busy you'd hardly know me. You'd meet lots of new people. But we'd be together. It would be – a compromise – but it would be something. And something is always better than nothing!"

She gripped his arm suddenly. "We'd have the time of our lives. I promise. Come on honey-bun, what's holding you?"

He didn't answer.

"Is there something holding you back?"

Still he said nothing. He didn't want new people, or hotels. Perhaps he did not want Ginnie, not honestly. Perhaps he was on the run to a future he could not even suspect. But no, all he really wanted was to have her to himself, alone, with her adoration, her excitement, her tenderness. He didn't want to move. He wanted them both to be locked up forever in some cottage in the middle of nowhere, where they couldn't be found. He wanted to go back, for things to be the way they were in Kerry.

"I – I don't know what's holding me," he said then.

The silence between them was broken by the heavy whisper of trees, and the wind rippling and shushing through the corn.

"And it wouldn't be like this. Not like Kerry either. You wouldn't have time for me," he grumbled.

"Of course I would, whatever gave you that idea?" She stifled a laugh.

"People would laugh. I don't want anyone sniggering behind my back!"

She took his hand, tugging until he looked her in the eye.

"Luke," she began seriously, "you fucking jackass.

277

They'll laugh anyway. They've slagged me for wanting to sing, they've sneered at the way I've performed. People love to break their asses laughing at someone else's risks. It means shag-all. It doesn't keep anybody awake at night because most people are too damned timid to do more than just laugh. Bloody hell. It's part of life. Anyway – "

She stretched her legs, then leant back on her arms. "After all this time in hospital, I know what I care about and what I don't care about. Funny how it took something like that to do it. Not something I'd recommend. I mean what's the use of changing and who the hell needs to be all that strong! I know about pain. My back. My skin. They still hurt. I've lost my – my *beauty*." She whispered the word as if it was unspeakable.

Her voice dropped again. "And maybe I've lost peace. My kind. The crazywoman kind of peace. That was mine. It belonged to me. Someone tried to kill it off."

He didn't interrupt, just watched her perplexed face, her eyebrows knitted.

"The worst thing was feeling just like a child whipped to within an inch of her life for something not her fault. That did something to me. Like being twisted. Having a piece knocked away. Something's missing from my mind, you know. It wasn't just the body. Maybe it doesn't show, but that's the truth. Not that I'm mad or anything. And even funnier, except it's not funny, I want to climb into the soft pockets of every kind man in the world, Luke. It's as if I've been crying inside myself all these weeks. So I don't give a shit who laughs at us, or why. They're not in my skin. They're not in yours. They can't *feel* for us. And maybe there's no reason why they should. But let them laugh if they want to."

Luke shook his head and dropped it into his hands. He flung the remainder of the bread into the ditch.

"Ginnie," he said hopelessly, "you shouldn't have had to change. I know I went on and on about change – last week. But you shouldn't have to change. Not you, not you. Not because of that Dunne bitch."

She took him in her arms and held him, felt his tears in the hollows above her collarbone, their slow dribble down her chest. It struck her as comical that after all she'd said, it should be she who comforted him.

"I'll always love you. There'll never be anyone else. It just isn't possible, it isn't, it isn't!" he protested.

She held him.

Gradually they undressed, shaded by an oak which rustled in the silence. She unbuttoned his shirt, her hands flying to his face and lips every so often, touching them, brushing his eyes. He undid her bodice, toyed with the blue feather in its silver clasp as it hung between her breasts.

"Like old times," he said, almost to himself.

"No. New times," she whispered, and brushed his jaw with the feather.

He removed her stockings, slowly unlaced her boots. Finally, she drew herself along the length of his body, then sat astride his pelvis. Her bodice was open but not removed. She wouldn't let him take it off. She thought fleetingly of *Frouwe Welt,* an image of worldly rottenness she'd once seen in an old poetry book of her mother's, a woman glorious to behold, her hair long and curling, her breasts, thighs and face unblemished and beautiful. She'd turned the page and seen the other side of *Frouwe Welt*, a hideous, sore-covered form, carrying the vanities and corruptibility of the world on her skin, like pestilence.

They made love slowly. It was slow and awkward. Luke didn't know where to place his hands for fear of hurting her. Ginnie leant forward, his torso within the spread of her knees, his pupils darkened in the shadow of her body as she moved over him, tilted forward, rhythmically and faster until he convulsed upwards and called out, his head rolling back. At the same time she lurched forward on his chest in the slow crush of orgasm, and lost herself with him, so near to total loss of self that she thought she could die there and then. That it would be all right to be so absorbed.

Afterwards, they lay still, foreheads moist, breathing harsh, the hair at the nape of their necks wet. Above, branches creaked. The sun flashed across their faces until they were dappled with light and they had to close their eyes against the glare. Ginnie rolled off Luke and lay on her side, her head against his shoulder, both of them forgetting why they had made love in the first place, the argument receding. She hoped they would always be able to forgive one another so easily. That they would be able to forget too. Injuries especially. What was always best forgotten.

She dozed, dreamt she was in hospital, then woke with a start.

"Oh Buddha-Buddha-Buddha!" she groaned, rubbing her fingers across her forehead.

"What is it?" he said sleepily.

"I don't feel so good. The light hurts my head."

"Yes," he answered, not hearing her. His body was softened, relaxed by the musky assaults of sex. He stared up at the sky and his head cleared. He knew himself to have been delivered, finally and completely, into manhood.

"Come on, Luke – you might change your mind. At least,

oh at least *think* about it!" she urged later, back in the centre of Malla as they stood behind the taxi.

"How can I tempt you? Let me see. Hmmm." She turned and looked into his face. "Think of the good things. That's all. Think of the good things. Don't pull back from them. People! Me! Love! Sex! Then there's food. Caviar on blinis, tequila cured salmon, foie gras on walnut toast, caramelised onions and pear bits!" She laughed as she rambled. "All of which you could have if you stay behind, but think of the way you could enjoy them with me – ah, bliss!"

She'd put the little hat with its circlet of peacock feathers back on her head. To Luke, as she teased him, she looked a dream in her velvet suit, the only sign of recent sex, on her mouth, which was too pink and full, slightly bruised about the edges from his final kisses. Her words were like a poem. He listened and he remembered.

"Ring me tomorrow morning. I'll be at Mick's place."

He said nothing, then jerked with a start towards his left.

"I don't believe it!" he murmured, more to himself.

Ginnie turned, then spotted the photographer who rapidly took a succession of shots before hopping back into his car.

"Oh shit. Ted Brogan. Bonnie Macbeth must've sent him."

"Does that mean we're going to be plastered all over *Now!?*"

"'Fraid so. Does that bother you?"

"Yeah. It still does. You know it does! I wish it bothered you."

"I'm used to it. Thicker skin. Whatever." She shrugged.

"Don't know if I'll ever develop it," he said sullenly.

She ignored the remark.

"Ring me? Promise?" She looked up at him under her eyebrows the way she always did when she wanted something. He didn't answer.

"And Luke? Sweetnuts? I like her."

"Who?"

"Kathleen."

"What has that got to do with anything?"

"Nothing. I suppose," she answered slowly.

She reached out and pressed her fingers to his lips, traced them slowly, then rushed forward and put her arms around him. If his heart didn't burst then, it never would. They held onto one another while the taxi driver stared, then looked away. In those moments, as his tongue found hers, Luke imagined sweet oils, spices, caught the warm flicker of amber, as he had so often seen it on her earrings, felt himself flooded through with love. She clung to him, her fingers caught tufts of his hair, stroked through his scalp, behind his ears, finally, brushed his hot cheekbones.

The car pulled away, and she was gone.

That night, he left his room in Kathleen Quinlan's flat and went out. The flat no longer seemed pretty and feminine, but cramped and dull. Kathleen had gone to a party with Tod Grimley. He could not face her, or anybody, just then. Tomorrow a picture of himself and Ginnie snogging would appear in the newspapers. Something else to damn them with. But then, as Ginnie said, people always found something to gossip about. Lies and hearsay kept many happy. As he walked the streets, the town nudged in on him, narrow and grey. Was this it? Had he chosen to live in an up-and-coming provincial town with two Chinese takeaways, an Italian restaurant, boutiques and bars, a converted arts centre and a condom-machine in every jacks? There was nothing that could possibly interest him, nothing that mattered a damn now.

He walked for miles, hands in his pockets. The moon

was up and eventually he found himself at Westross Castle where he sat and slumped against the wall of the old wine cellar and looked up at the sky.

He thought of Kathleen's wayward uncle, then the rivers. Imagined the Amazon, the Elbe, the Danube and the Mekong, the Mississippi, those swollen, certain waterways. So certain of direction, so certain of an out, of release into the oceans of the world.

Kathleen's uncle had done it. He'd lived life on his own terms. He'd let nothing get in the way of his dreams. He wondered what his father would have thought. Yet he couldn't imagine his father being much use. He knew that his father was too earth-bound for the pursuit of dreams. No, he was no inspiration at all. But his mother? They were peas in a pod, the pair of them, stubbornly clinging to what each believed to be right. Perhaps in her livid, stubborn way, she had set him in a mould that had left him wide open to the love of a woman like Ginnie. Perhaps they could forgive one another. One day.

Sounds echoed in his head, strange words, new phrases, feelings about the future that could yet burst out of him like an agitated, living stream too long dammed up. Every argument in existence fought for attention. In the end he still saw only Ginnie, whom he would always see, no matter what happened, because she was in his soul. He lay until dawn, tormented by the waning moon, by anger and fear and love; he waited and watched as the first strips of cloud were broken by light.

As he lay there, he knew he would phone her. He knew he would leave.

The End